Utah County Bookmobile
125 W. 400 N

HOLLY J. WOOD

Copyright © 2015 by Holly J. Wood

Cover Design by: Mythic Studios, Inc.

All rights reserved. No part of this book may be reproduced in any form by any electronic or mechanical means including photocopying, recording, or information storage and retrieval without permission in writing from the author.

All characters in this book are fictitious, and any resemblence to actual persons, whether living or dead, is purely coincidental. This work is not an official publication of The Church of Jesus Christ of Latter Day Saints. The views expressed herein are the responsibility of the author and do not necessarily represent the position of the Church.

ISBN-13: 978-1-940427-12-6
ISBN-10: 1940427126

Library of Congress Control Number: 2015905968

Book Website
www.hollyjwood.com
Email: hollyjwoodauthor@gmail.com

Give feedback on the book at:
hollyjwoodauthor@gmail.com

Printed in The United States of America

To Janelle, for believing.

ACKNOWLEDGMENTS

I'd like to express my thanks to my readers. I never planned on making this a series, so thank you for spurring on ideas for new books with your enthusiasm and support.

This book is dedicated to my sister, Janelle, for being the first to believe in my stories and always being willing to give feedback and encouragement. Love you, Nelly!

My heartfelt love and gratitude to family, friends and the women of the Silver Lake Ward who carried me through my weeks of bedrest. Each act of love and service has been recorded in my heart, and this story would not have been possible without you.

To Tammi Niederhauser and the Morgan High Troyettes, thanks for letting me be a fly on the wall during practice. What a fun and talented group!

I also want to thank Nicole Nielsen for letting me bounce ideas around, and for insight from a nurse's perspective.

A huge thank you to my beta readers: Susan Auten, Candice Toone, Jill and Sierra Evans, Hannah Price, Natasha Plyer, Christy Dorrity, Janelle Lehmann, and Joanna Purves. Your feedback was priceless.

To my editor, Jenette Hendricks, thank you for accomplishing fantastic feats under a tight deadline. You are fabulous, in every sense of the word.

High fives and hugs to the members of my writing group: Natasha Plyer, Christy and Devon Dorrity. My writing career would have died long ago if not for your support. Also a special thanks to Devon for the gorgeous cover design and formatting (again, under a tight deadline). I never cease to be amazed!

To Sierra Evans, you are beautiful. The end. Thank you for being such a gracious cover model. I'd also like to thank Aubrey Musso and Jen Eastman for their contributions to the cover.

Hugs to my in-laws, Don and LuAnn Wood, for their support and help with the kids when I needed it most.

To Mom, thank you for lighting the fire of family history work beneath me. And for loads of patience trying to explain how to do it. You inspire me in countless ways.

As always, a shout out to some truly "exceptional" individuals: Steve, Trevor, Lucy, Layla and Tyler. My world revolves around you. Thanks for reminding be on a daily basis what matters most, and showing me what lasting love looks like.

Finally, I must acknowledge the Lord's hand in my life. I've got a long ways to go, but I'm trying to learn. I'm so eternally thankful that because of Him I get to keep trying, and because of Him I get to have joy in the process. The blessings are too many to count.

CHAPTER

one

"No way did she just post that selfie." Alexis nudged my arm. "Courtney, you have to see this."

"Who is it?" I rolled onto my stomach and looked over her shoulder. "Oh. Wow."

She snorted as we gawked at the image of the girl on the screen. "You were so smart to break up with Kellen. I mean, any guy who would go out with a girl who posts pictures like that is not someone you'd want to be with anyway."

I nodded and propped my chin in my hands. I'd broken up with Kellen Bradley over a month ago, but talking about him still made me uncomfortable. It stirred memories of mistakes I was trying hard to bury.

After I'd dumped him he'd quickly rebounded and was now dating Veronica Mitchell, aka: Miss Selfie. I knew it was petty to make fun of Veronica, but I wanted to get my mind away from the painful thoughts Kellen's memory dredged up.

Alexis tried to keep a straight face as she continued analyzing the picture. "I mean, taking a selfie in a bikini is bold enough, but add to it that—" she let out a strangled sound as she struggled not to laugh, "expression." She lost the battle and fell into a fit of giggles. "I'm sorry . . . I just . . . can't." She barely choked out the words before laughter took over again.

I bit my lip and tilted my head. "I think the expression she was going for was sultry, but somehow it ended up looking . . . constipated?"

Alexis shrieked and I couldn't hold back anymore. We were both lying flat on my bed, laughing until we were wiping away tears. A knock sounded at my door a second before my mom looked in.

"What's so funny in here?"

I sat up as one last giggle escaped. "Nothing. Just a funny picture on Instagram."

Mom pursed her lips. "Mm-hmm." She didn't like when Alexis and I spent a lot of time on our phones. "You two had better call it a night. Court, you have drill practice in the morning and then I'll need your help setting things up for the reception right after school." She placed a hand over her round belly, a motion she seemed to do without thinking.

Alexis locked her phone and sat up. "Is there anything I can do to help?"

Mom smiled. "That would be great. Stop by tomorrow and we'll put you to work."

"Okay." Alexis picked up her keys and jangled the chain as she stood. "See you tomorrow, Court."

"See ya." I was still grinning in the aftermath of our giggle fest as she left the room. Alexis and I had been best friends since we were twelve. Now, four years later, she was still the kind of friend who could tell what I was thinking without my ever having to say a word.

"What have you been up to all evening?" Mom asked.

"Not much. Just hanging out," I answered, examining my nails. "Is Eliza home yet?" My older sister was getting married in two days. It was fun having her back home from college in preparation for the wedding.

Mom shook her head. "She and Luke are out, but I'm sure she'll be home soon. Do you want me to send her in to say good night?"

"No, that's ok. I'll see her tomorrow." I got up from the bed and went over to get some pajamas from my dresser. When I turned around, Mom was still standing in the doorway. I raised an eyebrow. "Is there anything else you need?"

She put a hand behind her back and shifted her weight. "Well . . ."

I frowned and gestured to my bed. "Here, come sit." Mom's unexpected pregnancy at forty-one put her in a high-risk category. She wasn't due for a few more months and though I tried not to worry, sometimes the strain of this pregnancy was evident on her face.

She nodded and shuffled to the bed. I bit back a laugh when the mattress springs groaned in protest beneath her.

"Your dad and I have been talking, and we think it might be time for you to find a part-time job."

"What?" All sympathy for her condition fled from my mind. "But I'm so busy with the drill team and school. How am I supposed to fit in a job, too?"

She gave me a wry smile. "You seem to find plenty of time to just 'hang out' with Alexis."

I rolled my eyes. "Mom, I'm a teenager. I'm supposed to have time to hang out with friends. It's healthy." I clenched my fists. "Do you expect me to fill every spare second I have? Because that's what will happen if I try to balance drill, homework and a job. There's just no way."

"We know how busy you are and we're not asking you to work full time. But when Eliza was your age she was expected to earn enough money to pay for insurance on her car, as well as help to pay for formals."

I shook my head. Of course she would bring Eliza into this. My parents were forever comparing me to my older sister. She never did anything wrong in their eyes.

Mom took in my expression and pinned me with a no-nonsense look. "It would also be good for you to help pay for some of the expenses of being on the drill team. Let's just see if you can't find something for a few hours a week, okay?"

I scoffed and looked at the wall, feeling only slightly guilty when I heard her struggle to get up from the bed and come to stand beside me.

She touched my shoulder. "We're not trying to punish you. Your dad and I just want you to learn the value of work. In a few years you'll be on your own and it's our job to prepare you for that as best we can."

I grunted and moved my gaze to the floor. "Whatever."

She dropped her hand. "We can talk more about this later. Are you reading your scriptures on your phone, or do you want to turn it in now?"

"I'll bring it in in a minute," I grumbled. It was my parents' rule that my phone had to be turned in each night before bedtime. I had learned to tolerate the rule, but tonight it added insult to injury. The only thing that earned me some extra phone-time was claiming that I liked studying my scriptures on it.

"Okay then. See you in a bit." I could hear the appeasing tone in her voice and felt a twinge of guilt.

After she closed the door I pulled on my pajamas and tossed my clothes in the direction of the hamper. I could tell without looking that they hadn't made it in, but I didn't care. The clock was ticking now.

I flopped on my bed and picked up my phone, logging back in to Instagram just as my phone buzzed. I smiled when I saw it was a text from Eli Jackson.

Eli: *Are you as excited as I am to see what the inside of a fetal pig looks like?*

I laughed.

Me: *Ugh . . . I've been dreading this day for weeks. Maybe I'll skip class tomorrow.*

Eli: *And leave me to suffer through it alone? I'm wounded.*

Me: *Haha. You know you secretly enjoy it, Mr. "I'm going to be a Dr. someday."*

Eli: *What? Now you're mocking me too? I was going to offer to do all the dissecting while you took notes, but I'm starting to reconsider . . .*

Me: *Come on, you know I was just kidding. You only hurt the ones you love.* ☺

There was a pause before he replied, but I knew I could tease him like this. Eli and I had the same biology class this semester and were lab partners. He was the type of guy I could joke around with and he would dish it right back. I enjoyed our little banters, but when he still didn't reply I wondered if he was done with the conversation. I was about to return to my Instagram surfing when my phone buzzed again.

Eli: *Alright, I'll do the dirty work tomorrow. But it's gonna cost you.*

Me: *Ooo, a bribe? I think we can arrange something . . . as long as you hold to YOUR end of the deal.*

Eli: *Which is?*

Me: *I don't have to touch the corpse, or come within close proximity.*

I glanced at the clock and realized I was running out of time. Mom would never believe I'd studied my scriptures for more than ten minutes.

Me: *Sorry to end this when things just started to get interesting, but I gotta go. We'll talk details tomorrow.*

Eli: *Ok. Good night.*

Me: *Nighty night.*

I smiled and then quickly went to Instagram. After a few swipes of the screen, I found who I was searching for: Tate Williams. I totally Internet stalked him, but I was sure I wasn't the only girl in school who did. His profile in all of its deliciousness was open to the public. Tate was a year older than me, a junior in high school. He was a star on the basketball team and was completely, utterly gorgeous.

He had this rugged surfer look, with blonde hair, tan skin and contrastingly light blue eyes. Tate had no idea who I was, although I liked to think he'd maybe seen me when he'd come to pick up Serena from drill practice. Their recent breakup had rocked the entire school.

Serena Powell was our drill team captain, and though she and her clique never gave me the time of day, I'd gathered from hallway chatter that she wasn't the one who ended the relationship.

I was disappointed to see he hadn't posted anything new since last night, but still scanned through the photos I'd already ogled a hundred times. My heart stuttered as I stopped to look at my favorite one. It was a close up of his face and dazzling white smile. I allowed myself to imagine that he was looking directly at me, and then held the phone to my chest and closed my eyes.

Maybe he would watch us perform during the basketball game next week, and there would be a moment when our eyes would meet. And he would smile, just like this. I glanced at his picture one more time and sighed before shutting off my phone. Time was up.

I shuffled down the hall to my parents' bedroom. No one was there so I set the phone on Mom's nightstand, relieved that I didn't have to pretend that I'd read my scriptures.

I padded back down the hall and noticed that the light was on in Eliza's old room. I heard her talking to Mom and decided to go in. Seeing the two of them sitting on Liza's bed and chatting away like friends caused a twinge of jealousy inside of me. Mom never talked to me like that.

"Courtney!" Liza turned to me with a big smile as I stepped into the room. She even looked like Mom with her brown hair and bright blue eyes.

I twisted a strand of long blonde hair around my finger as I sat on the bed beside them. "What are you guys talking about?"

"Just wedding stuff," Mom said as she pushed a bridal magazine aside to make more room for me. She had been ecstatic ever since Eliza got engaged. Planning this wedding had been all the two of them could talk about for the past several weeks. Frankly, it was getting a little old.

"What have you been up to, Court?" Liza asked.

I shrugged. "Not much . . . Mom and Dad are making me get a job." I threw an accusatory glance at Mom.

She sighed and looked at Eliza. "I merely said that it's time she took on a little more financial responsibility, just like you had to at her age."

"Liza wasn't on the drill team," I shot back.

"No, but she was still plenty busy."

Eliza held up her hands to ward off the mounting tension. "Mom, it's true. I wasn't as busy as Courtney is." She turned to me with a sympathetic look. "But I liked having my own money to spend. It might not be as bad as you think."

Mom relaxed her shoulders and smiled at Eliza, the love and admiration for her practically brimming from her eyes. My sister, the saint. She never lost her temper or was accused of being stubborn like I was. The worst thing she'd ever done in her life was probably forgetting to say "excuse me" after she sneezed. My stomach churned at the thought of how different I was in comparison.

Biting back a retort, I shook my head and stood up. "I'd better get to bed or I'll be too tired for practice."

"Okay, sleep tight." Eliza smiled.

"Did you turn in your phone?" Mom asked.

I nodded without looking back and then went into my room and closed the door. It had been over a month since I'd said my prayers so I barely had to ignore the impulse before climbing into bed. But somehow ignoring praying seemed to trigger the guilt that gnawed at my consciousness when I wasn't on guard. Thoughts of Kellen and the mistakes I'd made while dating him seemed to swarm in, filling me with turmoil as I tossed and turned, trying to find relief in sleep.

You broke up with him. You stopped doing that stuff, I repeated in my mind until I drifted into a fitful sleep.

It was the same dream; the one I'd been having for weeks now.

I stood on the bank of a small pond surrounded by trees, with emerald green grass stretching just beyond. The peaceful setting soothed me. I wouldn't mind visiting there so often, except for the girl.

She always sat near the pond, writing in what looked like a journal. Occasionally she would push back the wisps of blonde hair set free from her bonnet by a gentle breeze, or pause to stare at the pond.

The fact that she wore a dress and bonnet was weird, especially since she looked to be about my age, but it was her face that interested me most. Something about it fascinated me. She was a stranger, and yet she wasn't.

I stood rooted to the spot less than a yard from where she sat, but she never acknowledged me. I had tried everything from waving my arms to shouting at the top of my lungs to try to get her attention, but nothing ever worked. This dream was no different. After my usual antics to get her attention, I watched in frustration as she continued to write. Somehow I knew those words were important, if only I could get close enough to read them.

Sighing in defeat, I was about to sit in the grass when something unexpected happened. The girl looked up and stared directly at me. My heart beat rapidly at the intensity in her clear blue eyes.

"Lost."

I stared back in shock. Before my mouth could form a response, the dream shifted into something else and the girl vanished.

CHAPTER

two

"Okay, girls, I want one more run-through before practice is over," Coach Weaver said. She tapped her iPod and the music for our halftime routine filled the gym.

I wiped the sweat from my forehead with my upper arm and then moved back into starting position. Coach worked us hard at each practice; it felt like we'd already done this routine a billion times. But as tired as I was, my love of dance kept me going. I forced a smile on my face and pushed my muscles past the pain to execute each step as best I could.

This was a military number so I focused on keeping my movements sharp and precise. Adrenaline surged through me the way it always did when I got lost in a dance. Suddenly I wasn't counting out steps in my head. I was just dancing.

Before I knew it, the music was over. I held the end pose a few extra seconds on the gym floor before getting to my feet. Turning, I reached my hand out to my friend Janie. "Need a lift?"

She looked up at me and then groaned. "Ugh. Yes, please! Can you carry me into the locker room too?"

I laughed and helped her up. In spite of her complaints she practically bounced onto her feet. Janie was a petite little redhead with an electric smile.

Coach was always trying to make us "unified" as a team, but with thirty girls there were still cliques. I felt closer to Janie than anyone else.

"So, are you excited for your sister's wedding tomorrow?" she asked as we trailed after the other girls into the locker room.

I took a swig from my water bottle and wiped my mouth before answering. "Yeah, it's complete craziness at my house." We reached our lockers and I absently turned the combination dial. "I'm kinda sad Eliza's getting married and moving on—you know, because things will never be the same. But when I see how happy she is with Luke, it's impossible not to be excited for them."

Janie nodded. "That's understandable. But when you feel sad, just remember, 'you're not losing a sister, you're gaining a brother.'"

I snorted. "Did you seriously just say that?"

She laughed and I broke into a smile to show I was kidding.

"You think you can handle the 'shower challenge' today?" she asked, pointing to the towel I'd retrieved from my locker. Even with our first hour blocked out for practice, we usually ended up with only twenty minutes to get ready before class started. It was an ongoing challenge between us to see if we could handle a shower and still have enough time to finish getting ready. Most days showering wasn't really an option, but today I had to at least rinse the sweat off my body.

I grinned and gestured to my hair which was set in a tight bun. "Without washing my hair, I'm gonna finish the challenge in record time."

She paused with the towelette she was holding. "Oh yeah? Let's see it." She pretended to look at a stopwatch. "A-aand, go!"

I laughed and darted toward the curtained-off showers. I couldn't wait to get out of my sweaty spandex. The warm water did wonders to rejuvenate me as I let it pour over my skin, carefully avoiding my hair. Less than twenty minutes later I was dressed and even had time to apply some makeup.

Janie bowed. "You are today's champion," she said in an overly-exaggerated tone.

"I couldn't have done it without my fans," I replied with a flutter of my lashes. When she laughed I grinned. "See you tomorrow."

"Later." She waved a hand before turning back to the mirror as she worked a flat iron.

I hefted my backpack over my shoulder and barely made it a few steps out into the crowded hallway when someone bumped into me. I turned and saw that it was Serena Powell.

"Sorry," I said, even though it had clearly been her fault.

She pursed her glossy pink lips and shook her head as if shooing a fly before she continued walking. The hallway traffic had parted slightly for our exchange and I shrugged before turning to walk in the opposite direction.

"Hey!" a guy's voice called.

I kept walking, my thoughts focused on the dreaded dissection awaiting me in my next class.

"Hey . . . Courtney."

I wheeled around in surprise and felt all the air squeeze out of my lungs. Tate Williams was walking toward me. Serena had stopped partway down the hall and watched us as people continued moving around her.

I stood frozen in a trance as Tate smiled before he reached me. I had to crane my neck slightly to look up at his perfect face. *Could this be real?* I tried to look composed as he raised an uncertain eyebrow.

"It *is* Courtney, right?"

"Um, yeah," I managed, hoping I didn't sound as breathless as I felt.

"I think you dropped this." He gave me a sideways smile as he held out my teal hoodie.

"Oh. Thanks." I took it from him and felt myself blush. *Oh. My. Heck.*

"I'll see you around." He gave me a little head nod and then walked away.

I stood completely still for a few seconds before remembering to breathe. I sensed someone staring at me and turned to see Serena giving me a calculating look before she flipped her dark hair and moved down the hall.

I probably should have been bugged by her obvious irritation, but I was too ecstatic to care. Tate Williams knew my name! He touched my hoodie! I held the fabric up to my nose and took in a deep breath, sighing heavily as I lowered it again. Somehow my feet found their way to the biology classroom and I floated through the door with a silly grin.

Eli was always easy to spot in a classroom. Half-Argentine, his dark hair and features were hard to miss. He smirked as I sat down next to him at our lab table. "So . . . not only did you *not* skip class, but I don't think I've ever seen you looking so happy. What's up?" He titled his head as he studied me, his hazel eyes glowing with curiosity.

I tried to subdue my grin into an innocent smile. "Oh nothing. It's just such a beautiful day. Don't you think this is the best day ever?"

His lip twitched as he glanced out the window and then back at me. "It's snowing. You hate the snow."

I giggled. "I'm not talking about the weather, silly. It's just . . . a great day."

Eli eyed me suspiciously. "I was all geared up to work out the details of our 'arrangement', but I was banking on the fact that you'd be desperate and willing to submit to my terms. Your good mood is ruining everything."

I tried to look offended. "Sorry my happiness is such a disappointment to you."

He gave me a crooked smile, then faced forward as the bell rang. "We'll see how cheerful you feel after opening a jar of *that*."

I followed his gaze and grimaced at the rows of jars filled with baby pig fetuses lining the long black table up front.

"Oy." I wrinkled my nose and clenched my stomach, already smelling the formaldehyde. "Good thing I didn't eat breakfast."

Eli nodded. "Nothing like cold, slimy pig first thing in the morning."

I cast him a warning look and he chuckled. The jars were passed out and we were given instructions on how to proceed with the dissection. Not even my encounter with Tate could save me from the nausea I felt staring at the contents of the jar.

"Here." Eli handed me his jacket as he always did whenever we had dissection. Even though I could have used my hoodie, I accepted his offer and held his jacket over my nose. I secretly loved the way the leather mixed with the subtle scent of his body wash helped cover up the sickening chemical smell.

He reached to unscrew the lid and then stopped. "Oh wait. I think you wanted to do the hands-on stuff this time—or am I mistaken?"

I waited for him to laugh, but when he didn't, I lowered my eyes. "Come on . . . you're not serious?"

His gaze met mine and he nodded once, nudging the jar my direction. "Unless you'd like to work something out?"

I glared. "You must be pretty hard up for cash to stoop so low."

His eyes lit with amusement. "Who said anything about money?"

"Well then what do you want?" I folded my arms on the table and raised a skeptical brow.

"I'll let you know."

Our eyes locked together and something in his expression made my heart stutter before I shrugged and looked away. "Fine. You're not the kind of guy who would ask anything unreasonable." I sighed and pushed the scalpel toward him.

Eli smirked, revealing the dimple in his right cheek. "Sounds like we have a deal." He snapped on a pair of latex gloves. I shivered as he pulled the fetus from the jar, and then tried not to breathe through my nose as he dissected.

I glanced over at him a few times while I took notes. His dark hair fell slightly over his forehead as he intently studied his work. He was one of the best students in class, and I knew he really didn't mind doing the dissecting—so what was this bribe business all about?

"How come you don't want money?"

He gave me a weary look, as if I should already know the answer. "I work two jobs. I don't need your money."

My eyes widened. "How do you work two jobs and still manage to get straight A's?" *And how did I not know he worked two jobs?*

He smiled and I was momentarily distracted by the way the subtle bronze of his skin contrasted with the whiteness of his smile.

"I work at a body shop for a few hours after school, and then a couple nights a week I work at the movie theater."

I chewed my lower lip as I considered this information. I'd never realized he was so busy. "Don't you find it hard to never have, like . . . free time?"

The corner of his mouth lifted but he didn't stop what he was doing. "I have free time, but I have to be thinking ahead too. I've got my mission to pay for, and college. I'm hoping for a scholarship, but there's no guarantee. It's all gonna be here before we know it."

I knew Eli's parents were divorced. His dad had met his mom while serving a mission in Argentina. I didn't know any details about why they'd split three years ago, but I knew Eli lived with his mom now. I never realized how much responsibility rested on his shoulders.

After a few thick seconds passed, I twiddled the pencil in my hands. "My parents want me to get a job, but I don't know how I'll fit it in with everything else." I bit down on the pencil and chewed for a moment before realizing it was Eli's. I tried to take it out before he noticed, but it was too late. He glanced up and his face twisted. I removed the pencil from my mouth and smiled sheepishly. "Sorry . . . I'll get you a new one."

He looked confused until he noticed the pencil and shook his head. "Don't worry about it. I'm used to my chewed up pencils by now."

I blushed and forced a small laugh. "A bad habit, I guess. I'm always losing track of which one is mine."

Eli waved it off. "It's seriously no big deal." Something passed over his expression and he cleared his throat before continuing, "I was just going to say that I think there's an opening at the movie theater for a few nights a week. If you're interested."

"Really?" I sat up a little straighter. Working at the theater could be fun, and it would be nice to have a connection there. "What would I do?"

"Nothing glamorous. You'd probably be working concessions, like me."

"That's okay. I'd have to be free for drill performances though. Do you know what nights it would be?"

He tilted his head. "The supervisor is a guy in my ward. I can ask him, but I'm pretty sure he'll be flexible. He's been super cool about my schedule."

I smiled. "That would be great. Thanks, Eli."

He nodded once and then resumed his work with the scalpel. "I'll talk to him tonight and let you know." After a few moments he glanced at me out of the corner of his eye. "What if we end up working the same shift? Do you think you could handle that much awesomeness?" His mouth turned up at the corner. "I know being lab partners is overwhelming enough."

"I think I can handle it." I leaned back in my chair. "I mean, who doesn't want a friend who torments them constantly?" I smirked and stuck his pencil between my teeth for emphasis.

He shook his head and smiled, but his eyes tightened slightly before he glanced away. "Yeah."

I tilted my head, unsure what to make of his reaction. Before I could question him, Eli turned back to me and the expression was wiped from his face. "Class is almost over. Let's finish this thing."

CHAPTER

three

Mom and I were decorating reception tables when Rose Lawson caught sight of us.

"Vivian Moore, you sit down this instant."

"Rose, I'm fine." Mom tried to look irritated but couldn't quite manage it as she sat down at the round table and continued arranging the centerpiece.

Rose turned her stern look to me. "Courtney, you keep an eye on your mother. If she gets up from that chair you make her sit right back down, understand?"

I saluted as Rose bustled off to help direct the other ladies in the ward with the last finishing touches. Mom gave me a withering look. "I love that woman like a sister, but boy can she be bossy."

I shrugged. "You need someone to be bossy right now. I know you've been on your feet all day and you need to take a break. Besides, we're almost done. Let the rest of us finish up."

We took a moment to survey the reception hall and I got little flutters in my stomach. The room looked like a fairy tale, with soft white twinkling lights and glass votive candle arrangements on the tables just waiting to be lit. Mom and Eliza had worked hard to make their vision a reality, and it had paid off.

"Where do you want these?" Alexis appeared beside the table with a box of wedding favors in her hands.

Mom was about to answer when Eliza spoke up beside me. "Let's put them at the tables, one at each setting."

I turned in surprise. "Liza! I didn't think I'd see you until tomorrow. Mom told me you've been running around on last minute errands."

She smiled, her bright blue eyes shining. "Luke and I just got here, and I can't believe how fast it's all come together. Everything looks gorgeous!" She spun around and pressed her fingertips to her lips with a happy sigh.

"Between Rose and the other sisters in the ward, I've hardly been able to lift a finger. These women are decorating machines," Mom said.

"Rose is the Relief Society president. What did you expect?" I answered drily.

Eliza nodded and turned to Mom. "I'm glad to see you're sitting down. They were right to make you take it easy. With such a big day tomorrow, you should go home and put your feet up."

She scowled and shook her head. "Everyone is treating me like I'm about to shatter. I'll sit, but I don't want to leave. I'm fine." She patted her round belly and continued arranging the already perfect centerpiece. I knew she didn't want to miss a single part of this wedding, so I gave Eliza a look and shrugged.

Eliza twisted her mouth and was about to say more when Luke came up behind her and put his arms around her waist, kissing her on the cheek. Her face broke into an enormous grin as she turned in his arms to look up at him.

He bent his head down, staring into her eyes with a look of total adoration. "Where do you want these?" he asked, gesturing to another box of favors at his feet. By the way he was looking at her, his simple question seemed more like an intimate declaration of love.

Alexis nudged me in the side and whispered, "Sheesh, if they're this bad now, what's it gonna be like tomorrow?"

I giggled and raised my eyebrows in agreement. They were more in love than any other couple I'd ever seen, and they were picture-perfect at this moment; with her long, shiny hair cascading down her back and his strikingly handsome face gazing into hers. They looked like they belonged on a brochure for blissful relationships.

"Ahem," Rose cleared her throat.

Eliza reluctantly pulled her gaze away from Luke's but he didn't let her go, instead squeezing her tighter as Rose addressed them.

"Eliza, would you mind coming around and giving everything a final once-over? I think we're finished but let's make sure we haven't missed anything."

Eliza beamed. "Sister Lawson, you are amazing. Everyone has worked so hard and I couldn't be happier with the results. It's perfect."

Rose waved a dismissive hand. "The reception place did most of the hard work. We just got to do the fun part. Come see what you think."

Luke released Eliza, but quickly slid his hand into hers. It was like some part of them had to be touching whenever they were together.

Mom moved to get up and follow them, but one look from Rose sent her back into her seat with a huff. Rose pinned her with a warning glance. "You can see very well from where you are, Vivian."

Mom grumbled something under her breath and then directed her attention to Alexis and me. "Will the two of you start placing these favors at the top of each setting, like this?" She took one of the little glass jars filled with candies and placed it exactly center above the plate, then smiled in satisfaction. "*Now* the setting is complete. I'll finish this table if you girls will start on the others."

"Okay, boss." I picked up the box on the floor and then looked at Lexi. "Let's work together so we can talk."

She nodded and followed after me with another box. Once we were out of earshot I glanced at her and whispered, "I've been dying to talk to you all day. You'll never believe what happened to me this morning."

Alexis set her box down and blew a strand of layered brown hair out of her face. "We've been here for over an hour, and *now* you're telling me something juicy? What's the deal?"

I smiled and paused before arranging a wedding favor. "I had to wait until my mom wasn't listening. Guess who talked to me in the hall today?"

"Who?" She set down the glass jar she was holding and placed both of her hands on the table, her green eyes shining as she waited for me to continue.

I couldn't suppress my excitement as my smile burst into a grin. "Tate Williams! He picked up my hoodie that I'd dropped and actually called my name so he could give it to me. Lex, he knows my name!"

We squealed and bounced up and down before she rushed around the table and held onto my arms, looking me squarely in the eyes. "Tell me exactly how it happened. In detail."

With a quick glance over to my mom to make sure she wasn't watching, I pulled out chairs for us and we both sat down. I told Alexis the story, and then we analyzed my five second encounter with Tate for almost ten minutes before my mom scolded us to keep working.

"This is huge, Courtney," Alexis said as she resumed placing the jars. "I mean . . . just the fact that he knows your name is like a monumental sign."

"Whatever." I bit my lip and smiled while shaking my head. I secretly loved hearing those words and she knew it.

"I'm serious! He obviously noticed you before, and if he knows your name that means he was interested enough to find it out. It's not like you have a class together or any mutual friends. He had to have made some effort to discover who you are."

I shrugged, trying my best to downplay the situation but I couldn't keep the smile off my face.

"Hey there, Blondie," my dad said, startling me. He put his arm around my shoulder and kissed the top of my head.

"Dad, when did you get here?" I asked.

"Just now. I came over as soon as I got off work, but it looks like you all have everything under control, as usual." He smiled and then looked between Alexis and me. "What were you talking about?"

"Nothing," we answered at the same time, too quickly.

Dad raised an eyebrow, but before he could ask more questions, Mom called him over to her table. "Looks like I'm being summoned," he said with a wink. "Keep up the good work, girls."

Alexis smiled at me after he left. "I think it's so cute how he calls you Blondie. Where did your blonde hair come from, anyway?"

I shrugged. "Who knows? My dad used to tease my mom about the milk man."

She smirked. "I would joke that you're secretly adopted, but you definitely have your dad's dark eyes."

We continued moving around the tables until all of the wedding favors had been placed. Eliza and Luke came to see how we were doing.

"Thank you so much for your help. I think we're done now, so go enjoy your Friday night," Eliza said.

I took my phone out of my back pocket to check the time. "That didn't take as long as I thought it would." Glancing back up I asked, "How are you guys going to spend your last night of being single?"

Luke chuckled. "I wish I could spend the evening with Liza, but my buddies are taking me out for bowling and pizza."

"That's their idea of a bachelor party?" Alexis raised an eyebrow. "When my oldest brother got married, you don't even want to know what his bachelor party was like."

Luke gazed at Eliza and shook his head. "I don't need any party. I'd give up being a bachelor right now if it was up to me."

When Eliza beamed at him, Alexis turned to me and made a gagging gesture. I giggled, mostly because Luke and Eliza were so wrapped up in each other they didn't even notice.

"What about you, Liza?" I asked.

"Jill and my roommates are taking me out for pedicures and then dinner." She turned away from Luke to face me. "Do you want to come along?"

Pedicures would be fun, but I wouldn't have much to talk about with Eliza's best friends. "I'm good. Thanks, though."

"Okay. Come in and say good night if you get in after I do," she said, giving my arm a squeeze.

"I will. See you guys later."

Alexis and I watched them walk off arm-in-arm. "Maybe someday you'll be holding on to Tate like that," Alexis said, giving me a meaningful look.

I rolled my eyes and smiled. "Yeah right." But I'd secretly been hoping the same thing.

CHAPTER four

Okay, I used to want to get married in winter because I thought it would be totally magical, but now I've decided there's no way. It's too stinkin' c-cold!" Alexis rubbed her arms and hopped up and down.

I smiled. "At least it's not snowing. Look how the sun makes everything sparkle." I gazed around at the frost tipped trees near the Salt Lake Temple. Rubbing my gloved hands together, I trained my gaze back to the glass doors where the bride and groom would emerge. I was too anxious to see my sister and new brother-in-law to be bothered by the cold.

"Courtney, isn't this so exciting? I've been waiting for this day forever!" Morgan Matthews squealed as she came to stand beside me. Luke's ten-year-old little sister knew exactly how I was feeling. "And look at this—isn't it beautiful?" She reverently held out Eliza's wedding bouquet. "I'm in charge of holding it. Mom said she trusts me, but I have to be extra, extra careful with it."

I smiled and touched her arm. "You're doing a great job. It's gorgeous." I bent over the bouquet and gently inhaled the fragrant flowers. "Liza's going to love it."

Family and friends milled about in front of the steps by the glass doors. There was a tangible feeling of anticipation, and when the doors finally opened, a cheer rose up from the crowd.

My breath caught in my throat when I saw Luke and Eliza. I covered my mouth as tears formed in my eyes. They walked out hand in hand, both of them absolutely beaming. Luke was dashing in his black tux, but it was Eliza who held everyone's attention. She was positively elegant in her flowing white gown and her hair pulled up gracefully beneath her veil. Her vibrant blue eyes radiated a light I'd never seen in them before.

Luke couldn't seem to tear his gaze off of her. He picked her up in his arms and swung her around once. She laughed as cameras flashed and then the crowd cheered when he pulled her in for a kiss.

"What did I tell you?" Alexis said beside me. "It's already worse than yesterday." She shrugged and added, "But they're so cute together it doesn't matter."

I nodded before making my way toward them. I had to wait my turn to give Eliza a hug. When she saw me she beamed and rushed over. "Court, this is the best day of my life."

I was trying to be gentle so I wouldn't mess up her hair or makeup, but she squeezed me tight so I squeezed back. "Congratulations, Mrs. Matthews." A small tear escaped but I brushed it away.

Eliza pulled back and smiled. "I never knew I could be this happy." She looked off at something in the distance. I turned to follow her gaze but didn't see anything there.

"What are you looking at?"

She shook her head wistfully and then turned her gaze back to me, squeezing my hands. "I want you to feel this joy someday too. Promise me you'll make this your goal." She looked into my eyes and gestured toward the temple behind us.

I was caught off guard. Why was she saying this? Did she know? My insides squirmed but after an awkward beat I nodded. "I promise."

She smiled and touched my cheek before being pulled away by other well-wishers. I glanced around to find my parents, and saw Mom speaking with the photographer. I made my way over to her.

She turned from her conversation as soon as she saw me. "Courtney, you look lovely." She put her arm around my shoulder and kissed the top of my head. "Staying warm enough?"

I pulled my hands out of my dress coat and showed her the gloves. "Yep."

"Good. I thought you might like to help with the pictures. Will you carry this and give it to Liza between shots?" She held up a white fur wrap which I eagerly took from her.

"Gladly." I nuzzled the velvety softness against my cheek. "It's so warm."

"Yes, and with Eliza's short sleeves she's going to need it." Turning back to the photographer, Mom asked, "How soon will you be ready?"

The short, Asian man dipped his head slightly. "Anytime, Mrs. Moore."

"Great. Let's get started before everyone's noses are red."

He checked his equipment as Mom herded the group to the temple steps. I glanced around to find the bride and groom and spotted them talking to a group of their friends. Luke had his arm possessively around Eliza who was nestled against his side. *If there was such a thing as soul mates, it would be those two*, I thought.

Eliza had confided in me that staying worthy to be married in the temple had been a real challenge. Anyone who saw them together couldn't help but notice the chemistry oozing off of them. But temple marriage was a goal both she and Luke had been determined to keep. I was happy they'd finally made it to this day, but something inside me festered.

As my gaze traveled up to the temple spires, I thought about Eliza's words a few minutes ago. I'd always had a vague notion that I'd get married in the temple; it was just expected. But her request had caught me off guard. Would I be able to keep the promise I'd made?

Especially after what I'd done?

"Will everyone please turn their attention to the dance floor as Mr. and Mrs. Matthews share their first dance as husband and wife."

All conversation at our table stopped as we turned to watch Luke leading Eliza onto the dance floor.

"It's like they're in a world all their own," Eliza's best friend Jill sighed beside me.

I nodded but didn't say anything; I was too absorbed in the scene as their song began to play and Luke swept Eliza into his arms. Their foreheads touched as they swayed to the music and stared into each other's eyes. Eliza laughed at something Luke whispered to her, and I noticed the way his face lit up as he pulled her even closer.

"Does this mean they're going to kick off the dancing after this song?" Jill's boyfriend Aiden asked, breaking me out of my trance. He turned to Jill with a rakish grin. "Cause I got some moves you ain't seen yet, baby."

Jill snorted as the rest of us laughed. When Eliza's roommates and their dates began talking, Alexis and I turned to each other and exchanged a look. We were the only ones at the table without dates, so we weren't as enthusiastic about the dancing.

Jill noticed our exchange and put a hand on my arm. "Don't worry, girls. I've seen more than a few guys your age and I guarantee you'll both be out dancing before the night is over."

I rolled my eyes. "Yeah and most of them are in our ward. That's just weird."

Alexis looked at me and bit her lower lip. "Why is it weird?"

I instantly felt bad for saying anything. I knew that she thought Connor Hamilton was cute. He was one of the priests in my ward and a nice guy. Although Alexis wasn't a member of my faith, she still took seminary and came to church with me each week.

Jill shook her head. "It's not weird. I had lots of crushes on guys in my ward growing up. And if either of you gets asked to dance, you'd better say yes. It takes guts for someone to ask you, so don't discourage them." She gave me a pointed look.

I nodded for Lexi's benefit, but I didn't think I'd have to worry about it. The only guy in my ward who had ever shown interest in me was Nathan Adams, a boy I'd liked when I was thirteen, but that crush had faded years ago.

As the last notes of Luke and Eliza's song faded away, Jill picked up her fork and began tinkling it on her crystal goblet. I grinned and picked up my own fork as I turned to watch Luke and Eliza. They laughed as the rest of the room joined in until it sounded like a chorus of bells.

Luke gave Eliza a roguish smile before dipping her low and kissing her firmly on the mouth, causing the room to erupt in cheers and catcalls. When he brought her back up, she looked a bit breathless but was smiling from ear to ear. He gave her another quick peck on the cheek before he turned to our table and mouthed, "Thank you."

Jill grinned and dipped her head in a bow before turning to Lexi and me. "He told us to do that cue as often as we wanted. Hopefully he'll remember his gratitude and not want to kill us after he sees what we did to his truck."

We all laughed, remembering the shaving cream, balloon and tin can creation that awaited the happy couple outside.

"Now it's time for everyone to join the bride and groom on the dance floor. Let's see some dancing, people!" the announcer said.

A fast song began and everyone at our table jumped up. Lexi pulled me out of my chair. "Let's go!"

I grinned and allowed her to lead me onto the already crowded dance floor. We took turns doing ridiculous moves and laughing hysterically as each move got more outlandish. When the next fast song played, the group formed lines on each side while people took turns going down the "aisle". Eliza and Luke went first, creating an uproar with a bizarre semi-choreographed routine they danced down the line. More people followed and I couldn't remember when I'd laughed so hard, but when Aiden got in the center and did some break-dancing, I was impressed. He really did have moves.

The fast dancing seemed to end all too soon and suddenly it was a slow song. Alexis and I began to move off of the dance floor when I noticed Connor coming through the crowd. His eyes were trained on Lexi. I smiled and moved slightly ahead so he could ask her to dance. I turned around in time to see her beam at him and nod. She gave me a quick, wide-eyed look over his shoulder before they moved onto the dance floor.

I grinned and continued making my way back to our table, which was now empty. I thought about hitting the dessert table again, but I'd already had two servings of cheesecake. Besides, there was no shame in sitting alone. I was about to take my seat when I saw Nathan Adams making his way through the tables toward me. I liked Nathan as a friend, but I definitely didn't want to encourage anything beyond that.

Pretending not to see him, I turned around and was about to head off to the ladies' room when I ran smack into someone standing behind me.

"Leaving so soon?"

I looked up and my mouth dropped open. "Eli? What are you doing here?"

His eyes shone with amusement. "That excited to see me, huh?"

I laughed. "Just surprised."

"Me too." He looked around for a second and then raised an eyebrow. "Wanna dance?" His face held a look of uncertainty and I thought about what Jill had said.

"Sure."

The muscles around his eyes relaxed as he took my hand and led me onto the dance floor. I felt a small flutter at the touch of his warm hand in mine, then scolded myself. *This is Eli, Courtney. Don't be ridiculous.* Although I had to admit that he was more than just a little good looking in his white shirt and tie.

I discreetly glanced over my shoulder to distract myself from these thoughts and saw that Nathan was watching us. When he saw me he turned and walked back the other way. That had been a close call. I couldn't help being relieved that Eli had shown up just in time.

When we reached the dance floor, Eli took my hand and twirled me around once, then brought his other hand to rest on my lower back. I giggled and put my free hand on his shoulder. "You dance 'old school' style, huh?"

His mouth curved up in the corner, revealing his dimple. "Just following the crowd."

I looked around and noticed that most of the couples actually were dancing this way. He glanced down at me and my heart skipped a beat as he brought our hands up and placed my other hand at his neck. "Better?" he asked softly, bringing his other hand down until both of his arms encircled my waist.

I found it hard to breathe. I shook my head and brought my hand back to his, trying to disguise the way he was unsettling me. I smiled and tipped my head to the side. "I like dancing like this. It's fun to try something new."

His eyes met mine again as he nodded and looked away, resuming our first dance position. "So you never told me what you were doing here," he said.

"Actually, I believe *I* asked that question." I tilted my head to give him a smirk. "I have every right to be at my sister's wedding."

"Sister?" His brow creased for a moment and then he looked over to where Eliza and Luke were dancing and slowly nodded. "I thought her smile looked familiar," he glanced down at me, "and that would explain your bridesmaid dress. It's . . . you look, um—really pretty." He swallowed and then looked away again.

"Thanks." I bit back a smile as I silently blessed Eliza for having good taste in formal wear. "But you still haven't explained why you're here. Do you know the Matthews?"

Eli's shoulders relaxed at the change of subject. "My mom did some design work for them. She told us if we wanted to go out for dinner tonight we had to stop in at a reception after. The only way she could get my brothers to agree to wearing church clothes was to promise there would be dessert." He gestured over to the dessert tables. "They've been over there since we got here. I told them to go easy, but I have a feeling they didn't listen. I won't eat anything to make up for it."

I looked over and saw two boys with dark hair that had to be Eli's brothers eagerly swarming the dessert table. I looked back at him and shook my head. "Trust me, there's plenty. Eat as much as you want."

Our eyes met again and he smiled slowly. "Thanks."

The song was ending and I found myself disappointed it didn't last longer. As we pulled away neither of us seemed to know what to say. After a moment, I looked up at him through my lashes. "Thanks for the dance, Eli."

A corner of his mouth lifted. "I wasn't sure you'd say yes."

"What? Why?"

He shrugged. "You know . . . I wasn't sure if you'd want to dance with your lab partner."

I laughed and slugged him in the arm. "You're more than just my lab partner, you dork."

He pretended to wince as he rubbed his arm. "Yeah, apparently I'm also your punching bag."

I folded my arms across my chest. "Whatever. You know what I mean."

His face straightened as his eyes searched mine. "Do I?"

My pulse sped up, out of sync with the slow song that began to play. What was going on here? Eli and I had been friends the past few years, but nothing more. It seemed like one or the other of us had always been dating someone else.

Because of that, he'd always felt "safe". Safe to just be my friend. Talking to him was natural; comfortable. But now I sensed something changing. I wanted him to ask me to dance again.

He looked away and slid his hands into his pockets before pulling them out to snap his fingers. "I forgot—I have some good news."

I raised my eyebrows.

He tilted his head slightly. "Do you want to—?"

"Eli, sorry to interrupt, but I think it's time we got going."

I turned in surprise to see a striking woman about my mother's age with glossy dark hair and olive skin. She smiled at me but spoke to Eli. "Who is your lovely friend?"

He shifted his weight. "Mom, this is Courtney. Courtney, meet my mom, Daniela Jackson."

She reached out and took my hand, surprising me by pulling me in for an air kiss on the cheek. "I'm so pleased to meet you, Courtney."

I loved the subtle accent in her voice and the way her eyes danced in the same way Eli's sometimes did as she looked between us.

"It's nice to meet you too," I responded, blushing a bit under her knowing gaze as she released my hand.

"Are you sure you're ready to go?" Eli asked, casting his mom a quick look.

She shrugged and let out a sigh. "I'd like to stay, but I promised your brothers they could have friends over for a late night and they're anxious to leave."

As if on cue, the two boys I'd seen at the dessert table appeared at her side, both holding plates piled with goodies. One of them tugged on his mom's arm with his free hand. "Let's go," he whined.

Eli frowned at him and said something in Spanish. My eyes widened. I knew his mom was from Argentina but I had no idea he spoke another language.

The boy dropped his hand and turned to face me with a sheepish expression as Eli shook his head in exasperation. "Courtney, these are my brothers, Gabriel and Caleb."

"Nice to meet you." Gabriel, who looked to be about fourteen, stepped forward and took my hand in a firm shake. Except for the youthful roundness of his chin, he was the miniature version of his older brother.

I smiled. "You too."

His eyes lit up flirtatiously as he looked first at me, and then raised his brows at Eli.

Eli gave him a warning look and shook his head before clearing his throat at Caleb. The youngest who had been tugging on his mom's arm was absorbed in his dessert and didn't notice. Eli playfully cuffed him on the back of his head and scolded him in Spanish.

Caleb scowled at him before setting his fork down and reaching for my hand. "Hey," he said around a mouthful of food, irritation evident in his brown eyes.

I bit back a laugh as I returned the brief handshake. He seemed like a typical twelve-year-old boy to me. I liked all of them instantly.

Eli turned to me with an apologetic shrug. "I guess we have to go. I'll text you later, okay?"

"Sounds good."

"It was lovely to meet you," his mother said again as she placed a soft hand on my shoulder.

I smiled and nodded as she dropped her hand and the family walked away. I watched as she put her arm through Eli's and leaned in to say something to him. He glanced over his shoulder at me and I gave a small wave. One corner of his mouth lifted before he turned back to his mom.

I titled my head to the side. It was sweet the way he treated her; respectful and protective. I wondered what his father was like and how on earth he could have divorced such an exotically beautiful woman who also seemed genuinely kind.

I felt a tap on my shoulder and turned to see Nathan Adams looking hopeful.

"Wanna dance?" he asked.

I forced myself to keep my smile in place as I nodded.

The dance with Nathan wasn't as bad as I'd feared as he kept the conversation light and friendly. I realized I needed to stop jumping to conclusions about guys in general. How conceited was I to think he liked me more than a friend? I was making the same assumptions about Eli and even Tate for crying out loud! Most likely I was deluding myself—but as I remembered the way Eli had just held me in his arms—I secretly hoped I wasn't.

CHAPTER

Eli: *How was the rest of the reception?*

Me: *Good, but it went by too fast.*

I paused and thought about last night. It seemed like the dancing hadn't lasted very long before Luke and Eliza were cutting the cake, and then all at once they were running hand-in-hand through our archway of bubbles and sparklers, off on their honeymoon. My throat felt tight when I realized that things would never be the same now.

Shaking myself from these thoughts, I finished the message: *So what was the good news you wanted to tell me?*

Eli: *I talked to my supervisor & he thinks they can work around your schedule. He wants you to come for an interview this Tues after school. Can you make it?*

I grinned and did a silent fist pump.

Me: *Absolutely!! Thanks so much for setting that up for me.* ☺ *I'm excited!*

Eli: *No problem. Heading to church now. I'll talk to you later.*

Me: *K. C ya.*

I sighed and leaned back on my bed. At least our church didn't start until this afternoon. I still had plenty of time to get ready. I considered going back to sleep for a few hours, but then my stomach growled. I frowned and got up from the bed, pulling a warm robe on over my pajamas.

As I headed down to the kitchen I decided the problem with my drill practice schedule was that I had a hard time sleeping in anymore. I'd already been up early this morning to get my phone back out of my parents' room.

I smiled as I thought about this new job possibility. It had been so nice of Eli to arrange an interview for me. My heart did a tiny flutter when I thought about how handsome he'd looked dressed up last night, and how nice it felt when he'd held me on the dance floor.

"Morning, Blondie," Dad greeted from the kitchen table.

I gave a small wave and made my way over to the pantry.

"Do you want pancakes or something?" he asked.

I turned to see that he was already eating oatmeal. "No thanks." My voice sounded gravelly since I hadn't used it yet this morning. I poured myself a bowl of cereal and then sat across from him. "Mom still sleeping?"

"Yes. She's pretty worn out from yesterday, though she won't admit it."

I nodded before taking a bite of cereal. He set down the Church magazine he'd been reading and rubbed his eyes. "It was a big day for all of us . . . I can't believe my little girl is married now."

I set my spoon down and reached for his hand. Dad never got emotional, except when it came to his family. I'd noticed him brushing away a tear during his father-of-the-bride dance with Eliza.

"I've never seen her so happy before," I said, giving his hand a squeeze. "It was almost like she was glowing. And don't worry, they'll be here visiting all the time. I know Eliza wants to keep a close eye on Mom."

He grunted and gave a quick nod. "I feel the same way. Your mom puts on a brave face, but the doctor has warned her to take it easy. We'll have to get pushier if she doesn't take his advice."

I paused with my spoonful of cereal and grinned wickedly. "So you're saying I get a free pass to give Mom a dose of her own medicine?"

He chuckled and aimed his own spoon in my direction. "Don't get too excited. Hopefully it won't come to that." He picked his article back up and we resumed eating in silence. After a few minutes, he glanced up at me over the top of his magazine. "Mom told me she talked to you about getting a job."

I swallowed and nodded. "Mm-hmm."

"Well, I know how busy you are, and I've been thinking I might have some things for you to do around my office for a few hours during the week. How does that sound?"

I fought down the urge to smile as I looked up to meet his gaze. "Thanks, but I actually have a job interview this Tuesday."

He raised his eyebrows and set his magazine aside. "Really? That was fast. Where is this interview?"

"At the movie theater. I'll probably be working concessions, but there's a good chance they can be flexible with my hours." Excitement bubbled in my chest. "A friend of mine works there and told me about the opening."

"Which friend?"

"Eli Jackson. He's in my biology class."

Dad's expression quickly soured. "A boy?"

I sighed as I got up to rinse my bowl and put it in the dishwasher. "Yes, Dad, a *boy*. But he's just a friend. You don't have to worry."

"Hmph." He took a drink of juice and watched me over the top of his glass. After setting it down he said, "Well, we'll see what you find out after the interview. They might 'say' they'll be flexible, but after they find out how busy you are with your dancing, they may have second thoughts."

I snorted. "Thanks for the vote of confidence."

He raised a hand. "Sweetheart, I have no doubt you're more than qualified to work at the movie theater, and I admire that you went right out and got an interview as soon as we suggested it. I'm just asking that you keep the office assistant position in mind as an option."

"I will. Thanks."

He smiled and I headed back up the stairs to get ready. I appreciated his offer to let me work in his office, but I had a feeling he wanted to keep tabs on me more than anything else. Now that Eliza was married, I was afraid I was going to be the sole focus of my father's worries.

Alexis had to nudge me twice before I realized I was supposed to give the opening prayer. A few girls giggled as I stood up to walk to the front of the Young Women's room. My mind had been wandering all over the place ever since church began. Trying to ignore the sickening doubt of whether or not I should even be saying a prayer, I quickly said it and then sat back down.

"You're totally in la-la land today," Lexi whispered. "Daydreaming about a certain someone on the basketball team?"

I gave her a sideways smirk as we stood to repeat the Theme. I rattled it off and sat back down beside her. The last thing I wanted her to know was what I'd been thinking, so I changed the subject. "How did your dance with Connor go?"

She gave me a warning look and held a finger to her lips, turning slightly to make sure no one could hear, but when she looked back her eyes were brimming with excitement. "So good. I'll have to tell you about it later."

Sister Larsen, our Young Women's President, made some announcements and then dismissed us for classes. Alexis and I stayed in place with the other Laurels while the Mia Maids and Beehives left to their own rooms. Once we were all settled, Sister Larsen looked at us and smiled.

"Before we begin the lesson, I need a head count for how many of you can do baptisms for the dead on Wednesday?" She looked around expectantly as only two out of the six of us raised our hands.

Sister Larsen made a note of the girls' names, and then looked around again. "Is that all? None of the rest of you can make it?" Her gaze seemed to stop at me.

I squirmed slightly on the metal chair. "I don't think so. I have drill."

She nodded and her brow furrowed before she smiled and began the lesson.

Alexis looked at me out of the corner of her eye, but I avoided her stare. The uncomfortable feeling I'd had several times over the past few weeks surfaced again, but I pushed it down deep.

Lexi had met with the missionaries and wanted to get baptized, but her dad insisted that she wait until she turned eighteen. She was just finding her testimony. I couldn't confide in her about this.

Sister Larsen taught a lesson about family history work, and I zoned out. Whenever we looked up scriptures I would take out my phone and follow along, but then found myself checking Instagram in between. After all, scoping out social media was more polite than falling asleep in class, wasn't it?

After what felt like an eternity, Sister Larsen finally wrapped up her lesson. "Girls, this is an exceptional time in Earth's history. Never before has this work been easier or more accessible. I'd like to invite each of you to participate in some kind of family history work this week. For those going to the temple, that's definitely doing your part. For those who can't go," she glanced at Lexi and me, "maybe you can spend a little time indexing or looking at the Family Search website like we talked about. No matter how you're involved, you'll feel the spirit of this essential work."

She glanced at her watch and then looked up at us with a smile. "It seems I've ended early today, so let's leave a few minutes for testimonies. If any of you feel like sharing, I'd invite you to do so."

I felt myself squirm inside, the way I had during the Sacrament. Church was becoming unbearable.

Candice Newton popped out of her seat and I released in inward sigh of relief. One could always count on good ol' Candice to break the awkward silence. She was the oldest of our laurel class and practically bursting with her testimony. I predicted she'd have her papers in and leave for the mission field right on her nineteenth birthday.

As Candice bore her testimony, I noticed Alexis wiping a tear out of the corner of her eye. Seeing this made me happy and sick at the same time; happy that Lexi was clearly feeling the Spirit as Candice testified, but sick that I couldn't seem to feel anything.

After Candice sat down, there were several seconds of heavy silence. A glance at the clock told me there was still plenty of time. I picked at an imaginary piece of lint on my skirt and looked at the floor. An uncomfortable sensation formed in the pit of my stomach and I knew I had to get out of there.

When I stood, Sister Larsen and several of the girls around me looked up and smiled. My face flamed as I quickly shook my head. "Sorry, I just need to use the restroom." I darted out the door without looking back.

CHAPTER SIX

Dang."

I ran my fingernail along the edge of my pinkie toe where the bright blue polish had run over. It was Sunday night, and I was on my bed with ear buds in because I knew Mom wouldn't approve of the non-churchy music I was listening to.

I was readjusting the magazine beneath my foot when the music stopped, replaced by my ringtone. I looked at the screen and immediately pulled out the ear buds and accepted the call when I saw Lexi's picture.

"Hey, chica. What's up?" I asked.

"I've been looking at the Family Search website and had a question," she said. "Have you been on there yet?"

I grimaced. Alexis had actually listened to Sister Larsen's challenge—and was *doing* it? I cleared my throat. "Um, not yet. I had too much homework to catch up on. I can try and help you with it later, though."

"Yeah, you really should look into it. The website is way cooler than I thought, and since my mom doesn't come to church anymore and my dad isn't a member, there's tons of work for me to do."

"That's awesome, Lex."

She must have sensed my lack of enthusiasm, because she responded a bit defensively, "It is. Especially since I can't go to the temple yet . . . it makes me feel like I'm at least doing something."

I cringed. How selfish was I not to encourage her? I'd never considered how it must feel for her to be an "outsider," so to speak. For the thousandth time I wanted to be angry with her dad for not letting her get baptized until she turned eighteen, but I knew it was pointless. Instead I could at least give her my support.

"You're right—it's super important and I promise I'll look into it sometime so I can help you." Since I knew I didn't have any more motivation to give than that, it was time to steer the topic. "So, you never told me about your dance with Connor."

I could hear her smile through the phone. "Court, he is so sweet! He was totally nervous at first; he kept stumbling over his words, but after a little while we were talking like best friends."

"Hey! Don't you go replacing your best friend," I teased.

She laughed. "You know what I mean; it was totally comfortable. And, holy cow—his cologne smelled so good! I can still smell it on my dress." She inhaled and then sighed.

"Really? I wonder if I could still smell Eli's." I held the phone to my ear and walked to my closet to retrieve the bridesmaid dress.

"Eli? As in Eli Jackson?" Lexi asked in confusion.

"Yeah, he was at the reception last night and asked me to dance. Didn't you see him?" I pulled out my dress and took a deep whiff of the fabric. "Huh . . . no luck." Disappointment seeped through me. It would have been nice to smell his after shave or body wash, or whatever it was about him that smelled so insanely good.

"How did I not know about this?" Alexis demanded.

"Well, you were pretty wrapped up in your dance with Connor," I countered.

"True." She paused. "So you and Eli danced together, huh? Did he ask you?"

"Yep." The memory of Eli's hazel eyes seared into my mind, sending a tiny thrill up my spine.

"Hmm. That's interesting."

I smiled and rolled my eyes. "What? You know it's not like that. We're only friends, Lex."

"Well you guys are lab partners, and he's mega hot. If I were you I wouldn't be too hasty in saying there's nothing going on."

I had to admit, she had a point. "*Anyway,*" I cleared my throat, "I have news. Eli hooked me up with a job interview at the movie theater where he works."

"What?!" Alexis shrieked so loud I had to hold the phone away. "You've been holding back way too much information, girl. Start talking."

I laughed and put the phone back to my ear, telling her all about my excitement and anxiety over the job interview I had for Tuesday. Alexis lectured me for a few minutes on my lack of communication skills. After I apologized, we talked for another hour until I heard a knock on my door.

"Courtney, scriptures. Ten more minutes and then it's time to turn in your phone," Mom called through the door.

I glanced at the clock, sighing at how quickly the time had passed. "Lex, I gotta go. Phone check."

"'Kay. See you in the morning."

I was glad she never made me feel bad about my ridiculous phone curfew. "See ya."

I ended the call and stared at my screen, seeing that I had a notification from Instagram. I clicked on it, and almost dropped the phone.

Breathe, just breathe. It took several more seconds before I let out a shaky breath as I stared disbelieving: Tate Williams had sent me a follow request. *Me*. A follow request.

My heart thudded so loud I could hear it in my ears. Was it a mistake? Did he really mean to send the request to me? What if I accepted and he thought my pictures were lame? Were there any posts I should delete before I accepted him? Should I request to follow him back?

I'd already made up my mind in answer to the last question; Internet stalking him would be much easier if I were legitimately following him. *And technically*, I thought with a smile, *it wouldn't be stalking anymore*. I couldn't believe he had actually sought me out!

Scanning through my profile, I made sure there wasn't anything too embarrassing. I was fairly picky about my posts, so was relieved to find that nothing required immediate deletion. The clock was ticking on my phone-time, so before I could talk myself out of it, I accepted his request and then squeezed my stomach muscles as I sent one back to him.

I waited in agony for the next few minutes to see if he would accept right away, but no such luck. Time was up again.

Feeling too giddy to be frustrated, I practically skipped to my parents' room and found them both in bed, reading. I set the phone down on Mom's nightstand. "Good night," I said cheerfully.

Mom glanced up from her book and raised an eyebrow. "You seem chipper. Scripture reading was that good, huh?"

Dad lowered his paper and watched for my reaction.

I flushed. "Yeah . . . it's supposed to make you happy, right?"

Mom's blue eyes danced. "Absolutely. What were you reading about?"

I shifted to my other foot and then slowly backed toward the door. "Oh, I'm still in Nephi." That was true. I had started in Nephi many times, so technically I was still there.

My parents exchanged a quick glance before looking back at me. "Good night, sweetheart," Dad said, returning to his paper.

"Night."

"Love you," Mom called.

"Love you too," I answered from down the hall. I was going to have to make my story more convincing or they would never believe me and I'd lose those precious ten minutes of phone time.

I climbed into bed and pulled the covers up under my chin, thoughts of Tate successfully drowning out the faint reminder to say my prayers.

I wondered if I would see him in the morning. After making a mental plan of what I would wear, I got up again and quickly stuffed my clothes into my dance bag. I had to look my best tomorrow and couldn't trust myself to remember what outfit to pack in the morning. I also threw my books into my backpack for good measure.

Feeling satisfied that I'd gotten things ready ahead of time, I crawled back under the covers and thought about what I would say to Tate if I miraculously ran into him again. I drifted off to sleep with a smile on my lips.

CHAPTER

I opened my eyes and blinked twice. I was standing on a dirt road I'd never seen before. The dirt was frozen and rimmed with patches of snow along the edges.

"What's going on?" I asked the still morning air. Clearly I was having a dream, but it was unnerving that I could feel the cold beneath my slippers. I turned to look in both directions and spotted a cozy looking barn several yards down the road. It was the only sign of habitation in this rural place, so I wrapped my pajama-clad arms tightly about myself and headed in that direction. Where there was a barn there was bound to be a house close by.

Everything was calm and quiet as I trudged along and took in my surroundings. I guessed it to be early in the morning. The sun was still on the rise, leaving only a pale reminder of its warmth along the frosty winter landscape.

I maintained my focus on the barn ahead. Even with my brisk pace I was really hoping that barn would be warm. As I drew closer, I saw the light of a lantern shining in the window.

I reached the large barn door and raised my hand to knock, then paused. What if there was some kind of psychopath in there? No one would hear me scream in such a remote place. Wherever this *place* was. Even though this was a dream, I didn't want it to become a nightmare, as my dreams sometimes did.

I lowered my hand uncertainly until a sudden stiff breeze chilled me in places the cold hadn't reached before. Shuddering, I decided to risk it. I raised my fist to knock, but to my surprise my hand went right through the door. I gasped and pulled my hand back, staring at it for a moment. A slow smile spread across my face. *A dream where I had super powers to walk through walls?* Awesome.

I grinned and held my breath before stepping straight through the door. I laughed out loud at the thrill of what I'd just done before taking in my surroundings. The barn was cozy, with a few stalls occupied by two horses and a milk cow. The animals seemed unaware of my presence as they dozed. My gaze traveled to the hay loft above before a sound to my left made me jump.

I turned to see a girl sitting in a chair near the window a few feet away. Her back was to me as she pulled the blanket over her shoulders more tightly and sniffed again.

"Oh, you scared me!" I said, putting a hand to my chest. When she didn't turn I took a small step forward. "I'm sorry, it was just so cold outside . . . I didn't know anyone was in here." I held my breath as I waited for her to acknowledge me, but it was obvious she was either ignoring me completely or had no idea I was there.

After a few more seconds, I walked forward until I stood in front of her. When I saw her face, I gasped. It was the girl from my dreams. The one I'd seen sitting by the pond so many times. "Who are you?" I asked.

She was bent over a book, reading intently by the light that shone from a kerosene lamp in the windowsill. She looked a few years older than me. I studied her face, fascinated to finally see her up close. She wore the same kind of clothes I'd seen her in before, with a long, heavy skirt and a white blouse that buttoned at her throat. What I'd thought was a blanket over her shoulders was actually a shawl to protect against the cold.

Her hair was pulled up beneath a wool bonnet, with light blonde wisps framing the delicate features of her face. Bright blue eyes scanned the words as she read, and a faint smile touched her lips.

I craned my neck and saw that she was reading the Bible. Who was this girl and why did she keep popping up in my dreams? I waved my hand in front of her face a few times and she didn't even flinch. It was like I was invisible.

The latch on the barn door moved, catching us both by surprise. The girl looked up and I followed her gaze.

A young man poked his head in and smiled when he saw her. "Good morning, Hannah. I thought I might find you here." He stepped into the barn and tipped his hat, closing the heavy door behind him.

So her name was Hannah. That at least answered one question. Her face broke into a brilliant smile as she stood and dipped in a small curtsy. "Good morning, William. Charles is up at the house, having breakfast with Father, I expect."

I studied the young man. I'd seen pictures of men wearing top hats, waistcoats, breeches and boots, but I wasn't prepared for how good they looked in real life. Although, I was pretty sure not every guy could pull the look off as well as he did. No wonder Hannah's smile was so big.

William removed his hat, revealing wavy hair that was just a shade darker brown than his eyes. He gazed at Hannah as he stepped closer to her with a mischievous smile. He took her hand in his and kissed it. My pulse beat with the look in his eyes as his gaze never left hers. "'Tis not your brother I was hoping to see."

She flushed and pulled her hand away, placing it at her neckline. "Well you'd better hope Father doesn't catch you out here. You know it isn't proper for us to be alone." Even as she spoke, the look in her lively eyes revealed that she didn't mind.

William straightened and glanced down at the hat in his hands. "You're quite right. I won't be but a moment. I only wished to offer you the same invitation I've extended each Sunday." He looked up and waited until her gaze fixed with his. "Come with me, Hannah. I know you wish to," he said softly.

She bit her lip and turned from him. "You know I can't. I beg you not to ask again."

His brow furrowed as he stepped forward and took her arm, turning her gently until she faced him. "I will speak with your father. You're of age . . . you should be able to decide for yourself—"

"No." She placed a hand on his chest and looked up at him earnestly. "You mustn't, William. You know how he feels about the United Brethren. It will only cause discord and I couldn't bear—"

Her lip trembled as William looked down at her and ran the back of his hand down her cheek, but she shook her head and stepped back, folding her arms over her chest with the Bible still possessively in her grip.

"I couldn't bear it if Father were to banish you from our home. He only allows you to come now because you are Charles' closest friend. If Mother were still alive to pacify him, things might be different, but I dare not let you speak to him on matters of religion. It would only anger him. Especially if he knew of your intention to persuade me."

William's head jerked up, his eyes filled with hurt. "Hannah, I'm not trying to persuade you in any manner. It's you who have confided in me your desire to hear the Brethren; to find a faith that speaks to your heart."

Her face softened as she stepped closer to him. "I'm sorry. I didn't mean for it to sound that way. You are the only one to know my true feelings," she looked at the floor, "but regardless of what I feel, I am the rector's daughter. Father has already lost a good portion of his parish to the United Brethren, and if I were to abandon him also . . ." she paused and looked up, her eyes empty but determined. "It's simply not a possibility. Please don't speak of it again."

William dropped his head, the firm line of his mouth indicating he wanted to say more. After a moment he nodded once and then glanced up at Hannah with a sad smile. "As you wish."

They stared at each other in silence for several seconds and I almost wanted to say something to break the tension. Hannah fiddled with the edge of her Bible and looked out the window. "It seems it will be a lovely day today."

He raised an eyebrow and smiled. "I think only you could find winter in England lovely."

So this was England. I thought their accents sounded British.

William's face softened as he took the Bible from her. "What are you reading this morning?" He flipped open to where she'd stuck a small piece of paper for a bookmark. He fingered the marker for a moment and her face flushed.

"I know I should have a proper marker. I've been meaning to embroider one . . . sometime."

He gave her an impish grin. "Yes. I know how dearly you *love* needlework."

She laughed and then let out a sigh. "One of the many areas in which I fail to be a refined young lady."

"And thank heaven for that. I detest refined young ladies; entirely too dull for my taste." His expression was earnest though he still smiled. She blushed, but before she could respond he glanced at the page in front of him. "You're reading in Proverbs?"

She nodded. "It's one of my favorite passages—"

"Trust in the Lord with all thy heart," he said, without looking at the page.

Her mouth hung open for a moment before she closed it with a wry smile. "How is it you always seem to know what I'm about to say?"

He regarded her with a look of longing for a moment before suddenly tapping his hat against his thigh. "Your father will be expecting you in shortly. I believe it's almost time for your church meeting. And knowing you, I'm certain you've not yet had breakfast."

Hannah blushed. "Yes. I'm afraid I've lost track of time."

He shook his head and smiled. A light shone in his soft brown eyes as he gazed at her. "You always were a morning lark."

Her blush deepened. "I suppose you know a great deal of my secrets; Charles always teases me so."

William stepped closer to her and lifted her chin with his finger. "Your secrets are safe with me, Hannah."

The air in the barn grew very still. I wondered if I should turn away; the moment seemed too private to intrude on, but I had to see if they were about to kiss.

Hannah's clear blue eyes stared up at William as he gazed down at her a moment longer. Then, almost abruptly he dropped his hand. "I'll be off then." His movements seemed forced as he replaced his top hat and opened the barn door.

Hannah remained rooted to the spot as she watched him, her delicate brows furrowed in confusion. It seemed to take her a moment to find her voice. "Take care, William."

He nodded and stepped outside. She stared after him as the door began to close. The sad longing in her eyes suddenly brightened as it opened again.

William's gloved hand gripped the doorframe as he looked at her. "I'll not ask you to come to the services with me again, but might I inquire if you plan to attend the county ball on Saturday next?"

Hannah's face bloomed into a smile. "Yes."

"Good." William's grin reached his eyes as he tipped his hat, and was gone.

CHAPTER

I startled awake at the sound of my alarm and slammed down on the Snooze button. It took me several seconds to register where I was as I stared at the neon numbers on the clock. 5:15. *Drill practice.*

I rubbed a hand across my eyes and tried to shake myself back into reality. I had been so deep into the dream that the weight of sleep felt even heavier than usual. Forcing myself into a sitting position, I pulled off the covers and shuffled over to my dresser.

As I changed into my dance clothes, images from the dream still lingered in my mind: Hannah's bright blue eyes and friendly smile, the way William had gazed at her . . . that strange conversation they'd had about United Brethren.

Normally I could only remember fragments from my dreams, if that. But every detail from last night was etched into my memory. I even felt sad that it had ended. I really wanted to see Hannah and William dance together at the ball.

Another glance at the clock pulled me out of my thoughts. I always slept in until the last possible minute, so I didn't have time to stand here in a daze. Pulling a hoodie over my dance clothes, I ran into the bathroom to brush my teeth and tie back my hair. Coach would kill me if I was late.

After throwing on some tennis shoes and grabbing my backpack and dance duffle, I tiptoed out into the dark hallway. Mom used to get up and make me breakfast before I had practice, but as her pregnancy progressed she'd eventually stopped trying. I was glad; she needed her rest and I'd never liked dancing on a full stomach anyway.

A quick raid of the pantry resulted in a package of Pop-Tarts, a banana and a bottle of apple juice. *Breakfast of champions.*

I slipped out into the garage and hit the button to open the automatic door. The dim light on the ceiling flickered on, illuminating my burgundy Buick. I sighed in response to the sight of my underwhelming vehicle and then climbed in before the frigid February air could hit me full force.

Normally I blasted the radio on the drive to school, but I found myself mulling over thoughts of my dream in silence. Why had it felt so different from my other dreams? What was it about seeing Hannah that had impacted me so strongly? I couldn't seem to shake the images I'd seen.

After a matter of minutes, and a few less-than-full-stops at stop signs, I was parked and jogging into the gym. Bright lights and warm-up music hit me as soon as I stepped through the doors. I slipped off the tennis shoes, replacing them with my soft leather dancing shoes.

Most of the girls were scattered around the gym doing stretches. I spied Janie yawning into a leg stretch on the floor and walked over to join her. She looked up and gave me a sleepy smile. "Morning."

I sat on the floor and mirrored her stretch. "Morning." Neither of us were very talkative in the mornings, and I was fine with that. The silence was comfortable and I liked quietly relaxing into my stretches. Taking a slow breath, I reached for my other leg and stretched my body over it, allowing my head to drop comfortably on my knee.

"Hey girls, mind if I join you?"

I lifted my head, trying to fight down irritation at being interrupted in my peaceful stretch, but the irritation turned to shock as Serena Powell plopped down on the floor beside me.

Janie cast me a quick confused look before smiling at her. "Hey, Serena. Sure . . . you can join us."

I nodded and continued stretching. Never mind the fact that Serena hadn't waited for an invitation. There were a few moments of awkward silence as Janie and I exchanged glances. I knew we were both wondering why she had unexpectedly started noticing our existence.

Serena flipped a glossy chestnut ponytail over her shoulder and stretched her arm across her chest. "So how are you guys feeling about the halftime dance? I have to admit, I'm a little nervous about that combination at the end. I can never seem to get it right."

I turned to her and tried not to gawk. *Was she kidding?* Everyone knew Serena's technique was flawless. She was the best dancer on the team. I raised my eyebrows and stretched into my other leg. "I definitely need more practice."

Janie nodded. "Yeah, that last segment is tricky."

Serena seemed to ignore Janie's comment as she turned her full attention to me. "Whatever, Courtney! You're always so good. I'm sure you'll nail it." She flashed a huge smile.

"Um, thanks." Now I knew something was up. Not only was she paying attention to me, but suddenly she was acting like we were besties.

I turned to Janie. "And I don't know what you're talking about. You had it down last Friday." With my face turned away from Serena, I gave Janie another look that conveyed how weird this situation was.

"So, Courtney," Serena forced my attention back to her. "I had no idea you knew Tate so well." She stared at the floor as she did a shoulder stretch. It was obvious she was trying hard to sound disinterested.

My stomach bunched into a ball as the pieces began to fall into place. I shook my head. "I don't. Why do you say that?"

She trilled a little laugh and I tried not to flinch away when she put her hand on my knee. "It's okay. I totally don't care. I was just curious. I hear he's been talking about you and I noticed that you guys are suddenly friends on Instagram. I just didn't realize you knew each other. He never said anything about you when we were dating."

She pinned me with her gaze and I felt paralyzed. I was stuck on the fact that Tate had been talking about me. With whom? About what? I couldn't show how excited the thought made me feel, especially with Serena's hawk-like radar tracking my every reaction.

I raised my eyebrows and shook my head again. "I'm sorry, but I really don't know what you're talking about. Yeah, he followed me on Instagram, but I'm sure he follows dozens of people every day. Don't we all?"

Janie watched the two of us like she was observing a tennis match. She quickly interjected, "Yeah, I follow people all the time." She offered a weak smile in an attempt to defuse the tension.

Serena smiled back, but her eyes were calculating. "Tate doesn't. He's very selective in who he follows." She turned to me. "If I didn't know any better, I'd say he was interested in you, Courtney." She tried to make the words sound light, but they held a threatening undercurrent.

I shook my head more forcefully, cursing the telltale flush that was creeping up my neck. "I'm sure you're wrong. Whatever you've heard is just rumors."

Coach Weaver called us to start our warm-up jog, saving me from further scrutiny. Serena flashed me another smile but said nothing as she jumped up. After taking a few steps backward she said, "You should hang out with me and my friends at lunch today . . . Janie too. We're going to the Tasty Freeze. See you guys there?"

I glanced nervously at Janie. "Um . . ."

"Sure. We'll see you there," Janie answered quickly.

Serena nodded before jogging away to catch up with her clique. After they were a good distance ahead, I turned to Janie as we jogged. "Why did you tell her we'd go? That was one of the most awkward conversations I've ever had. It's like she's out to get me," I whispered.

Janie nodded. "Exactly. If you'd said no she would have been even more suspicious. You've got to stay on Serena's good side. I've known her since grade school and I've seen the kinds of devious things she's capable of." She took a few breaths as we jogged around the gym before continuing, "If what you said is true and there's nothing going on between you and Tate, then there's nothing to be afraid of. Just clear the air with Serena and she'll leave you alone."

When I didn't respond right away, Janie slowed down and turned to me. "Wait . . . *is* there something going on between you guys?"

I scrunched up my brows. "Not technically . . ."

She stopped jogging. "What?! Are you serious?"

"Shh!" I pulled on her arm to keep her going before Coach caught us. "Here's the deal, I honestly don't know what's going on. Last week Tate stopped me in the hall because I'd dropped my hoodie. That was the first time I realized he knew my name. Then, last night he started following me on Instagram. I'm sure it's nothing, but if what Serena said is true and he's been talking about me, well . . ." I bit my lip and tried to rein in the excitement fluttering in my ribcage. "Let's just say if Tate was interested, I wouldn't discourage him. I've been crushing on the guy since last year."

Janie's eyes bulged. "Oh my . . . *wow*!" She blew out a breath and then panted a laugh as we kept jogging. "I wish I would have known that before agreeing to meet up with Serena for lunch. Sorry, Court."

I held my side where an ache was starting to form. "No worries. You didn't know. I just hope it goes well and I can get her off my case."

She nodded. "You know what they say: keep your friends close and your enemies closer."

"You're always so full of wisdom . . . or cheesy clichés." I nudged her. "But maybe you're right. Maybe being Serena's 'frenemy' is the best thing to do."

I turned to glance across the gym where Serena led a pack of her friends in the jog. She definitely had a competitive side. And with her picture perfect—well—*everything*, I was willing to bet she usually got what she wanted in the end.

CHAPTER

I was on my way to biology when I heard my name.

"Courtney, wait up."

My heart did a crazy staccato as I turned slowly and saw Tate coming toward me down the hall. I was far away from the locker room by now, but I still glanced through the crowded hallway for any sign of Serena. If she saw me talking to Tate, lunch would be a nightmare. Luckily there was no sign of her.

I tried to act casual as I waited for Tate to catch up. He somehow pulled off that tousled look with his sandy blonde hair and made whatever he wore look good. *Really good.* My stomach squeezed in anticipation.

When he reached me he smiled and I was instantly lost in his marine-colored eyes.

"I noticed we're usually headed the same direction this period. Mind if I walk you to class?" he asked.

The spicy scent of his cologne made me feel a bit lightheaded. "Sure. What class do you have?" *Did I just manage to sound calm and collected?* Maybe it was the fact that I was wearing my favorite outfit and had paid extra attention to my makeup that gave me a boost of confidence . . . or the fact that I'd heard Tate had been talking about me. Whatever the reason, I congratulated myself on my composure.

Tate fell into an easy stride next to me. "I've got Trig. Where are you headed?"

"Biology."

He nodded. "I liked that class last year, dissecting all kinds of crazy stuff."

I wrinkled my nose. "Yeah, I actually don't love the dissecting, but the rest isn't so bad."

"Well if you ever need help, you know, studying . . . I did pretty well in that class."

His broad shoulder accidentally bumped into mine and the contact, coupled with his unexpected offer, almost knocked me off my feet. I stumbled and he reached out an arm to catch me. "Whoa. Sorry about that."

I laughed and fought the heat rising to my cheeks. "I'm okay, just kind of a klutz, that's all."

He kept his hand on my arm for a few seconds after I was steady and then dropped it. "I've seen you dance. You're not a klutz."

"You've seen me dance?" I continued walking, too flustered to look him in the eye.

"Yeah. I've noticed you on the drill team and you're really good."

"Um, thanks." I didn't like thinking about the drill team. It reminded me of the fact that he and Serena used to be together. We were almost to the biology room so I slowed my pace and turned to him. "And thanks for your offer to help me study. I might take you up on it sometime."

He gave me a crooked smile. "I hope so." He slid his hands into his pockets and straightened his shoulders, making him look even taller. "Maybe I can walk you to class again tomorrow?"

Just then Eli showed up behind Tate. He glanced quickly between the two of us, his face a mask. "Hey, Court."

"Hey, Eli." I smiled at him.

Tate turned to see who I was talking to.

Eli gave him a head nod. "Mind if I get past?"

Tate seemed to size him up for a second. "Sure." He stepped out of the way and Eli moved past us. Tate stared after him and then looked back at me. "So . . . tomorrow?"

I glanced up and smiled, my stomach doing little flip-flops. "Yeah. Tomorrow sounds good."

He nodded and gave me another smile before moving off down the hall. I stood motionless for a moment and then walked into the biology room. I noticed Eli watching me as I entered, but he looked away as soon as we made eye contact.

I sat down in my seat and busied myself with getting out my book, all-too-aware of the tension practically radiating off of my lab partner.

"So, you and Tate Williams, huh? When did that happen?" His tone held too much of the Serena "pretending-not-to-care-but-really-caring" thing that I was starting to get tired of. I rolled my eyes before reaching back into my bag for a binder. "He walked me to class—big deal. What is this, junior high?"

He raised an eyebrow. "You seem kind of touchy about something that's not a big deal."

I gave him a look and he smiled faintly before opening his notebook. "I'm just thinking he might be the reason why you came to class so happy last week, and I heard him ask to walk you to class tomorrow, so I just figured . . ." he let the words trail off as he wrote the date on the top of his page.

When I didn't respond, he flicked my pencil. "Come on, you used to always talk to me about your relationships."

"Only because you talked about yours."

His head lifted in surprise and I blushed. Where had that come from?

I shrugged. "Sorry. I guess I am a little touchy, but it's because there's nothing to tell. I hardly even know him." Why did it bother me to talk about this with Eli? He was my friend. I should be able to confide in him, but a big part of me didn't want to. In fact, a big part of me wanted to tell him there was nothing going on with Tate and that I was available. Why was I so mixed up?

Class started and saved me from having to continue the conversation. I wanted us to get back to our usual, joking-around selves, but Eli remained silent for the rest of the class. When the bell rang he gathered up his bag.

I reached for his arm. "Eli, I never told you how grateful I am that you got me the job interview. I'm really excited about it."

He looked down at my hand on his arm. When his gaze finally met mine, there was something unreadable in his hazel eyes. I wished I could dissect his thoughts.

"It's no big deal. Just something any friend would do," he said.

Even though his tone had been neutral, the words stung somehow. I attempted a smile. "Well, still . . . thanks again."

He nodded and then walked away. Normally we left class together. I frowned as I followed him with my gaze and then picked up my bag, wondering what other ups and downs awaited me today.

"I still don't see why we have to do this," Alexis complained. "Let's just ditch and you can come up with an excuse why you couldn't make it. The last thing I want to do is eat lunch with Serena Powell and her groupies."

Janie laughed from the backseat. "Amen to that. But it's just one lunch. Hopefully there won't be room to sit by them and we can have a booth to ourselves."

I hoped Janie was right as I pulled into the parking lot of the Tasty Freeze. A gnawing sensation formed in my stomach as I saw Serena's sporty SUV. I put my Buick in park and turned to face my friends. "Guys, there's something else."

"What?" Alexis asked.

"Tate walked me to my class this morning. He offered to help me study for biology, and then asked if he could walk me to class again tomorrow." I gripped the steering wheel as the words came tumbling out. I still couldn't believe it had happened.

Both girls squealed.

Alexis grabbed my arm until I faced her. "Oh. My. Goodness. Courtney, there's no question now—he totally likes you!"

A grin spread across my face as I looked first at her and then at Janie. "I think you might be right. I still can't believe it, but he was definitely acting that way."

We all squealed for a few more seconds before I reined it in. "But you guys, what does that mean about Serena? She's going to murder me. In cold blood. I don't think I can sit through another interrogation and pretend there's nothing going on."

"It's not like she has any claim on him. They broke up, so he's fair game. I don't see why you think you have to be her buddy. Let's just get some drive-thru and then you can dish all about what happened." Lexi's eyes danced excitedly.

I looked back and gave Janie a questioning look.

She bit her lip. "Well, you can't run forever—being on the drill team together and all. But after what you just told us, I have to agree that lunch with Serena may not be a good idea right now. In fact, let's get drive-thru somewhere else in case she sees us."

Alexis turned in her seat. "You're seriously scared of her, aren't you?"

Janie gave a half-hearted shrug. "I just know how nasty she can be. But don't worry, Courtney. If you and Tate like each other, we'll back you up."

"Thanks, guys." I blew out a breath and put the car in Reverse. "Now let's get out of here. I already feel like I'm being watched."

We pulled back onto the street and decided on a nearby taco joint for lunch. Janie wanted to eat inside. As soon as I walked in, I froze.

My ex-boyfriend, Kellen, was sitting with his girlfriend Veronica at one of the tables. They had their heads bent together across the table as he stroked her arm. I cursed my bad luck. I should have remembered he liked to eat here.

Alexis gave me a strange look. "What's wrong?" She followed my gaze and then frowned. "Uh-oh. Let's go . . . we can find somewhere else."

Janie looked between the two of us in confusion. "What is it?"

I shook my head. "Nothing. Just an ex-boyfriend situation, but it's no big deal. Come on, let's order." I knew we wouldn't have time to go somewhere else and I'd already caused enough drama at the Tasty Freeze. I would just pretend I didn't see them and enjoy lunch with my friends.

Alexis gave me another look before following me into the order line. We got our food and then found seats as far away from Kellen and Veronica as possible.

I looked out of the corner of my eye and saw him staring at me, his jaw clenched.

Veronica tossed a glare my way before turning Kellen's attention back to her.

"Okay, I have to know the story here," Janie whispered.

I took a sip of Sprite and looked at my food. "You remember that guy I broke up with a little while ago?"

She nodded.

"Well, that's him. His name is Kellen Bradfield, and it won't take long to tell you our story." I took a bite of my burrito and then swallowed before continuing, "We got together at the beginning of the year. I met him right after Christmas break, and he was super sweet and thoughtful. We dated for a few weeks, and everything was going great. I actually thought I was in love with him." I gave a short laugh and took another sip of my drink.

"I remember how obsessed you were," Alexis added.

"Yeah . . . I was pretty pathetic."

"Well, he is cute, so I don't blame you," Janie said. "So what happened?"

Alexis turned to me, waiting for an explanation. I'd never told her the true reason I'd ended things with Kellen, and I wasn't about to open up in the middle of a fast food place.

I shrugged. "He just turned out to be kind of a jerk. He wanted to push things in a physical direction I wasn't comfortable with." I took another bite of food to avoid having to say more. I couldn't tell my friends that I'd made mistakes with Kellen before finally breaking up with him. It would be too humiliating. I'd ended the relationship, had committed to myself not to do those kinds of things anymore. So everything was fine now.

"Wow, he *does* sound like a jerk. Good job for ending it," Janie whispered as she sat back in her chair.

Alexis eyed Kellen across the room. "No wonder he got together with Miss Swimsuit Selfie," she whispered. "Looks like she's perfect for him."

I glanced over at Veronica's revealing shirt and ultra-tight skinny jeans. She did have a bit of a bad reputation. She and Kellen were playing footsie under the table and they had their heads together. I wasn't sure if they always acted like this, or if they were putting on a show for my benefit. Either way, it was nauseating.

"Well . . . at least it's been an entertaining lunch break," I said, attempting to change the subject as I turned to my friends with a half-smile. "But that's enough from me, why don't you guys talk now while I finish eating?"

I was relieved when they didn't object, and did my best to focus on the conversation as I tried to drown out the emptiness and guilt that lingered whenever I thought about what I'd done. *Everything is fine. You stopped—that's enough.* I just had to stay busy. That was the key to keeping the sick feeling from lingering. And with all that was happening in my life, staying busy wasn't a problem.

CHAPTER

ten

I waited until I hit a red light to read the text I heard on my phone.

Eli: *Good luck with the interview. Bryce is super chill so don't stress, you'll do great.*

I smiled, happy that Eli was communicating with me. After Tate walked me to class again this morning, Eli had hardly said anything to me during biology. I'd tried joking with him like we used to, and even though he'd joked back, something had changed.

I wasn't sure if it was because he didn't like Tate, or if something else was going on in his life that was causing him to be distant. Or maybe—I hardly dared to believe it—but it was possible he was jealous. Whatever the reason, I was eager to make things right and get our friendship back to where it used to be.

Me: *Thanks, I needed a pep talk.* ☺ *Be there in a few.*

I put down my phone before the light turned green. I let off the brake and willed myself not to drive too fast. There was plenty of time, no need to rush. My palms felt sweaty as I rehearsed the answers to the questions Eli had told me his supervisor, Bryce, would probably ask.

It was ten minutes to six when I pulled into the parking lot of the movie theater. It was already dark outside, but I was grateful that at least it wasn't snowing. I grabbed my purse and locked the car, hugging my coat around my shoulders.

I walked through the parking lot slowly, having to catch myself a few times from slipping on my heeled boots. I should have thought about the ice and worn my less-stylish but more practical Sherpas. Nothing screamed, "Hire me!" like hobbling in on a twisted ankle.

After a few more close calls, I managed to make my way through the front doors of the theater. A blast of warm air filled with buttery popcorn smell hit me. I looked toward the concession stand and saw Eli helping a line of customers. He must have sensed my gaze because he looked up and gave me a head nod and encouraging smile.

When I smiled back and his eyes lit up a bit before he returned his attention to the woman he was serving. Somehow he even looked good in the black polo and nametag he wore.

My attention was diverted by the cute blonde who was suddenly at his side. She looked my way and seemed to analyze me for a moment before whispering something to Eli. He nodded and she looked at me again before helping another customer in line.

Hmm . . . funny he never mentioned working with *her*, I thought, surprised by the flame of jealousy that seemed to ignite out of nowhere.

"Are you Courtney?" a man asked, walking toward me with a purposeful stride. He looked to be in his mid-to-late twenties, with average height and thick-rimmed black glasses. He wore an identical polo to Eli's and I could see the name Bryce on his nametag.

"That's me." I smiled and stretched out my hand, realizing a second too late I probably should have removed my knit gloves first.

Bryce shook my hand and then gestured to a nearby table. "Glad you could make it. Have a seat."

I took off my gloves and stuffed them in my coat pocket. More than a little nervous that our interview would be public, I began to feel overly hot and slipped off my coat, placing it on the back of my chair before sitting down.

As Bryce placed a paper on the table I noticed his wedding ring and remembered that Eli had said Bryce's wife had recently had a baby. I'd have to remember to ask him about that if I needed a conversation filler.

He looked up at me with a friendly smile. "Eli has told me lots of good things about you, so that's already working in your favor."

I willed myself not to glance over to Eli. "That's good to hear," I said with a nervous giggle that sounded ridiculously juvenile. I cleared my throat and straightened my posture to try to counteract the silly schoolgirl persona I was afraid I was giving off.

Bryce nodded. "Why don't I outline the responsibilities you'd have as an employee here, and then you can ask whatever questions you'd like."

"Great," I answered in my most mature tone. I folded my hands on the table and listened attentively as he rattled off a list of duties my job would entail. I could feel Eli and that girl watching me as the six o'clock crowd thinned out, but I forced myself to stay focused on what Bryce was saying. From what it sounded like, this job would be nothing I couldn't handle.

"So that's it—at least all I can think of right now. Any questions?" He stared at me through his thick-framed glasses.

"Um, I think it all sounds really good," I said. "The only question I have is about scheduling. I'm not sure if Eli told you that I'm on our high school drill team, but I have game nights every so often that I'll need to be available for. Is that something you think you can work with?"

He leaned back in his chair and put his arms behind his head. "Yeah, Eli told me about that. It shouldn't be a problem, as long as you know your schedule a few weeks ahead of time so I can figure out which shifts to put you on."

"Absolutely. I can get you a print copy or email our drill schedule right now if you'd like." I felt a tiny swelling of pride that I sounded so prepared.

"Cool. If you've got it on your phone just shoot me an email and I'll look it over." He leaned forward again and wrote his email address on the paper in front of him, sliding it across the table to me.

As I typed the address into my phone, he continued talking, "I have a few more questions for you, but if everything looks good on your schedule I'm fairly confident we can find a spot for you here."

I looked up from my phone with wide eyes. "Really? That's awesome!" So much for pretending to be mature, it was all I could do to hold back a squeal.

He smiled. "These interviews are more of a formality. I like getting referrals from employees I know I can trust. You're lucky Eli thinks so highly of you. He's one of my best workers." He glanced Eli's direction before turning back and winking at me.

I felt myself blush. Just what exactly had Eli said? I quickly sent the email and answered a few more of Bryce's questions, which were mostly about things I'd filled out on my application.

"Well, this is all looking good," he said. "Why don't we go over and I can show you around the concession stand and employee room." He stood and I followed him over to where Eli and that girl were watching from behind the counter.

Eli waited until Bryce wasn't looking and raised his eyebrows, giving me a questioning thumbs up. I smiled and shrugged. It had to be a good sign that Bryce was showing me around the place, right?

"This is where you'll be working," Bryce said, opening a small door to allow us behind the counter.

"Does that mean she got the job?" Eli asked.

Bryce smiled. "Yes, Courtney's officially hired—if she wants the job?" He turned to me.

I beamed. "Absolutely! Thank you so much."

Eli grinned, the smile reaching his hazel eyes.

The girl with the blonde hair didn't look happy as she crossed her arms. "She might not want it after realizing she'll go home smelling like popcorn every day."

Bryce laughed and gestured toward her. "Courtney, this is Ashley. You'll be working with her and the other six employees from time to time. Most of you are part-time, but a few of my employees work full-time during the day."

He turned to Ashley. "And as for the popcorn smell, isn't that what people love about coming to the theater? Consider it job security," he teased.

Ashley smirked. "Yeah right."

Bryce laughed again and I realized he must be as laid-back as Eli had said. I would never have dared to talk to my boss that way.

He looked around and then sighed. "Well, I would show you the ropes, Courtney, but I have some other work to do and Eli will do a better job than I would anyway. He trains most of the new employees." He turned to Eli. "That okay with you?" There was a teasing glint in his eyes as something seemed to pass between them.

"Sure," Eli answered with a shrug. He gave Bryce a quick warning look when he must have thought I wasn't looking.

"So I guess that means I have to man the counter alone—is that it?" Ashley's full lips twisted into a pout.

Bryce gave her a humoring half-smile. "You'll be fine. The next rush won't come on for at least twenty minutes. Eli can give Courtney a walk-through and then he'll be back to help."

He turned to me. "Just ask Eli whatever questions you might have. Your first shift will begin this Thursday. I've got Eli working that same night so he'll be able to train you on the job. Glad to have you on the team, Courtney." He smiled and then started walking away before turning around again. "Oh, and Eli, make sure to get her a couple of shirts." He looked at me and scratched his head. "I'm guessing small?"

I shrugged. "That probably works."

He nodded. "We've got a few on hand. I'll get a nametag ordered tonight. See you Thursday."

"Okay. Thanks again," I said with a smile.

He nodded and then walked off in the direction of the ticket counter. I turned to Eli with a grin I'd been holding back the past several minutes. "I can't believe it! I didn't expect to get the job so fast."

He grinned back, his hazel eyes dancing. "I knew you would."

Without thinking, I reached over and gave him a hug. "Thank you so much for your help. I owe you big time."

He seemed to stiffen for a moment and then hugged me back, sending delicious shivers down my spine as the firmness of his chest pressed into me.

"You're welcome," he said quietly into my ear. Feeling his warm breath on my neck was causing my heart to beat in a frenzy, so I quickly pulled away. When his eyes met mine the electric feeling was still tangible. "Now I guess you owe me twice," he said, tilting his head to the side.

I frowned and then remembered. "Oh right . . . our dissection deal. Good to know you're keeping track." I gave him a teasing roll of my eyes.

"Ahem," Ashley cleared her throat, her face sour. "Sorry to interrupt, but you guys had better do that walk-through before the crowds start showing up." She gave Eli a pointed look and I silently cursed her gorgeous, flawless complexion.

"Right," Eli said. He straightened his shoulders and turned back to me. "Let's start in the employee room. We'll find you those shirts."

I followed him out from behind the counter, feeling Ashley's eyes on my back the entire time. When we rounded a corner out of earshot, I said, "You never told me about Ashley."

He glanced sideways at me. "What about her?"

I shrugged. "That you work with her . . . or, anything, I guess."

One corner of his mouth lifted. "I work with lots of people, Courtney. You wanted me to tell you about all of them?"

I reddened. "No. It just seems like it might have come up, that's all." I looked at the black carpet dotted with neon stars. "I've never seen her before. Does she go to our school?"

Eli stopped outside a door marked "Employees Only" and opened it, gesturing me inside. "Nope. She goes to Ridgeline."

"That's cool," I said in a neutral tone. Somehow knowing she attended our rival high school didn't make me feel any better.

"So this is where you'll come at the beginning of each shift to clock in, and then out when you're done. You can also come in here during break time. Depending on your shift, you'll probably get at least two fifteen-minute breaks."

I looked around the drab room with faded white walls. There was a couch of questionable sanitation and an old tube-style TV in the middle of the floor. Another corner boasted a fridge and microwave.

Eli took in my expression and laughed. "It's not much, but sometimes it's nice to have a place to go and unwind."

I smiled and shook my head. "It's fine."

He showed me where the time clock was and helped me fill out a new punch card. Then we found a box of work polos and Eli dug through it until he found a couple in my size. "Here, these should fit."

As he handed me the shirts wrapped in plastic, I suddenly became hyper-aware of the fact that we were alone. Eli's eyes found mine as if he sensed it too. My breathing became shallow and I tried not to think about how good he smelled as I looked away.

"Thanks for showing me around."

"No problem." We stood in silence for another moment before he cleared his throat. "Well that's pretty much all there is to see in here. Do you have any questions?"

I looked up at him. "Nope. Not at the moment anyway."

"Okay." He seemed reluctant to leave. I felt it too, but we could only stand there in silence for so long before things got awkward. "Let's head back out to the concession stand then," he said.

I nodded and followed him toward the door, but before opening it, Eli stopped and turned to face me. "I'm not sure why you were asking about Ashley, but just so you know, there's nothing going on between us."

My mouth opened but before I could respond, he added, "Not like it is with you and Tate anyway." He tried to say it jokingly but his eyes held no humor.

"Wh-what?" I stammered. "Where did that come from? I already told you, there's nothing going on between me and Tate."

Eli shrugged. "You can stick to whatever story you want, but obviously there is. A guy doesn't walk a girl to class every day without it meaning anything. Especially a guy like Tate."

"What is that supposed to mean?" I asked, crossing my arms.

He raised his hands. "Look, I'm not trying to start anything. I'm just making an observation." He turned and opened the door, gesturing for me to go out first.

I glared at him as I moved past and then continued to fold my arms as we walked down the hall. "Well *you* used to walk me from biology all the way to my next class. So what does that mean, Mr. Observation?"

Eli flushed and I smirked, knowing I'd just pinned him in a corner.

"It means that I had a class in almost the same direction, so it made sense to walk with you."

I nodded, trying not to smile. "It's only logical."

"Exactly."

"Just like Tate has a class close to our biology room that hour."

Eli gave me a look and then shook his head. "You just keep telling yourself that, Court."

I secretly loved when he used my nickname, but I wasn't about to let it show. "So why did you stop walking with me after class?"

He turned and looked at me. I was fascinated by his eyes; sometimes they were more brown, sometimes more green or even gold. In the dim lighting of the hallway they appeared the color of rich chocolate. "I didn't want to get in the way of—you know—you and Tate."

I sighed. "You're totally jumping to conclusions."

He raised an eyebrow. "So you're saying there's really nothing going on between you two?"

I shook my head, causing my hair to tumble over my shoulders. "We're just starting to be friends. I've never spoken to him before last week." Why was I so set on convincing Eli about this? I was holding back some truth and while a part of me realized it wasn't really fair, I couldn't seem to help it.

He leaned back on his heels and slid his hands into his pockets. "Okay." He smiled and I watched as the light slowly came back to his eyes.

"Eli!" Ashley called.

We turned and I saw a line of customers at the concession stand.

"Dang. Guess I lost track of time." He turned to me. "I'll show you the stand on Thursday. It should be a slow night. See you in biology tomorrow?" His lip titled up in a crooked smile.

"Yeah. See you—and thanks again." I smiled back and then watched as he turned and jogged the rest of the distance to the stand.

Ashley sent me a scathing look before handing a bucket of popcorn to an older man waiting at the counter.

I ignored the look and made my way out of the theater, clutching my new work shirts and feeling excited about what the next few days would bring.

As I pulled into the garage and turned off the ignition, I heard my phone buzz. I looked at the screen and saw a text from a number I didn't recognize.

Hey, Courtney, it's Tate. I've been thinking about you . . . how did the interview go?

I gawked at the screen and read the message several more times before saving his number in my contacts. I vaguely wondered how he got my number, but didn't care enough to ask. He was actually texting me!

Me: *It went great! I got the job.*

Tate: *Sweet. Looks like I'll have to start spending more time at the theater.*

I covered my mouth to hold back a squeal. He was totally flirting with me! Could this night get any better? I tried to think of a response to his text, but came up blank. Thankfully my phone buzzed again.

Tate: *I heard you guys are performing halftime at our game this Friday. You planning on going to the dance after?*

I smiled and sucked in a breath.

Me: *Yeah, I'm planning on it. How about you?*

Tate: *I am now. See you in the morning.*

Me: *See ya.*

I locked the screen and dropped my phone in my lap, leaning my head back on the headrest to bask in the moment. Tate Williams was interested in me. There was no doubt about it now. I stared blankly out the windshield and then squealed out loud. I had to tell someone.

I picked up my phone again and was about to dial Lexi when Eli's face popped into my mind, causing the giddiness to drain away. I'd just told him that nothing was going on between Tate and me. I couldn't deny that what I was starting to feel for Eli was more than just friendship, but even though I suspected he might feel the same way, he hadn't made any moves. Tate was making his feelings pretty clear, and I was definitely attracted to him. So where did that leave things?

"Argh," I groaned, holding the phone against my forehead.

A tap sounded at my window, startling me. I glanced up and saw my mom standing outside my window with a concerned look on her face. Smiling sheepishly, I opened the door a crack, waiting until she moved out of the way before opening it fully.

"Hey, Mom," I said. "You scared me."

She wrapped her arms tightly around herself. "Sorry. I just heard the door open and wondered why you hadn't come in yet. How did the interview go?"

I leaned back into my car and hit the garage door button on the visor, closing the door to block out the cold. I grabbed my purse and new work shirts, emerging from the car with a grin. "I got the job!"

"Honey, that's great!" She leaned over her round belly to give me a hug. "I knew you would."

I pulled back and smiled. "Thanks. I think it's going to be fun, and they're willing to work around my schedule."

As we walked back into the house, I started telling her about the interview, but I couldn't help noticing how hard she was breathing after taking the few short steps to get inside.

"Mom, are you okay?"

She waved a hand. "I'm fine. Keep telling me about the interview." Although she tried hard to disguise it, her words came out a little breathless.

I frowned. "Okay, but sit down first. Where's Dad?"

"He had some meetings at the church. He should be back soon."

I nodded. My dad was a counselor in the bishopric, so he was often busy with meetings. I got my mom a glass of water and then told her how the rest of the interview had gone.

As we were talking my phone buzzed again. I picked it up and my heart thudded when I saw who the message was from.

"Is everything okay?" Mom asked after a few seconds.

I glanced up. "Yeah, why?"

"You just look concerned. Who is that message from?"

I shook my head slightly to jar myself back to our conversation. "It's just a message from my friend who got me the job. He wanted to tell me congrats." I smiled in what I hoped was a convincingly casual way.

Mom gave me an appraising look and then nodded. "That's nice." She must have sensed that I wanted a change of subject. Tracing her finger along the bottom edge of her glass, she said, "I saw on the email Sister Larsen sent out that you guys are doing baptisms for the dead tomorrow. That should be fun."

Ugh. That wasn't the change of subject I'd been hoping for. I looked down at my phone for a second as I tried to collect my thoughts. "Yeah. I really wish I could go, but I have this huge biology test Thursday that I'm totally not prepared for and I kind of already joined a study group." I glanced up and met Mom's eyes with the most regretful look I could manage. If I held her gaze, she wouldn't suspect I was lying.

She frowned. "Courtney, you know how I feel about you missing activities. Especially one like this. Nothing could help you more in your life than spending time in the temple. They were asking for a few priesthood volunteers and I was thinking it would be nice if Dad could go with you. He used to go with Eliza and it was really special for them."

I'm sure it was. I loved my sister, but I wished my parents would stop expecting me to be her carbon copy. I would never live up to that.

"I think you should change your study group time to make this work." Mom's eyes searched mine.

I stood up from the table. "Sorry, but I really can't. I'll go with Dad some other time to make up for it. We'll have a daddy-daughter date."

She frowned and gave me a skeptical look.

I held up my hands. "I promise."

She continued looking at me and I hated seeing the disappointment in her eyes. After a few moments she sighed. "Okay. It's your decision. But I hope you realize how serious a promise is."

I nodded and grabbed an apple from the bowl on the counter. "I do." Twisting the stem in my fingers, I said, "I'd love to stay and chat, but I still have tons of homework to catch up on."

Mom nodded and I didn't hesitate before bounding up the stairs to my room. Guilt seemed to trail my every step, along with that same sick feeling I'd been trying to ignore the past month.

I pulled my phone out of my pocket as I took a bite of the apple. I still needed to reply to Eli's text. As I entered my room and looked at the stack of books waiting on my bed, I debated whether or not to start on my homework before texting him back. It only took me a second to make a decision.

The homework could wait a few more minutes. Besides, thinking about my current boy issues was the quickest way to push the emptiness to the back of my mind where it belonged.

I flopped onto my bed and texted Eli. After a twenty-minute conversation that mostly revolved around the theater and biology homework, Eli texted that he had to study.

I locked my screen and held onto my phone as I rested my head on my arms. I needed to study too . . . and I planned to get to it right after a quick power nap.

CHAPTER

Hannah sat beside a fireplace in a room lit by candlelight. She held a book in one hand while scratching behind the ears of a calico cat with the other. It was a cozy scene, with snow falling softly outside and the ticking of a clock the only sound. I let out a happy sigh and plopped down into a chair across from her. A dream in Hannah's simple world was just the thing I needed to unwind.

The front door opened, letting in a blast of cold air. Hannah snapped her book closed and jumped up from her chair to assist the man coming into the house.

"Father, you're home early. Let me help you with your coat."

"Confound it, girl, I don't need any help," he snapped, banishing the peaceful mood that had filled the room. He removed his hat, revealing gray hair and thick, bushy sideburns.

Hannah waited patiently as he handed her his hat, gloves, cane and overcoat. For someone who didn't need help, he sure treated her like a servant. But she didn't seem to mind.

"How was your visit to Mrs. Cavendish?" she asked.

Her father huffed and made his way over to the chair by the fire. "That infernal woman will outlive the lot of us. This is the third time I've been summoned to her 'dying bedside', and mark my word if I'm not called again next week. I wish she would hurry up and get on with it, and leave me in peace."

Hannah's lips pressed into a line as if to keep from smiling as she hung her father's things on a coatrack. She went to the sideboard to pour him some tea.

His sour expression didn't waver as he took the cup of steaming liquid from her. "Is supper ready?"

She clasped her hands in front of her. "Yes. Mrs. White has prepared a hearty stew for us. It should be just the thing to warm you after a night out."

He grunted and glanced at his pocket watch. "If Charles is not here within five minutes we'll begin without him. Your brother must learn to respect mealtimes and be punctual. He's taken to coming home late and I'll not tolerate such behavior in this household."

Hannah bit her lip and glanced at the clock. "I'm sure he'll be here, Father. He cannot help it if the mill requires he work a bit longer than usual."

"If that is, indeed, the reason for his tardiness," her father grumbled.

Hannah stiffened. For the first time I caught a spark of anger in her clear blue eyes. "Charles' integrity is beyond reproach. If he gives work as his reason, then that is the case."

Her father eyed her coldly, but before he could reply, the door opened again. Two young men stood on the porch, laughing and stomping off their boots before entering the house.

"Close the door before we catch our death of cold!" Hannah's father bellowed.

The young men stopped laughing and closed the door behind them. I recognized William as he turned and removed his hat. "Forgive the intrusion, Mr. Walker. Miss Walker." He bowed to Hannah's father and then darted a quick glance at Hannah. She blushed and bobbed a small curtsy. Mr. Walker made no reply as he scowled at William.

"Father, it's quite a storm out. I've invited William to dine with us while the worst of it passes," the other young man said. His face was similar to his father's, but the kindness in it made him handsome. His dark eyes were the same shape as Hannah's.

"And just when did you feel at liberty to invite dinner guests without consulting me, Charles?" Mr. Walker demanded. The immediate tension in the room was so tangible I was mortified, but before anyone could respond he shook his head. "However, I suppose we can't very well turn him out in the storm. I only hope there will be enough stew to feed us all."

"Mrs. White always makes a large pot," Hannah responded.

Her father glared at her before making his way to the dining table. "Tell her to bring it out then."

Hannah nodded. She glanced over her shoulder at William, a smile evident in her eyes before she disappeared into the kitchen. He watched her go, but as soon as she was out of sight he shifted uncomfortably, glancing at the door more than once.

Charles put a hand on his shoulder. "Have a seat, William. I daresay we've both earned some rest after that long day at the mill."

They sat down at the table, then all the men rose again when Hannah entered the room. She was followed by a plump woman in a white cap and apron whom I could only guess was Mrs. White.

Charles moved Hannah's chair out for her, seating her next to William. After he slid her chair in all of the men sat back down.

I was amazed by what gentlemen they were. Even that troll Mr. Walker had shown respect by standing when a lady entered the room. It was a far cry from most of the guys I knew, and the ladylike charms Hannah possessed were pretty much nonexistent in my world. Sure, maybe things were a little too formal here, but I wouldn't complain if a guy treated me with the respect these men gave Hannah.

Mrs. White arranged the serving dishes on the table as Charles and William carried on a quiet conversation. Mr. Walker blessed the food and then everyone began eating as Mrs. White bustled back and forth to the kitchen.

My stomach growled as I smelled the stew and freshly baked rolls and I wished I could have a taste. There were some definite drawbacks to being a silent observer.

"So, Father, how did your evening visits go?" Charles asked.

Hannah tried to warn him with a look, but she was too late. As Mr. Walker went into another rant about Mrs. Cavendish's blatant refusal to die, I saw William discreetly pass a note into Hannah's hand. Both of them kept their eyes forward, but I watched as the hint of a smile played at Hannah's lips as she slipped the note into the pocket of her dress.

The moment was so intimate and romantic, I grinned in satisfaction that I had caught it. *Way to go, William*! Curiosity burned through me as I wondered what the note said.

The rest of the meal was finished quietly and a glance outside showed that the storm had nearly stopped. After thanking the Walkers for the meal, William left out into the cold night. Hannah watched him go before asking to be excused for bed.

She carried a candle upstairs and I followed her into her bedroom. It was small, but cozy, with a dormer roof and window. A fire was already blazing in the hearth, keeping the chill out. Hannah closed the door and went over to a small writing desk beneath the window. She removed the note from her pocket and read by candlelight.

Convincing myself I wasn't eavesdropping, I stepped forward so I could read what it said.

By lantern's glow she ponders, m'lady of the morning.

My shoulders slumped. I'd been hoping for a steamy love letter at the very least, but this cryptic note? What was that all about? I watched Hannah for her reaction, but she didn't seem disappointed at all. In fact, she looked downright giddy.

A knock at the door caused her to jump as she quickly slipped the paper beneath the book on her table. "Come in," she called.

Charles' face appeared in the doorway. "Am I interrupting anything?"

She shook her head. "Not at all."

He raised an eyebrow and entered the room, closing the door behind him. "Are you quite certain? No poetic riddles from a secret admirer to occupy your thoughts?" He grinned and Hannah's face broke into a smile.

"Not that you would know anything about it." A light danced in her eyes.

He held up his hands. "Not in the least. Nor would I do you the disservice of offering any hints."

She shook her head. "I've made that mistake before."

His face softened as he watched her. "I'm sorry for the way Father treated William tonight."

The light faded from her eyes as she turned away. "So am I." Her face was pensive a moment before she looked back at Charles. "Father was in a bit of a temper about your coming home late these past few weeks. I explained that you can't control your hours at the mill, but he was still cross."

Charles stared down at his hands and Hannah furrowed her brow. "Charles . . . it *is* the mill that has been detaining you, isn't it?"

He glanced at her and smiled. "Not to worry, Hannah. It is something that relates to my work, if that's what you're asking."

Understanding filled her eyes. "Your carpentry?"

He nodded. "Promise you won't tell Father. I've been able to sell a few pieces already. It's what I love to do, Hannah."

She stood from her chair and moved to a dresser in the corner of the room. Running her hand along the top of the grain, she smiled. "You have a gift. Of course I won't tell Father."

His shoulders relaxed as he approached the dresser and leaned in to examine it more closely. "When I finished this piece I was sure it was my best work, but now all I can see are the flaws." His hand rubbed over a knot in the grain that was almost heart shaped. Something about that knot stirred a vague memory in the back of my mind, like a speck of dust floating just out of reach.

Hannah laughed. "You are entirely too critical, Charles. The dresser is perfect. It's the loveliest gift I've ever received. And you know I've put the little compartment to good use." She winked at him. "Someday you'll be a famous carpenter living the life of luxury in America, I'm sure of it."

Charles straightened and smiled tenderly at his sister. "Well if you are sure of it, then I'll not question you." He squeezed her hand and turned to leave the room but stopped before opening the door, the spark of mischief back in his eyes. "I may not give you a hint about the riddle, but I will tell you that Father has retired for the evening . . . should you care to venture out in search of your treasure, that is."

Hannah grinned and nodded before he winked and left the room. She bit her lip excitedly and glanced out the window. After reading the note again, she blew out the candle, grabbed her shawl and headed quietly downstairs. I followed behind and watched as she peered into the empty drawing room and then made her way to the front door.

With just the moonlight to guide her, Hannah picked her way through the snow. I was freezing, but my adrenaline kept me warm as I followed her into the barn which was only slightly less frigid than outside.

Hannah wasted no time going over to the chair where I'd found her reading her Bible in the last dream. The moonlight filtered through the small window, illuminating a piece of woven silk ribbon lying on top of a note.

Hannah beamed and picked up the scarlet ribbon which had her name beautifully embroidered in gold thread. She slid it through her hands tenderly before picking up the note.

Now you have a proper place marker for your reading. Don't forget your promise to attend the ball. I expect you to save me a dance.

She held the note to her chest and sighed a moment before quickly hiding it in the pocket of her dress. I followed her out of the barn and back to the house, impressed by how stealthy she was.

I was willing to bet this wasn't the first time she'd snuck out, and I would know. I'd snuck out a few times when I was dating Kellen—until I got caught. That hadn't been pretty. I hoped for Hannah's sake that her father really was asleep like Charles had said.

She tiptoed through the dark and up the stairs into her bedroom, pausing to light a candle before moving to the dresser again. She carefully slid open the top drawer and removed an armful of petticoats, placing them on the bed.

I took a step closer, curious as to what she could be up to, when suddenly she popped out a piece of wood from the bottom of the drawer. I gasped. A false bottom! I stepped even closer until I was practically leaning my chin on Hannah's shoulder in an attempt to see. The little compartment was filled with notes like the one she'd found in the barn, along with trinkets of all kinds. A small leather-bound book caught my eye.

"Hey, is that your journal?" After so many dreams of watching her write in her journal I was dying to know what was inside. I willed her to pull it out, but instead she stepped back and removed the note from her skirt.

She brought the paper up to her nose and inhaled deeply, a smile on her lips as she placed it into the compartment. She carefully replaced the false bottom and petticoats before reaching back into her pocket for the bookmark.

Her face glowed as she opened her Bible and removed the scrap of paper she'd been using to keep her place. The ribbon looked beautiful against the worn pages. Hannah admired it a moment before taking it out to hold as she read her Bible by candlelight.

"Reading your Bible again, huh?" I sighed and slumped into a chair. I'd been hoping for something a bit more exciting when Hannah had gotten the note—like maybe a secret meeting with William. But now it was clear the excitement was over.

This girl really had a thing for her scriptures.

CHAPTER

I woke with a start and noticed something hard beneath my hand. My textbook. I glanced at the alarm clock. In exactly one minute, my alarm would go off. Great. So much for my "power nap" last night. I threw off the blanket Mom must have placed over me and quickly got ready.

On the drive to school I thought back over the details of my dream. Why was I having these dreams? What was my subconscious trying to tell me? Hannah and William were in love, but her father stood in their way of being happy. That didn't add up in my life. Sure, my dad was a bit overbearing when it came to boys and dating, but he wasn't extreme.

A thought popped into my head and I gasped. *William.* Tate *Williams . . .* was my brain trying to tell me something I wasn't even aware of yet? Was I in love with Tate? Was Serena the one standing in our way?

Thinking of Serena made my stomach churn. I was going to have to face her and come up with an excuse for bailing on lunch yesterday. I put my car in Park and turned off the ignition, gripping the steering wheel as I stared at the gym doors. I had to face her sooner or later—might as well get it over with.

I opened the car door, bracing myself against the cold as I hurried into the school. Janie was stretching out on the floor. She waved me over as soon as she saw me. I looked around but didn't see any sign of Serena. Smiling in relief, I made my way over to Janie.

Just before I reached her, Serena's voice stopped me in my tracks. "Hey there, Courtney."

I cast Janie a quick, helpless glance before turning to face Serena. "Hey, Serena," I offered the most sincere smile I could manage as my mind raced to come up with an excuse for why I'd never shown at lunch. Maybe I'd get lucky and she wouldn't mention it.

"So, we waited for you yesterday. What happened?" Serena's large blue eyes held an edge of accusation as she waited for my response.

I swallowed. "Yeah, I'm really sorry about that. You see—"

"It was my fault." Janie suddenly appeared at my side. She smiled apologetically. "We were planning on meeting up with you guys, but then I started feeling sick. Courtney was nice enough to hang out with me while I rested in her car."

Serena looked at me and all I could do was nod and shrug in response.

She raised an eyebrow. "Huh. That's funny, because I could have sworn I saw your car in the parking lot."

Crud. My mouth opened but no words seemed to come.

"Well that's because we were there, about to go in, when I told Courtney I felt like I was going to hurl," Janie explained. "She wanted to go in and tell you guys, but it was kind of an emergency situation."

Serena eyed her for a moment. "It's good to see that you're feeling better today. Must have been a pretty quick bug."

"I think it was just something I ate for breakfast. I'm good now." Janie patted her stomach for emphasis.

Coach Weaver called us out to start our warm-up laps and I released the tension I'd been holding in my ab muscles. *Bless you, Coach.*

Serena jogged a few steps away before flipping her dark hair over her shoulder to look at me. "Rain check?"

"Sure." I plastered a smile on my face while my head screamed, No! Why wouldn't she just leave me alone? The more Tate contacted me, the more Serena seemed to want to cozy up and be best buds, and the more I had to worry about facing her wrath if I ever got together with him.

Ugh!

After practice I booked it down the hallway as fast as I could, trying to make sure I was well out of Serena's sight before Tate caught up to me. When he touched my shoulder, I jumped.

"Hey, what's the rush?" he asked with a half-smile. "Are you trying to give me a hint?"

I turned to him and shook my head. "No. Sorry, I just . . ." I bit my lip and debated telling about Serena's antics, but then decided against it. "I just didn't want to be late for class."

"Oh. Have I been making you late?" He tilted his head down to look at me and I found myself drowning in the pools of his gorgeous blue eyes.

"No . . . I mean, not yet. I just have a big test tomorrow and I didn't want to be tardy." I bit my lip and continued walking, hoping I didn't sound as stupid as I felt.

Tate kept pace alongside me. "A biology test? You know, my offer to help you study still stands if you want to take me up on it."

I paused a step and turned to him as a light bulb went off. "Really? That would actually be super helpful if you wouldn't mind. I need all the help I can get." I looked up at him hopefully.

His lopsided grin was charming. "Sure. Since your test is tomorrow how about we study tonight?"

I did a quick calculation as I mulled this over. I'd told my mom that I couldn't do baptisms because my study group was planned for the same time. Our youth group was supposed to meet at the church right after school.

"Tonight works if it's the only time you're free, but this afternoon would be even better. Would after school work for you?"

"That depends. Do you have a hot date tonight or something?" Tate raised a playful eyebrow.

I blushed. "Yeah right. Just more studying to do."

The corner of his lip lifted as he nodded and we kept walking. "After school sounds good. How about we meet up at my car and go to the Tasty Freeze?"

I cringed inwardly. The Tasty Freeze made me think of Serena. It was also the most popular hangout in our school and I was sure to be spotted, but I didn't want to make any more fuss than I already had. "Sounds good," I answered with a smile.

We reached the door to my class and Tate gave me a nod. "See you after school then. Do you know what my car looks like?"

"Yeah. I've seen it before." I hoped that didn't sound too stalker-ish, but who wouldn't notice Tate's super cool hot rod?

He smiled and nodded again before moving down the hall. I walked into the classroom, looking for Eli, but he wasn't sitting at our table.

I took my seat and watched the doorway, but when he still didn't show after the bell rang, I felt my heart sink. Eli almost never missed class, but when he did the hour dragged painfully on.

As Mr. Sanchez began our test review, I pulled out a notebook to take notes, but secretly texted Eli beneath the table.

Me: *Where are you?*

Eli: *Naughty girl. Shouldn't you be listening to Mr. Sanchez?*

Me: *I'm excellent at multi-tasking.*

Eli: *I hope so. I'm counting on you to take good notes. They were short-handed at the body shop today and asked if I could fill in.*

Me: *Ditching school for work? How will you ever maintain your 4.0?*

Eli: *It's just a one-time deal. Speaking of those notes—if I can talk you into studying with me tonight, I'll make it worth your while.*

I sucked in a deep breath as I felt a twinge of guilt I couldn't explain. It shouldn't be a big deal that I was already planning to study with Tate, but I couldn't bring myself to tell Eli about it. I really did need to study for other classes tonight, but maybe I could swing it to study with Eli too. I decided to stay neutral for the time being to see how the evening played out.

Me: *Ha! Look who's bribing whom now.*

I paused, considering how to word the text.

Me: *I'd love to study, but I'm buried up to my eyeballs in homework. I'll keep you posted, but I promise to email the notes.*

I thought better of it after a moment and sent another text: *If you're willing to erase one of my "debts" that is . . .*

It was almost a full minute before he responded. I could practically feel his disappointment and it killed me.

Eli: *No worries if you can't study. I guess I'll consider erasing one of the debts in trade for the notes, but you still owe me for one. Now quit texting and pay attention, or your notes will be useless to me.*

Me: *Yes, sir! Talk to you soon.*

I locked the screen and slid my phone discreetly back into my bag. I had to focus on what Mr. Sanchez was writing on the white board, but I couldn't shake the feeling of disappointment that had settled in my gut. Little did Eli know that if I ended up taking crummy notes, it was all his fault.

CHAPTER

thirteen

I deliberately took my time going out to the parking lot after school. If luck was with me, Serena would be gone by the time I met Tate at his car. I was retrieving books from my locker when I felt two hands pinch me around the waist.

"Hey!" I spun around to see Alexis grinning. I sighed. "I should have known it was you. What's got you in such a good mood?"

Her green eyes were bright. "Connor just invited me to come to the temple. He said we could walk around the grounds or he'd sit in the waiting area with me and we can just hang out until everyone's done. Isn't that the sweetest?"

I attempted a smile and returned my attention back to my locker. "Yeah, that's really cool of him. So you guys will just sit outside while everyone else does baptisms?"

She titled her head. "I'm not actually going to take him up on it, silly. I'm going to bring some scriptures and read while I wait. I don't mind waiting alone. It will be fun."

I turned and raised an eyebrow, but she took hold of my arm. "I'm serious, Court, I want to go. And I'm forcing you to come." She pinned me with a look. "I know you don't have practice tonight."

I shook her arm off. I hated the fact that my best friend was turning into a major Molly Mormon. And she wasn't even a member of the Church yet. I should be happy that she wanted to go to the temple, but instead I was bugged. How many times was I going to have to get out of this activity?

"Sorry, Lexi, but I can't. I'm studying for a huge biology test," I paused for dramatic emphasis, "with Tate."

Her eyes widened. "Seriously? When did this happen?"

"This morning. I wish I could come with you guys, but it just isn't a good time for me." I pretended to arrange things in my locker, even though I was done.

Alexis frowned. "Well, that stinks. I was really hoping we could go together. But have fun with Tate."

I turned and faced her, arranging an apologetic look on my face. "Sorry. For sure next time."

She nodded and pointed a finger as she started walking backward down the hall. "Details. I want to hear how it goes."

I smiled and then gave her a meaningful look. "Likewise." I closed my locker and shouldered my backpack as I headed out to the school parking lot. My bag felt heavier than usual, but I was pretty sure my conscience had something to do with it.

Deep down I knew why I was bugged about the Alexis situation. She seemed to be moving upward in her life, and she was happy. Really happy. Meanwhile, I was struggling to keep my head above water. I felt like every day I was losing another piece of myself to the void.

As if to pour salt in the wound, I rounded a corner and ran into Kellen and Veronica making out in the empty hallway. They pulled apart and stared at me. Something ugly sparked in Kellen's eyes. He smirked and then put his hand behind Veronica's neck, pulling her in for a deliberate kiss. She smiled into his lips.

I felt sick as I stumbled past them and moved down the hall as quickly as I could. Kellen was a total jerk, and I had fallen for him—had allowed myself to think I had actually loved him. I'd thought that my feelings for him were more important than anything else, that the power of my love could outweigh the mistakes. And now, even though I'd ended the relationship, I couldn't shake the painful reality of how wrong I'd been.

I burst through the metal doors and out into the parking lot, taking a deep breath of the crisp winter air. There were only a few cars left and I spotted Tate blowing into his hands as he stood beside his Mustang.

I held onto the straps of my backpack, struggling to keep it from tipping me over as I hurried to meet him. His shoulders relaxed when he saw me approach.

"Man, I was starting to worry you were going to stand me up."

"I'm so sorry," I huffed, sending a puff of steam into the air. "I got caught talking to a friend and didn't realize how long it had been."

He opened the passenger door and I realized that the car was running. The engine sounded powerful even when it was idling.

"You should have waited in your car instead of outside," I said with a worried look.

He shrugged. "Maybe."

I'm sure he hadn't expected to be waiting so long. I felt like a total jerk.

After he got in the driver's side and buckled his seatbelt, he turned to me. "Still good with the Tasty Freeze?"

I nodded. "They sell some yummy hot chocolate. My treat."

"Sounds great." He gave me a sideways smile as he put the car into gear. The engine purred as we pulled out of the parking lot.

"This is pretty much the sweetest car I've ever ridden in," I said, running a hand along the leather interior.

Tate grinned. "Thanks. She was my dad's baby from his high school days. I couldn't believe it when he gave her to me for my sixteenth birthday."

A tiny thrill ran through me as I realized I was sitting in the passenger seat of the coolest car in the parking lot, on my way to study with one of the hottest guys in school. I was the luckiest girl alive. I decided to relax about Serena and just enjoy myself.

Tate and I talked and laughed on the drive. The conversation was nice, but still felt a little forced on my end as I grasped for topics. Talking to Tate didn't come as easily as it did to Eli, but I decided it was because I hadn't known him as long. Thinking of Eli made me uncomfortable so I pushed thoughts of him from my mind.

We pulled into the parking lot of the Tasty Freeze and Tate turned off the car. "Did you bring your biology book?" he asked.

I nodded and reached into the backseat, careful not to smack the back of his head as I hefted my backpack over. I hesitated and turned to him with a questioning look. "Are you sure this won't be boring for you? I mean, I feel bad that you won't get anything out of this deal other than some hot chocolate."

He looked at me and one side of his mouth lifted. "I think I'm getting more out of this deal than you realize."

My heart thudded to a halt at how close his face was to mine and the look that was in his eyes. I turned to grab the door handle in an attempt to hide my blush. "Well, I'll make it an extra-large hot chocolate. That way I won't feel so bad."

He laughed and we made our way inside. Luckily, it wasn't very crowded today. I ordered two cocoas and a large basket of fries to share. Tate offered to pay, but I refused to let him. It was the least I could do to show my gratitude.

"I'll go find us a booth, then," he said.

"Okay." I smiled and couldn't help but watch him for an extra second as he walked away. There were a few other girls in the place who did the same. I noticed how they would look from him to me and then whisper to each other, but I tried not to care. We were only studying together; let them talk.

As I waited by the order counter, I overheard a hushed conversation going on in a nearby booth.

"Holy cow, Kiersten! You guys have only been dating for like three weeks."

"I know, but I've never felt this way about anyone before."

Curious, I glanced around the giant cardboard milkshake blocking my view to see Kiersten Jennings talking to another girl. I'd known Kiersten since we were in Kindergarten and we were sort of "hallway friends". We'd run across each other at different parties and sometimes shared classes together, but nothing beyond that. I knew it wasn't polite to eavesdrop, but I was intrigued by the intensity of the quiet conversation.

"Well if it's only been three weeks and you guys are already moving past first base, where do you think you'll stop?"

My jaw dropped open and I edged closer to the sign. Had I heard right? Kiersten had always seemed like one of those goody-goody type girls.

She sighed. "Honestly, Katie, I'm not sure. Being with Ryan just feels so amazing. All my life I've done the 'right thing,' but now I finally know what it's like to be in love. My parents would flip if they knew, so promise you won't tell anyone, okay?"

"I promise."

"Order thirty-two," a voice called, breaking me out of my eavesdropping with a guilty lurch.

I walked to the counter in a daze and picked up our tray. If someone like Kiersten Jennings could make such a small deal out of moral standards, what was I so worried about? Maybe I'd been beating myself up over nothing.

I balanced the tray and made my way over to Tate. His broad shoulders looked great beneath his fitted navy Henley as he watched out the window, hands clasped in front of his chin.

"Sorry that took so long," I said, placing the tray on the table.

He turned to me with a smile. "Actually, it was pretty fast." He reached for a hot chocolate. "Thanks again. Next time we go somewhere, I'll treat you."

My stomach did a double flip. "Okay." I slid into the bench opposite him and we ate fries and talked for a few minutes before I realized time was going fast.

"I hate to say it, but I think I'd better study or I have zero chance of passing this test."

"No problem." Tate pushed the tray out of the way. "I'll come over there so I can see what you're looking at." He stood up from the bench and slid in next to me, close enough that our elbows touched.

My pulse raced at the contact. As I pulled out my biology book and notes, I noticed that the curious glances from onlookers had turned to full-on stares. Studying in a public place had probably been a bad idea.

Tate pointed at the chapter heading I'd flipped to in my book. "Awesome. I totally remember this chapter. Let's see your notes."

I forced myself to ignore the stares and whispers and focus on the subject matter. After a few minutes, I was absorbed enough in studying to drown everything else out, until Tate's ringtone went off. He pulled out his phone and glanced at the screen. Frowning, he silenced it and slid it back into his pocket.

I didn't want to be nosy, but I couldn't help myself. "Who was that?"

He shook his head. "Nothing important. I can call them back later."

I nodded but my insides burned. I could have sworn I'd caught a glimpse of Serena's face on the screen. I tried to turn my attention back to my notes, but then I heard what sounded like a message notification chime on Tate's phone. I glanced at him but he shook his head again.

I debated pushing the topic, but decided against it. We were having fun. I didn't want to ruin it by bringing up past relationships. We studied for a few more minutes before my phone buzzed. I pulled it out and saw that I'd missed two texts. The first was from Alexis. It was a picture of a sunset above the temple and the message said: *Wish you were here!*

I closed out of it, deciding to respond later. The second text was from Janie and made my stomach drop.

Check your Instagram. Now!!

I furrowed my brow and quickly clicked on Instagram. There, smack at the top was a picture of Tate and me sitting together at our booth. The caption read: *"Somerset High's newest couple?"*

My eyes practically bulged out of my head as I glanced around, wondering who had sent the anonymous post.

Tate watched me curiously. "What's wrong?"

I swallowed and held up the screen for him to see. "This."

He took my phone and his eyes widened a second before he laughed. "That's hilarious. I wonder who posted it." He handed the phone back to me, smiling as if it was all a funny joke. "At least it's a good picture of us."

I raised my eyebrows. "You don't mind?"

He shrugged. "Stuff like this is always being tossed around. Besides, a rumor that you're my girlfriend is more of a compliment than anything else."

My heart melted and I had no idea how to respond. "That's, um . . . that's really sweet of you to say . . . and I feel the same way." I hesitated and felt the beginnings of a blush. "It's just, well . . ." I was going to have to say it. No more beating around the bush. "The thing is, Serena has kind of been asking me lately if there's something going on between you and me. She seems jealous, and I have to know—are you guys still together or something?"

Tate frowned and tilted his head toward me, but before he could say anything I rushed on.

"Because if you are, it's totally cool. It's just that I probably shouldn't hang out with you if—you know—things are still going on between you two. That way people won't get the wrong idea." *And Serena won't strangle me with her bare hands.*

Tate blew out a breath and turned until his blue eyes locked with mine. "Courtney, there is nothing going on with me and Serena. We broke up weeks ago."

I nodded and hunched my shoulders slightly, afraid to pose the next question. "Okay . . . but wasn't that her that just called you?"

He smiled stiffly and looked down at his hands. "Yeah, it was. She still calls me sometimes. I thought we could be friends, but I'm starting to realize that's not going to be an option." He glanced up at me. "She seriously asked you if there was something going on between us?"

I nodded. "To be honest, I'm a little bit scared of her." He snorted and I gave a small laugh, biting my lip before I continued, "I know, it sounds stupid, but she really intimidates me. She's been wanting to get together for lunch and is always asking questions that feel more like an interrogation. It's just hard when we're in drill together, you know?"

Tate leaned his head back against the seat. "I'm so sorry. I had no idea. I'll talk to her."

I shook my head. "No. I really don't want to make a big deal out of it." I gestured to my phone. "I mean, I'm sure she's seen this post and I'll have to explain it to her, but I'll just be honest. She can't be mad that we're studying together."

Tate looked at me and leaned forward, resting the side of his head on his hand until his face was close to mine. "The thing is, I'm not sure if that's all there is to it. Are you?" he asked quietly.

I could feel my pulse in my skull. I met his gaze and suddenly my throat felt dry. I licked my lips. "I guess not."

He gave a half smile and touched my arm. "Then let's not worry about what Serena or anybody else thinks and just see where this takes us."

I lowered my lashes, suddenly too unsettled to meet his gaze. "Okay."

When I finally looked up, his eyes seemed to communicate a dozen messages before he sat back and placed his hands on the table. "Great. Now that that's settled let's get back to the fascinating topic of Binary Fission."

I laughed and turned back to my notes.

CHAPTER

It was dark outside when Tate pulled up beside my car in the school parking lot.

I turned to him with a smile. "Thanks so much for your help. I actually feel like I have a chance of doing okay tomorrow."

He smiled back. "Anytime. I'd rather study with you than do my own homework anyway."

I blushed and shook my head. "Well, thanks again." I opened the door and grabbed my backpack. "Guess I'll see you tomorrow?"

Tate nodded and opened his door. "Hold on a second. I can at least walk you to your car."

I held back a smile as he walked me the few steps to my car, thinking maybe I'd found a gentleman like William after all.

"Here, let me get the door for you," he said.

I hit the unlock button and he opened the back door. After placing my bag on the backseat and closing the door, he turned to me and said, "You're all set."

"Thanks."

There was a moment of something unspoken between us as our eyes met.

Tate's gaze never left mine as he stepped forward and drew me into a hug. My senses exploded like each nerve had been infused with gunpowder. Before

I knew what was happening, he pulled his face back a few inches and suddenly we were kissing. Our lips connected as though they were created just for this purpose. I couldn't think, could hardly breathe as he continued to kiss me and I kissed him back.

Before I knew what was happening we were leaning against my car. As soon as my back hit the cold metal it seemed to jar me back to reality. This was moving too fast.

I pulled away from him and we stared at each other, my racing pulse making me breathless. Tate smiled and ran a hand gently through my hair. "I'll definitely be seeing you tomorrow." He kissed my forehead and then walked back to his car.

I stood motionless for a moment before numbly climbing into the driver's seat of my Buick.

Holy. Cow.

I forced myself to put the key in the ignition and start the car. Then I turned and gave Tate a small wave. He waved back as he waited for me to pull out first.

I followed the roads back to my house on autopilot as I alternated between squeals and hyperventilating. No one had ever kissed me the way Tate had; not even Kellen. It was like having an incredible out-of-body experience. Tate Williams had kissed me!

I floated into the kitchen and Mom had to repeat herself three times before I noticed her standing at the stove.

"Courtney, are you alright? How did your study session go?" she asked.

I gave her a blank stare before shaking my head to clear my thoughts. "It went really well."

She lifted an eyebrow. "Judging by the silly grin on your face, I'd say it went better than that. Was there a cute boy in the group or something?"

My smile widened. "Yeah. But don't worry, I still studied. I'm going to ace this test."

She started to smile, then suddenly winced, dropping her wooden spoon into the pot of boiling pasta as she doubled over in pain.

"Mom?" I rushed over and put my arms around her shoulders. "Are you okay?"

She nodded, but was clearly in too much pain to speak. I urged her over to the table. "Here. Sit down. I'll call Dad."

She shook her head as she sat in the chair. "No . . . I'm sure it's nothing. Let me sit for a minute and it will pass."

I frowned at the discomfort lining her face. "I don't think so. You need to at least call the doctor's office. If you're in pain, that's a bad sign. The baby isn't due for two more months."

She took a long breath before nodding. "The doctor's office is closed by now, so I'll have to call the after-hours nurse line."

I quickly handed her cell phone to her and then turned off the stove. I poured her a glass of water, trying not to freak out when I could tell she was having another round of pain. As she spoke with the nurse I sent my dad a text telling him to come home ASAP.

". . . Alright. I'll be there in a few minutes." Mom ended the call and I moved to help her up.

"They want you to come in?" I tried to keep the concern out of my voice.

She nodded. "They just want me to come in to the hospital to get checked out. I'm sure it's nothing and I'll feel silly for causing so much trouble."

I shook my head. "Better safe than sorry. I'll help you into the car and then come back for your purse." My hands trembled as I helped her into her car. I could tell she was in a lot of pain and trying to be brave.

Please say she's not in labor, please say she's not in labor. Images of helping deliver a baby on the side of the road filled me with terror.

I grabbed our purses and we were on our way to the hospital.

"I texted Dad to come home. Once we get to the hospital, I'll call him and tell him to meet us there."

"Easy on the gas, Court," Mom warned as she clutched the sides of her stomach. "We don't have to speed."

I wrinkled my brow and glanced at her, unconvinced that everything was as "peachy keen" as she made it sound.

"I'm glad you texted him," she continued, "but until they're done at the temple he won't have his phone on him so you'll probably just have to leave a message." She paused to breathe deeply again. "Whatever you do, don't make it sound like an emergency. I'm sure these are just pesky Braxton Hicks contractions and they'll send me back home within the hour."

I hoped she was right.

After parking as close to Labor and Delivery as possible, I escorted Mom into the hospital. She was whisked into a wheelchair and carted down the hall by a nurse who must have been a former track star. Both Mom's purse and mine bumped against me as I tried to keep up.

Hospitals had always made me uncomfortable. I swallowed back tears as Mom emerged from a bathroom dressed in a hospital gown. She gave me a reassuring smile, but she looked so helpless as she was assisted back into the wheelchair. This was not the strong, always-in-control mother I knew. I desperately wished my dad was here. I'd left him a message while Mom was changing and hoped he would get it soon.

I followed after the nurse as she pushed my mom into a curtained-off area with a hospital bed and monitors.

"Let's take a look and see what's going on, shall we?" the middle-aged woman in scrubs said. She helped Mom onto the bed and I looked away as Mom was strapped with monitors and covered with a sheet. When she was all settled, I sat in a chair by her bed and held her hand.

She smiled and gave my hand a reassuring squeeze.

The nurse stared at the monitor and began typing things into a keyboard. She made friendly chit-chat with my mom as she typed, but I could see a small crease in her brow as she glanced at the monitors. Another nurse came in and whispered something to her. Mom continued to squeeze my hand.

After the other nurse left, the older woman turned to my mom. "Mrs. Moore, I'm going to give your doctor a call. Would you like a drink while you wait?" she asked.

"Is everything all right?" Mom's voice trembled slightly.

The woman gave her a kind look but didn't smile. "You're definitely having contractions, but I need to speak with your doctor before I can give you more information. I'm going to have Cathy bring you some water, okay?"

Mom nodded and squeezed my hand, more tightly this time.

The few minutes we waited felt like hours. Mom had another contraction, which I could see charted in red on the monitor. She breathed deeply and I stroked her hair.

"Everything's going to be okay," I said. "Just grip my hand as hard as you need to."

She could only nod.

I was trying to put on a brave face, but I couldn't stop the tear that slid down my cheek. The steady rhythm of the baby's heartbeat sounded from the monitor, both reassuring and terrifying at the same time.

"Do you think I should call Eliza? I feel like she should know what's going on," I said, wishing Dad would call back. I wanted to comfort Mom, but I was so not qualified. Eliza would know exactly what to do or say in this situation.

Mom shook her head. "Absolutely not. We're not going to call Eliza on her honeymoon over something like this. I'm sure everything is fine."

I wished I could believe her. The red lines on the monitor seemed to glare at me.

Cathy entered holding a foam cup with a straw. "Drink as much as you can," she said as she handed it to my mom. "How are you feeling?"

Mom exhaled as the contraction subsided. "Like I'm going into labor."

Cathy frowned and glanced at the monitor. "The nurse is talking with your doctor now. She'll be here any second."

As if on cue, the nurse stepped back through the curtained partition. "Dr. Lloyd wants me to give you some medication to get these contractions stopped." She handed Mom some pills and waited until she'd swallowed them. "We're going to check and see if you're dilating, and then we'll keep monitoring your contractions. I want you to drink as much as possible in the meantime."

Again Mom could only nod. Normally in stressful situations she would be talkative and try to put everyone around her at ease. Her pensive silence worried me more than anything else.

"Dr. Lloyd also asked me to give you a shot to help with the baby's lungs. It's just a precaution, but at this early stage, it can only help." She pulled out a needle and my head swam.

Mom turned to me and put a hand on my arm. "Courtney, why don't you go out into the hall for a minute?" She knew I was bad with needles.

The nurse glanced at me. "Are you okay, sweetie?"

I nodded, but couldn't even look at her in case I saw the needle again. "Yeah. I just need to use the restroom." I squeezed Mom's hand. "I'll be back in a second."

"I'm fine, take your time."

Without waiting for further response, I darted out of the curtained room and into the hallway. The sight of more nurses and suffering pregnant women being carted around in wheelchairs made my stomach turn.

I scanned the hallway for a restroom and then booked it down the hall when I saw the sign I was looking for. It was a private bathroom, so I locked the door and moved to the sink. One glance in the mirror at the greenish hue of my face confirmed that I was going to have to either calm down, or lose whatever Tasty Freeze treat was left in my stomach.

I splashed cold water on my face and took several deep breaths. It was pathetic that I was hiding out in the bathroom trying not to puke while my mom was the one who needed help. I had to get back to her as soon as possible.

Another tear escaped before I blotted my face with a rough paper towel. How was this happening right now? I had no idea if my mom and the baby were going to be okay. More than anything, I wanted to pray. I *needed* to pray, for Mom's sake and the baby's. But I didn't feel worthy to ask for anything.

The realization brought on more tears and I covered my face with the soggy paper towel, allowing silent sobs to shake my body until I forced myself to pull it together.

Maybe I couldn't bring myself to pray, but I could at least try to be there for her. After splashing a bit more water on my face—this time to hide my tears—I dried off and combed my fingers through my hair. *You can do this, Courtney.*

I took a deep breath and then left the restroom. I spied Dad down the hallway standing at the nurses' desk and rushed toward him. "Dad!"

He turned and his features relaxed slightly as he pulled me in for a quick hug. "Where's your mom?"

"She's back here." I led him to the curtained monitoring room.

As soon as she saw my dad, Mom's face crumpled. "Grant."

He was at her side in an instant, stroking her hair as the nurse filled him in on what was happening.

I slumped into the nearest chair, feeling an enormous weight lifted from my shoulders. My dad was here. Everything would be okay now.

It was almost two in the morning when we finally left the hospital. Dad had given Mom a blessing which I knew brought her comfort. Her doctor prescribed some medication that was successful in getting the contractions to stop, and she was being allowed to return home with strict orders for bedrest.

Through bleary eyes I focused on Dad's taillights as he drove Mom home through the empty streets. I'd been awake for nearly twenty-four hours and I had to unroll the window a few times so the biting air would keep me from falling asleep.

I'd convinced Dad that I wasn't too tired to drive, but as I pulled into the garage in a daze, I realized I probably shouldn't have taken that risk. The adrenaline rush had worn off now that Mom's condition was stable, and it was all I could do to make it up to my bedroom.

Without bothering to change into pajamas, I fell onto my bed and was asleep before my head hit the pillow.

CHAPTER fifteen

"Slow down, dearie, or I daresay you'll have to leave me in the snow on the side of the road."

"I'm sorry, Mrs. White." Hannah slowed her pace as the two women walked down the snow-encrusted road. I walked beside them, grateful it was at least sunny in this dream.

"I thought perhaps we ought to hurry in case Father comes home early for tea. You know how cross he gets when things don't run on schedule." Hannah shook her head. "I should never have agreed to go into town on such a silly errand."

Mrs. White looked at her and huffed, sending a vapor of steam into the air. "'Tis not silly at all! If your dear mother were alive, she'd have made sure you had a proper new dress for the ball. You should use the money Charles gave you for material to make a gown, as he intended."

Hannah looked at her companion. "Charles will need that money if he ever hopes to sail to America. My blue dress will be perfectly suitable. Besides, I have Mother's lace gloves and you've convinced me to buy new ribbon for my hair. I should think you would be happy."

Mrs. White shook her head. "I'd be happy if we had proper conveyance into town, that's what," she grumbled.

"Father needed the carriage to pay visits to his parish." She took Mrs. White's arm. "The exercise is invigorating, don't you think?"

We reached the edge of town and I was surprised to see cute little shops lining the main road. It was a cheerful scene with a few people milling about the streets in the afternoon sun.

Mrs. White was making a retort when she suddenly stopped mid-sentence. "Look there—who is that walking with Mr. Benbow?"

Hannah held up her gloved hand to shield the sun. "I couldn't say. I've never seen him before."

Two men were walking down the street toward a carriage, but I didn't notice anything unusual about them. This had to be one of those small towns where everyone knew everyone and strangers were a big deal.

Mrs. White pulled on Hannah's arm. "Come, let's hurry and see if we can't get a better look."

Hannah smiled at her sudden enthusiasm and they picked up their pace, but they were too late. The carriage pulled down the street before they could get close enough to see inside.

Mrs. White let out a disappointed sigh. "Ah well. If there's anything to be found out, Mrs. Henshaw will know of it." She turned to Hannah. "We must hurry to the shop at once!"

Hannah laughed. "Why, Mrs. White—I don't believe I've ever seen you move quite so quickly."

The older woman winked as she let go of Hannah's arm and bustled into the shop across the street. I trailed behind the two women, enjoying the chance to look in the store windows and at the people passing by. It was like being in one of those Jane Austen movies my mom was always watching.

"Good day to you, Mrs. White, Miss Walker," a lady said from behind the shop counter as we entered.

"And good day to you, Mrs. Henshaw," Mrs. White replied. There was an eager gleam in her eyes as she hurried over to the counter.

The two women were soon absorbed in gossip. Hannah smiled and shook her head before browsing through some ribbons. I stood beside her, watching to see which one she would choose.

The front door opened again but Hannah was too preoccupied to see who it was.

"Good afternoon, Mr. Hornsby," Mrs. Henshaw called.

Hannah took a sharp intake of breath and looked up. I watched curiously as she tried to hide behind some bolts of fabric.

The man who had entered was tall, with light red hair and a deep brow which gave him a bullish look.

"Good day, Mrs. Henshaw," he said, removing his hat.

"Is there something I might help you with?" she asked with a barely contained smile. This was clearly a ladies' shop.

He cleared his throat. "Thank you, no. I just happened to be passing by and noticed Miss Walker, so I thought I would pay my regards."

Both women's eyes lit up as they turned to look at Hannah. I grimaced for her sake as she slowly raised herself from her hiding place, pretending to just now notice his appearance.

"Good day, Mr. Hornsby," she said with a small curtsy.

"Miss Walker." A smile formed on his thin lips as he made his way to her. "I trust you are well this afternoon?"

"Perfectly well, thank you," she replied. It was obvious by her posture that she wanted to be done with this conversation as fast as possible. I didn't know anything about this guy, but I couldn't blame her. He gave off some major creepy vibes.

"I see you are browsing for a new ribbon. Might I be so bold as to assume you are making the purchase in preparation for the county ball? I do so hope you'll attend." His eyes were intense as he looked down at her.

She shrank back. "You assume correctly, sir. I'm afraid I haven't much time and must get back, so if you don't mind . . ." She grasped the blue ribbon in her hand and took a step past him to move toward the counter.

He reached for her arm. "Ah, but you have chosen perfectly. That shade will just match the color of your eyes. You must allow me the pleasure of purchasing it for you."

Hannah tensed and looked down at his hand where it held her arm, slowly removing it with a forced smile. "Thank you for the offer, but I'm afraid I cannot accept. Now if you'll excuse me, I must get home before my father returns from his visits."

His face hardened for a moment before he forced a tight smile. "Of course."

Without looking back, Hannah moved to the counter. She was taking out coins from her reticule when Mr. Hornsby's voice caused her to stiffen.

"As it happens, I've just had the pleasure of visiting with your father. Such an agreeable man; we're very fortunate to have him as our rector. I'd like to invite the both of you over to dine sometime very soon . . . and Charles, of course."

Without looking at him, Hannah replied, "That's very kind of you, Mr. Hornsby." She quickly paid for the ribbon. "Thank you, Mrs. Henshaw."

The woman nodded. "Have a fine day, Miss." She cast a quick glance over Hannah's shoulder at Mr. Hornsby before winking at her.

I felt so sorry for Hannah; the gossip was really going to fly now.

Hannah blushed as her mouth formed a line. "Come along, Mrs. White. We must hurry."

Mrs. White nodded and gave a farewell to Mrs. Henshaw, but that rotten Mr. Hornsby wasn't taking any hints. He followed them out of the shop.

"Might I offer you a ride home, Miss Walker? I'd hate for you to fall ill from exposure."

Mrs. White gave her an imploring look, but Hannah's back stiffened. "You're very kind, sir, but—"

"Hannah!"

Her face instantly dissolved into a smile as she turned and saw William crossing the street.

"Addressing you by your Christian name? Who does he think he is?" Mr. Hornsby said in distaste.

Hannah glared at him. "William and I are very good friends, Mr. Hornsby."

I laughed at the way she said his name, emphasizing the formal title. That ought to take him down a few notches.

William finally reached them, his face darkening at the sight of Mr. Hornsby. He titled his hat at the women. "Ladies, you're both looking well today. What brings you to town?"

Hannah's eyes lit up at his smile. "I just came to purchase a new ribbon and am on my way home for tea." She angled her posture so that her back was turned to Mr. Hornsby. "What are you about, William?"

"Yes, shouldn't you be working at the mill?" Mr. Hornsby cut in with a sneer.

William's jaw tightened. "It just so happens we've finished our work early for the day." He turned his attention back to Hannah and his brown eyes searched hers. "I'd be honored to escort you and Mrs. White home, if you'd like."

Hannah beamed up at him. "That would be lovely." She turned to the gaping Mr. Hornsby. "I appreciate your offer, Mr. Hornsby, but as William's home is much closer to mine it's only reasonable that he should accompany us on our walk. Good day."

Mr. Hornsby fumed as William tipped his head and took Hannah's arm. Mrs. White cast a regretful look at Mr. Hornsby's carriage before trundling after the others.

"I shall look forward to seeing you at the ball, Miss Walker," Mr. Hornsby called after them.

Hannah glanced over her shoulder and dipped her chin slightly before turning back around and grasping William's arm tighter. I quickened my pace to hear what they were saying.

"If that blackguard thinks he's going to dance with you at the ball, he's sorely mistaken," William growled.

"Shh, he'll hear you," Hannah giggled.

"To think we could have ridden back home in a nice carriage, and here we are traipsing through the snow," Mrs. White complained as she caught up to them. She paused a moment to catch her breath while playfully scowling at Hannah.

Hannah grinned and touched her arm. "You are a dear, Mrs. White."

"Well you're just in luck that I've heard news to put me in a pleasant temper," she retorted.

"What news might that be?" William asked.

Mrs. White straightened and her merry eyes glimmered as she walked alongside them. "That man we saw with Mr. Benbow? He's a missionary come from America. He's staying with the Benbows and has preached to them. I've just had it from Mrs. Henshaw that John and Jane Benbow have already been baptized!"

Hannah and William stopped walking to look at her.

"But John is a member of the United Brethren," William said, his brow deeply furrowed.

"*Was* a member, Mr. Lucas," Mrs. White corrected. "And I've not even told you the most surprising news—apparently this preacher claims he has new scripture." She paused for dramatic emphasis and lowered her voice. "Says he has a book in addition to the Bible."

Hannah's mouth dropped open. "Scripture to replace the Bible? Mrs.

White, how could you entertain such talk? It's shameful! And you employed by the rector." Her cheeks took on color as she stared indignantly at the older woman.

Mrs. White stiffened. "Didn't say 'replace,' now did I? The way Mrs. Henshaw put it, this scripture is supposed to be in *addition* to the Bible." At Hannah's frown she continued, "I'm not saying I believe it, mind, but it is a piece of news, isn't it?"

"It is, at that." William put a placating hand on Mrs. White's shoulder and smiled. "You know how fiercely Hannah loves the Bible. The news has simply come as a shock to her, and rightly so."

Hannah placed a hand on her hip and gave him a look. "I hope I'm not the only one who loves the Lord's good word, William Lucas. At least enough to defend it in the sight of heresy."

He lifted his hands, a teasing glint in his eyes. "Ah, you see, Mrs. White? She's taken to calling me by my full name. Now we know it's serious."

Hannah scoffed as the tips of her ears reddened with indignation. She bent down and scooped up a handful of snow, forming it into a ball and launching it at William with impressive speed.

He darted out of the way, laughing at her outrage for having missed. Before he could retaliate, she threw another snowball, hitting him square in the face. He stopped laughing and wiped the snow off with his sleeve.

Hannah covered a grin with her gloved hand, then squealed as William bent down to get a handful of snow.

"If it's a fight you're wanting, Hannah Walker, 'tis a fight you'll get," he said.

"Now you've done it," Mrs. White laughed. "Best make a run for it, Miss." She shook her head and watched as William chased the squealing Hannah down the road, each of them throwing snowballs and laughing in turn.

"Heaven help us to try and turn that girl into a proper young lady," Mrs.

White mumbled. She smiled and blew out a breath before trudging after them in the snow.

CHAPTER
sixteen

When I awoke the next morning, it took a while to get my bearings. I was in my room, but there was way too much light coming through the windows. I turned and looked at my clock.

"Oh crud."

I threw the covers off and ran in the bathroom to brush my teeth. I'd missed drill practice, and my biology test. Was there really any point in hurrying now?

Coach would understand when I explained about my mom and the hospital, and I was pretty sure Mr. Sanchez would let me make up the biology test. Hopefully.

I headed back to my bed and climbed under the still-warm covers. Stretching my muscles, I thought over the events of the night before and wondered how my "Energizer Bunny" mother would handle five weeks of couch arrest. Things were going to get interesting around here.

With all of the craziness last night, I hadn't had to do my nightly phone check-in. Grabbing it off of my dresser, I looked to see if there were any messages. I wasn't disappointed, but the first one sent from Eli last night made my heart sink.

Any chance you'd be willing to send me your notes? I'd ask if you were up for studying, but it looks like you already took care of that.

Had he seen that stupid Instagram post? Of course. What else would he be referring to? I squirmed and continued to scroll through my messages.

Alexis: *Um, I saw the post. What the heck, woman? I need info—stat!!!*

I also had two missed calls from her. She was going to kill me for taking so long to get back to her. The next messages were from this morning.

Janie: *Where are you, Courtney? It might be best if you lay low . . . Serena did NOT look happy this morning. The entire school is buzzing about you & Tate.*

I cringed. I definitely wasn't ready to be the center of school gossip.

Janie: *Oh, and make sure you have a dang good reason for not being at practice, otherwise you can't perform at halftime. Coach was ticked.*

Tate: *Hey, I was hoping to walk you to class. Where are you?*

Eli: *Is everything ok? You remember we have the test, right?*

"Ugh!" I flopped back on my pillow and put a hand across my eyes. At least one thing was for sure—I was glad I hadn't heard my alarm this morning.

With trepidation, I signed into Instagram and found the post of Tate and me. I had to admit, it was a pretty good picture. Seeing the two of us looking cozy in a booth studying made my heart flutter, but the number of comments on the post instantly seized any warm fuzzies.

I knew there were bound to be negative comments and I almost didn't have the courage to read through them. But curiosity got the better of me. I scanned through the comments, many of which were from people I didn't even know. There were some nice things, but almost as many not nice things.

Who's that girl?

What is Tate thinking?? He can't do better than Serena.

Rebound!

My face flushed hot and I logged off, tossing the phone across my bed. How humiliating. Was that how people would see me if Tate and I got together?

As some pathetic, not-nearly-as-good-as-Serena rebound? Tears burned my eyes as a knock sounded at my door.

"Honey, can I come in?"

"Um, yeah." I swallowed and ran a hand over my face in an attempt to banish the tears.

The door opened and Dad walked in balancing a breakfast tray. The smell of bacon made my stomach rumble and almost helped me forget about the nasty comments.

"I just took a tray in to your mom and thought you might be hungry," he said with a smile.

"Thanks, Dad." I sat up taller in bed and took the tray from him. "I was just about to go check on her. You stayed home from work?"

He nodded. "I wanted to get things squared away around here so your mom can stay down." He put a hand on my knee. "We already blessed the food, so you can eat."

I guiltily paused the hand that had already been reaching for the toast. "Oh, okay." Waiting another second for good measure, I picked up the piece of bread sprinkled with cinnamon sugar and nibbled on it. "How is she?"

A line creased between his brows. "Tired. The medication they gave her wiped her out pretty good, but at least the contractions have stopped." He sat down on the edge of my bed. "I just got off the phone with Rose Lawson. I'm pretty sure you and I can handle some extra responsibilities around here for the next few weeks, but Rose is organizing help from the ward where it's needed."

The piece of toast in my mouth suddenly felt dry and I struggled to swallow it down. As much as I liked Rose, I knew what a drill sergeant she could be sometimes. The thought of her invading our home and taking charge didn't sit very well.

"I can definitely step up and help out more. In fact, I don't think we even need to get the Relief Society involved."

Dad patted my knee again. "I'm glad you're willing, and I know you'll be a big help, but I also know your mother. More than anything else, she's going to need some policing to stay down while you're at school and I'm at work. Not to mention some company. With my work and calling and your school, drill and new job, she's going to get lonely. I don't like the idea of asking for help, but we have to be realistic and admit that you and I are too busy to offer all the help she's going to need."

I furrowed my brow. "I guess you're right." After taking a swig of juice I asked, "So what's the plan?"

He smiled. "Rose is ready to take over the household, but I told her a few specific things for now and she's sending around a sign-up sheet. Knowing our ward, we're going to have more help than we'll know what to do with, and we need to accept that help graciously. Sometimes being willing to receive service is harder than giving it, but it's important that we do."

I shrugged, still not liking the idea but I would go along for Mom's sake. "Okay."

Dad ruffled my hair the way he used to when I was little and stood up from the bed. "Come in our room and see your mom when you get a minute."

I nodded but stopped him before he left. "Dad, will you call the school and excuse my absence today? I sort of slept through my alarm."

He put his hand on the doorframe. "I could have woken you, but figured you needed to catch up on your rest. I'll call."

"Thanks. I also missed a big biology test, so I might need you to write a note for my teacher so I can make it up. And a note for Coach Weaver so she'll let me perform this week even though I missed practice."

"I'll write the notes."

I relaxed back into my pillow. "Thanks."

He nodded and closed the door behind him. I smiled as I took a bite of bacon. He hadn't even suggested that I finish the school day. I definitely wasn't happy about Mom's situation, but there might be a few silver linings—like the fact that Dad was too distracted to worry about me the way he normally did. A little extra freedom never hurt anybody.

"Be so glad you're not here today," Alexis said ominously. "There hasn't been this much gossip going around since Tate and Serena broke up."

I'd called Alexis as soon as lunch break started. I frowned and adjusted the phone to my ear. As much as I wanted to hear what kind of gossip it was, I'd learned my lesson from reading the Instagram comments. I bit my lip, forcing myself not to ask for more information. "Yeah, it's nice to have a day away from the madness. Who are you going to eat with?"

"Actually, I've gotta run. I'll talk to you tonight, okay?"

"Oo-kay?"

"See ya, Court."

Click.

I frowned again and stared at the dead screen. It wasn't like Alexis to be so cryptic, or abrupt. Something was definitely up with my best friend.

I stood from the kitchen table and was about to make myself some lunch when my phone buzzed. I expected a text from Lexi, apologizing for the quick conversation, but it was from Tate.

Hey, I was hoping to meet you for lunch but I'm thinking you're officially not here today. Everything ok?

My stomach flipped. I had texted Eli this morning, apologizing for the lack of note-sending and bringing him up to speed on my mom's situation, but I hadn't texted Tate. I was afraid that he would have changed his mind about me after reading people's comments and all the gossip flying around. Was it possible he still liked me in spite of the fact people were saying I wasn't 'as good as Serena'?

Me: *Yeah, I'm home today. It's been a little crazy, but everything is okay.*

I briefly explained what had happened last night, but before I could read his response, the doorbell rang. It was probably Rose. Dad had said she'd be stopping by. I moved into the living room and opened the front door. My eyes widened in surprise.

"Eli!"

He stood on the porch with a bouquet of flowers in his hands. His hazel eyes were uncertain. "Hey . . . I just thought maybe your mom could use some cheering up, so I brought these. How's everything going?"

I reached a hand up to my messy hair. Why oh why had I not changed out of my pajamas? I cleared my throat and gave him a warm smile. "That's so nice of you. Come on in."

The fact that Eli was thinking of my mom was too sweet for words. He'd never even met her before. He stepped into our living room and I closed the door.

"Have you had lunch? I was just about to make a sandwich."

He shrugged. "I'm good."

I took the flowers. "I'll put these in a vase. Come into the kitchen and eat with me, I won't take no for an answer." I tried my best to sound bossy, but when he smiled I knew he wasn't buying it.

"Okay. Thanks." He glanced around as he followed me into the kitchen. "Your house is really nice."

"Thanks." There was a bit of awkwardness between us that I was afraid had nothing to do with the fact that he was in my house and everything to do with a certain Instagram post. "Have a seat and I'll get you some food. Turkey or PB and J?" I glanced over my shoulder at him.

"Either one." He avoided eye contact.

Just then Dad came into the kitchen. "I thought I heard the doorbell . . ." his voice trailed off as he caught sight of Eli.

"Dad, this is my friend, Eli Jackson. He's the one who got me the job at the theater."

Eli stood up from his chair and reached out to shake my dad's hand. "It's nice to meet you, sir."

He was nearly as tall as my dad and I was impressed by how effortless his manners were. A sudden stirring from my dreams and how William acted rendered me almost breathless.

Dad also seemed impressed, but I could tell he was working to hide it. "Nice to meet you, Eli." He darted a look my way and I hurried to step forward with the vase.

"He took his lunch break to come here and bring Mom some flowers. Isn't that nice?" I handed the vase to Dad. "Will you take them up to her? I'm just going to eat lunch here with Eli." I gave him a pleading look, which he miraculously seemed to understand.

"Well that was thoughtful." Dad glanced between the two of us. "I'll take them up, but she's probably going to want to meet you, Eli."

He nodded. "I'm glad to hear she's doing okay."

Dad took another second to size Eli up and then made his way upstairs. "Enjoy your lunch," he called over his shoulder.

I let out a small sigh of relief. That had gone way better than expected. I turned to Eli with a smile. "Sorry, I know you don't have much time. I'll be fast."

His hazel eyes finally connected with mine. "Can I help with anything?"

I shook my head. "Nope. Just have a seat and tell me how the biology test went. Was it hard?" I busied myself with finding lunch meat and cheese. He'd said he didn't care what he ate, but I could make a mean sandwich and I wanted to impress him.

"It wasn't too bad. I talked to Mr. Sanchez after I got your text. He said he'll let you make up the test if you bring a note from home."

I paused the hand that was reaching for the mayo and turned to look at him. "You did that for me?"

He shrugged. "It was no big deal."

I straightened and tried not to notice how good he looked today. "Well it means a lot to me. Thank you." I wanted to say more, but he glanced away again.

"Sure."

I turned back to my task and made small talk with Eli until our plates were ready. I set the food in front of him and watched in delight as his eyes widened.

"Wow. That's quite the sandwich."

I smiled. "Hope you're hungry." I placed a bag of chips and two sodas on the table.

He waited for me, so I took a bite of my sandwich. He seemed to hesitate another second, and then said, "Mind if I say a blessing? It's kind of a habit."

The food in my mouth almost choked me as I tried to swallow. There was no hiding the fact that a prayer hadn't crossed my mind so I just nodded and closed my eyes.

Eli said a blessing and then started eating. His prayer had been short but sincere, not rushed or awkward. I felt stupid that I hadn't been the one to suggest it.

"Are you still planning on coming in to work tonight?" he asked.

The carbonation from the soda burned my throat as I quickly swallowed to answer, "Of course. I promise I'll be dependable."

His eyes searched mine across the table and my heart sped up. I could tell he wanted to say something, but didn't. We finished the rest of our lunch in silence and I missed the way we always joked around.

There was an elephant in the room, and I wasn't about to be the one to drag it into the spotlight. My phone had buzzed a few times and I felt a guilty twinge knowing it was Tate. I'd left him hanging, but I wasn't going to text him back with Eli there. Whenever I was around him I found myself wanting to avoid the whole Tate subject.

When Eli finished, he picked up his plate and stood. "Thanks for lunch. Now that I know how you are with food, I may have to rethink the terms of our 'arrangement.'"

My heart sank a little. I'd secretly been hoping he was going to ask me out when we'd made that agreement, but instead he was distancing himself. And could I blame him? From all aspects it looked like Tate and I were on the fast track to getting together.

I took Eli's plate before he could make it to the sink. "I like to cook, so I'm happy to make something for you anytime."

His hazel eyes adopted the teasing glint I'd been missing. "Maybe that's making things too easy for you then."

My pulse sped up as I realized how close we were suddenly standing to each other, and how much I liked it. "What else did you have in mind?"

His face grew serious as he watched me. His eyes searched mine a moment before travelling quickly to my lips and up again. I couldn't breathe.

Then, all at once he took a step back and his face turned expressionless.

"Thanks again for lunch. I'd better get back." He looked away and slid his hands into his pockets. "Were you planning on coming for the last half of school? I could give you a ride."

It took me a moment to shake off my disappointment. "Thanks, but I think I'll stay. I have to go in and talk to Coach Weaver after school, but I'll be on time for work."

He nodded. "Good luck with that. And tell your mom sorry I didn't have time to meet her."

"She'll understand. Maybe next time you come over." I glanced at him hopefully but he only gave a brief nod in return.

"See you tonight, then."

"See you." I opened the door for him and watched as he strode to his car parked at the curb. How was it that I'd never noticed how much I liked the way he walked? It wasn't a swagger, but it was confident and just . . . nice. Again I was reminded of Charles and William, the way they carried themselves with good posture and confidence. When Eli turned and saw me standing there, I felt my face flush.

He smiled and gave a small wave before getting into his car. I waved back and then closed the door. My phone buzzed in my back pocket, reminding me of the texts.

I got out my phone and scanned through them on my way up to my mom's room. Tate was asking if I had plans tonight. I should have been excited by this, but found that I was relieved to have an excuse not to hang out. My heart was all mixed up at the moment. I texted a quick reply apologizing and explaining that I had to work, then headed into Mom's room.

She smiled when she saw me and sat up a little in bed. Dad fluffed the pillow behind her before she leaned back. I'd never seen her looking so worn out.

"Is your friend still here? I wanted to thank him for the flowers."

I sat at the foot of her bed. "No. He told me to say sorry he had to leave, but lunch break was almost over. Maybe you can meet him another time."

She nodded. "I hope so. That was really sweet of him." She turned and touched the tip of one of the daisies and my heart warmed to Eli all over again. My mom loved flowers.

"How are you feeling?" I asked.

"Fine. I'm sure once the side effects of the medicine wear off I'll be able to get up and about today."

Dad and I exchanged looks and I put a hand on her leg. "Mom, I know you hate being down, but that baby needs you to take it easy, and there's nothing wrong with that."

"Exactly what I've been saying," Dad added with an arch of his brow.

The doorbell sounded downstairs and for a split-second I hoped Eli was back.

"That will be Rose. She just texted that she was on her way," Mom said.

I felt a little deflated but brushed it away. *Get a hold of yourself, girl.*

"I'll get it." Dad stood from the bed and left the room.

"I heard you missed practice this morning, so I've already written you a note." Mom reached for a piece of paper on her nightstand and handed it to me.

"Thanks. I'm sure I can work it out with Coach." I smiled to reassure her. "I asked Dad, but since you're here would you mind also writing one for my biology teacher? Eli talked to him and he'll let me make up the test, but he wants a note."

Mom looked at me out of the corner of her eye. "The same Eli who got you the job and brought me flowers?"

I nodded and traced the pattern in her bedspread.

"So is he your boyfriend now?"

I rolled my eyes and couldn't help but smile. "No. He's just a good friend."

"Uh-huh." She smiled back as Rose and Dad's voices could be heard coming down the hallway. "Keep me posted on that, okay? If I'm going to be stuck in bed I need to at least feel like I know what's happening in your life."

"Okay."

Rose entered the room with her usual flourish. "Vivian, I'm so glad Grant called me. We've got everything under control."

I moved out the way so she could give my mom a hug, fully expecting Mom to wave off her concerns. To my surprise, I watched several tears escape Mom's eyes as she hugged Rose back. "Thank you so much for coming."

"There's no place I'd rather be. Now you just take it easy and I'll tell you what we have organized so far," Rose said, pulling back from Mom with a tender smile. She turned to Dad and me. "We've already got more offers for help from the ward members than you'll probably need so I want your input too. That way we can come up with a schedule that works for everyone."

Dad and I nodded and stayed quiet as Rose rattled off the list of meals, cleaning, and errands that had been offered over the next few weeks. As hard as it was to accept all of this help, I felt a renewed sense of relief with each family name listed to pitch in.

Mom was wiping away so many tears by now that I handed her a box of tissues, but I knew part of what she was feeling. With the members of our ward rallying around us, everything was going to be just fine.

CHAPTER

seventeen

It was kind of weird walking into school a few minutes before the final bell rang, but I wanted to make sure I didn't miss Coach Weaver before she left for the day. I found her office and was relieved to see her sitting at her desk.

"Hey, Coach," I said, knocking on the doorframe.

She turned in her swivel chair and raised an eyebrow. "Look who showed up today. Where were you this morning?"

I took a deep breath and walked in. "I had to take my mom to the hospital last night. She was having contractions and showing signs of preterm labor. We didn't get home until really late, and I slept through my alarm." I handed her the note from my mom and then held my breath as I waited for her reply. Coach was a stickler for rules, but I hoped she'd cut me some slack just this once.

Her blue eyes revealed no expression as she read through the note, and then she finally looked up at me. "Well, Courtney, you know the rules: if you don't show up for practice, you don't perform that week. If I don't hold you to it, what message does that send to the girls who had to abide by that rule?"

I lowered my head in disappointment. "I understand."

"However . . ."

I looked up, not daring to hope.

"This is an extenuating circumstance, and you've always been good at making practice a priority. I think you've got the routine down enough that you should be fine to perform tomorrow."

I blew out a sigh of relief. "Thanks, Coach. I'll go over the dance a few times at home tonight too—just to be sure."

She nodded. "Tomorrow morning at practice I want you to explain to the team what happened and the reason I'm allowing you to perform. That way there shouldn't be any bitter feelings."

"Okay." Too bad nothing I said would erase the bitter feelings Serena had for me at the moment.

Coach seemed satisfied and then directed her attention to my outfit. "Is that a work shirt?"

I glanced down at my black polo. "Yeah. I just got a part-time job at the movie theater."

"Great. A little extra responsibility never hurt anyone." She smiled and pointed a manicured fingernail at me. "Just make sure it doesn't interfere with our drill schedule."

"It won't." I smiled back at her and waved before heading out the door.

The familiar smell of popcorn greeted me as I entered the movie theater. I nervously adjusted the polo beneath my jacket and made my way to the concession stand. Eli was already behind the counter. He smiled when he saw me and I couldn't help but smile back. I'd been looking forward to working with him more than I realized.

"Are you ready for this?" he asked as I approached.

I glanced around and arched an eyebrow. "It doesn't look like we'll have much to do. Nobody's here."

One corner of his mouth lifted, revealing his dimple. "It's early. We'll probably see some customers for the evening shows." He handed me my time card over the counter. "I've already filled this out, so just head into the break room and punch in like I showed you. Do you remember where the hooks are for your jacket and stuff?"

I nodded as I took the time card. "Yeah, I think I got it."

"I can't leave the counter unattended, but come back and let me know if you have any trouble clocking in."

"Okay." I was determined not to have any trouble though. The time clock had seemed pretty self-explanatory and I wanted Eli to know that I was all sorts of capable when it came to this job. "I'll be back in a second."

He nodded and I walked off in the direction of the break room. A glance at my phone told me it was still a few minutes before my official starting time, so I waited until it was exactly 4:30 on the dot before placing my time card into the machine. I drew it back and saw with satisfaction that the stamp was perfectly centered on the line. This job was going to be a snap.

I placed my card back in its holder and then hung up my purse and jacket before heading back out to the concession stand.

Eli was restocking rows of fountain cups when I joined him behind the counter.

"All squared away?" he asked.

"Yep."

"Good." He straightened and handed me a slender magnet. "Here's your nametag."

I took it from him and smiled at my name printed on the shiny surface. "That was fast."

"You must have made a good impression on Bryce. He normally has a week or two trial period before ordering a nametag."

"Well don't I feel special?" I said as I clipped the tag onto my polo.

"Just don't let it go to your head," Eli teased.

"Why? Are you worried I'm going to get promoted before you do?" I smirked and loved the returning spark in his eyes.

"Yeah, you better watch it because I'm looking to climb the corporate ladder." He lowered his voice, "Rumor has it the janitor position might be available soon and I don't want some underdog to swoop in and steal it out from under me."

My eyes widened. "Did you just call me a dog?"

He stepped back. "No! Haven't you ever heard—"

"Kidding," I said, holding up my hands.

He shook his head and tried not to smile. "And to think I brought this on myself."

I laughed. "Too late now. You should have thought things through before telling me about the job, because now you're stuck with me."

"Guess so." His face slowly straightened as his eyes met mine. There was something unreadable in his expression that made my heart speed up.

"Um, excuse me?"

We both turned to see a middle-aged woman standing at the counter.

"Can I get a large popcorn and soda?" Her scowl was unmistakable.

Eli snapped to attention. "Absolutely."

As he helped her I observed each step closely so I would be able to do my job. I admired his natural friendly manner and the way the woman walked away with a smile on her face.

"You're good with people," I said after she'd gone.

He turned to me with a questioning look. "What do you mean?"

I pointed at the woman's retreating back. "She was kind of grumpy a minute ago and now she's smiling. You did that."

"Nah. She was just glad to get her popcorn before the movie started." He looked down at the ground for a second but I caught the hint of a smile on his face.

I shrugged. "Well, I tried watching what you did, but I guess I'd better get some proper training so I can help you if we get a rush."

"Good point."

Eli spent the next hour teaching me how to use the register and where to find all of the supplies. A slow trickle of customers came in as the evening wore on, mounting to a pretty big rush just before the seven o'clock showings.

I tried not to stress, but I felt bad when I had to ask Eli for help at the register more than once. He was always patient, and I had to confess I kind of loved how close he stood as he helped me complete the transactions.

After the rush started to die down, I was so busy restocking the candy tray that I didn't notice what was happening at the counter until Eli said, "Courtney, there's someone here to see you."

The sudden coolness in his tone caught me off guard. I glanced at him in confusion before turning to see Tate standing at the counter with a playful grin.

"Hey there, miss. Could I please buy some popcorn?"

My face flushed as I tried to collect myself. "Tate. What are you doing here?"

He shrugged and leaned forward on the counter. "Me and a couple friends wanted to see that new action flick." He turned and gestured to a group of guys waiting behind the line. I recognized some faces, and it looked like most of them had dates. Tate turned back to me and gave a cajoling smile. "Any chance you're getting off soon and can come see it with me?"

I swallowed, sensing Eli's tension even though I knew he was pretending to be busy helping a customer.

"I can't. I don't get off for another hour." I tried to look as apologetic as possible while hiding how uncomfortable this situation was making me.

"Oh. That bites." Tate's expression fell as he glanced back at his friends again.

"Sorry." I twisted the hem of my shirt and willed myself to stop blushing.

"But I've heard it's a great movie . . . do you still want popcorn?" I was trying not to be rude, but there was a line behind him and I didn't want to get in trouble on my first night on the job.

Tate smiled. "No problem. Maybe I can catch you after." He darted a glance at Eli and then back at me. "Yeah, I'll take a large popcorn. What's your favorite candy?"

I tilted my head, not sure I'd heard right. "*My* favorite candy?"

He nodded and I realized I couldn't hold up the line any longer. "Um, I really like Swedish Fish."

"Okay. I'll take a box of those too, then."

I gave him a strange look and then handed him his order. He paid for it and I was mercifully able to handle the transaction without any help.

Tate handed me the box of candy and winked. "Good luck on the job. It looks like you're doing great."

I smiled at the sweet gesture. "Thanks. Enjoy the show."

"I'll try." His marine colored eyes looked regretfully at me for a moment before he took his popcorn bucket and walked off to meet his friends.

I blew out a quick breath and then greeted the next customer in line.

"Wow. If it was that busy on a Thursday night, I can't imagine what the weekend is like," I said as I held my time card under the clock and waited for the stamp.

"Yeah. It gets pretty crazy," Eli answered without expression. He'd been distant ever since Tate's unexpected appearance, but we'd had such a steady stream of customers that I hadn't had time to worry about it.

Wanting to get back to the way things had been before, I chattered on about the customers and how the night had gone. He gave one or two word responses as we got our coats.

Finally I couldn't take it anymore and turned to face him. "Eli, what's going on? I'm sorry Tate showed up like that. I promise I won't be inviting friends to come see me and interfere with work."

His hazel eyes flashed. "Friends? Come on Courtney, you guys are more than that. Why won't you just admit it?"

I looked away. "You saw that Instagram post, didn't you?"

He scoffed. "Everyone in the school saw it. But it's not just that. I'd have to be blind to not notice the way he looks at you. He walks you to class; he invited you to the movie and bought you candy. If that's not the way a boyfriend acts, then what is?"

I sighed and shook my head. "Okay, so maybe he likes me, but it's not like we're officially together."

"*Yet*," Eli added.

I looked at him and folded my arms. "And why do you care?"

"I don't." He held my gaze but his jaw was firm.

I continued to stare at him, trying to hide how badly that statement hurt.

Finally he sighed and ran a hand through his dark hair. "I just think you can do better, that's all."

I raised a disbelieving brow and Eli dropped his hand to his side.

"Tate's one of those guys that has everything: he's the basketball star, drives the sweetest car in school, and now he almost has . . . almost . . ." his voice dropped off in frustration but I was too curious to let it go.

"Almost has what?"

His brows furrowed. "Nothing. He's one of those guys that is used to having girls swarm all over him and I just think you can do better." He looked at me and the light was gone from his eyes. "But it's your life, Courtney. None of this is any of my business."

Well then make it your business, dang it! I searched his eyes for a moment and then turned and left the break room. I made it all the way to the exit doors before he caught up to me.

"Hey, hold on."

I stopped but didn't turn to face him.

"Aren't you going to wait around?" he asked.

"For what?"

He shoved his hands in his pockets. "Aren't you going to meet up with Tate after his movie? I was going to tell you that you can wait in the break room if you want."

I lifted my chin. "No, I'm not waiting around another hour so I can hang out with Tate. I have homework and early practice in the morning."

Eli looked pensive. "Are you sure? Because you could meet him in the theater right now and finish the movie. We get in free, you know."

I placed my hands on my hips and glared at him. "Eli, you're making absolutely no sense. First you tell me I can do better than Tate, and now you're practically shoving me at him. What's the deal?"

He frowned. "Nothing. I just feel bad about the way I reacted a few minutes ago and want you to know that whoever you choose to date is totally cool with me."

"Good to know." I stared him down while trying to ignore how his close proximity made my pulse race.

He opened the glass door and we stepped outside. "Can I walk you to your car?"

I wanted to say yes but felt I had something to prove. "It's fine. I'm not parked far."

"I don't mind." He fell into step beside me and I was secretly happy he was insisting. Dark parking lots always freaked me out a little.

We walked in silence to my car, but before I clicked the button to unlock it, Eli suddenly took my arm, turning me to face him.

"Courtney, here's the thing—I do care who you date. Probably more than I should. So I'm just asking for the truth—are you guys together?" His warm eyes searched mine as he waited for my answer.

My mouth opened slightly and a small puff of steam escaped on a staggered breath. My heart was beating frantically. His hand felt delicious on my arm and I wanted to drink in the look in his eyes.

I knew I could change things between Eli and me right here, right now if I wanted to. And I *did* want to, but would that be fair? I couldn't pretend the kiss with Tate had never happened, or that I didn't have feelings for him too.

After several seconds, I swallowed and finally found my voice. "Eli, I can honestly say that Tate is not my boyfriend . . ."

"But?" He filled in the word that he sensed was coming, dropping his hand as his eyes tightened slightly.

I looked at the ground. "But I don't know which way things are headed—with anyone. I know that's a lame answer, but I'm just a little confused right now. Can you be patient with me?"

He gave a half-smile and I had to cross my arms to keep from wrapping them around his neck. He looked so handsome and vulnerable in that moment it was almost irresistible.

"Sure. I can be patient." A mischievous spark slowly ignited in his eyes, replacing the hurt from a moment before. "But don't forget, you still owe me on that deal we made."

I rolled my eyes and smiled. "Right. You want me to cook something for you."

He shook his head and stepped closer, leaning in until I could smell the tantalizing scent of his body wash as he whispered in my ear. "I've got something else in mind."

I shivered and waited, every nerve on high alert as I impulsively hoped he would draw me into his arms for a kiss. But to my disappointment, he pulled away.

"See you in class tomorrow."

I stood motionless for a second before answering. "Okay." I fished out my keys and unlocked the door. Eli opened it for me, waiting until I was situated before he shut it. He smiled and waved and then walked off between the rows of parked cars.

"Oh boy," I said, turning on the ignition. My mind raced in a thousand directions as I pulled out my phone to send Tate a text letting him know I wouldn't be able to meet him after the movie.

The song, "Fallin' for You," came on the radio. I cranked it up and allowed my thoughts to linger on Eli as I pulled out of the parking lot, heading for home. What I needed was a good night's sleep. Hopefully everything would make a little more sense in the morning.

CHAPTER eighteen

"See how lovely the moonlight glistens on the snow." Hannah sighed as she gazed out the carriage window.

I felt a surge of excitement as I realized I was dreaming in Hannah's world again. I sat beside her on the small seat as we bounced along in the dark. The moon was just bright enough to see the outline of her face.

"Lovely if you're enjoying it alongside a warm fire," her father grumbled from the seat across from us. Even in the dark I couldn't miss his sour expression.

Charles sat next to him. In the dim light I could see his fair hair beneath his top hat and that his eyes were shining with amusement. "Father, surely you know Hannah sees beauty in everything around her. Let's not spoil her enjoyment of the evening. After all, every pretty young girl deserves to be excited for a ball." He smiled at Hannah and gave her a wink as Mr. Walker muttered something under his breath.

Hannah smiled back faintly. "Thank you, Charles." She turned to her father with pity in her eyes. "It will do you good to be out among your parishioners in a setting other than church." She patted his knee, trying to coax a smile as she looked at him. "I'd not be surprised if you see more attendance tomorrow once people see you enjoying yourself tonight."

His frown deepened. "I'll not put myself on display in order to gain more attendance at church. Those who have left us for the so-called United Brethren should repent of their evil ways and come back of their own volition."

I was startled by the sudden fierceness of his tone. I turned to watch Hannah's reaction, but she only smiled more sadly as she dropped her hand and gazed out the window again.

Her father folded his arms across his chest, staring down both of his children even though neither of them would meet his gaze. "I'm not attending tonight for any reason other than to make sure my children do not associate with the traitors in our midst. There will be absolutely no dancing with any member of the United Brethren, do I make myself clear?"

Hannah gave an imperceptible nod as she trained her gaze out the window.

Charles' mouth hardened as he watched her and then turned to his father. "But surely you'll make an exception for William. He's like an older brother to Hannah, and I've asked him to watch over her tonight to keep her sheltered from the scads of eager young chaps who'll undoubtedly seek her attention."

Hannah turned to look at Charles as something unspoken passed between them. When she glanced at her father I could see how hard she was trying to hide the hope in her eyes.

Mr. Walker huffed and shook his head. "I make an exception for William as your friend, Charles, but that is all. Hannah has you for her chaperone. If she is in need of a dance partner, I expect you to fulfill that duty."

Hannah's face fell. "Father, it is hardly fair to ask Charles to miss out on the company of young ladies from our parish in order to keep me entertained." She swallowed and looked down, studying her lace gloves. "These balls are so seldom, after all."

Mr. Walker put up a hand. "Your brother may call on any young lady of his interest if that is his desire. He does not require a ball to begin a courtship."

Charles' jaw tightened as he looked away from his father, but the man seemed oblivious as he continued, "Besides, Charles will have plenty of opportunities to dance. It is my personal understanding that Mr. Hornsby desires to occupy much of your time this evening, Hannah."

I felt her cringe beside me as Charles blurted, "Frederick Hornsby? The fellow with the red hair and fiery temper? Father, you must be joking."

Even in the darkness I could see Mr. Walker's face harden as he thumped his cane on the carriage floor. "I most certainly am not. Mr. Hornsby is one of the most dedicated members of my parish. He is a fine man and one of the few who truly understands the dangers of what is happening amongst our flock. He has made his intentions toward Hannah quite clear, and I have given him my approval."

Hannah looked sick. All of her earlier enthusiasm had vanished as she stared at the carriage floor. I wished I could put a comforting hand on her knee. Who knew there were dads as awful as this? I wanted to take that cane of Mr. Walker's and bonk him right on top of his head.

The rest of the ride was silent until the carriage finally rolled to a stop. I looked out the window to see a pair of cheerful lanterns brightening the path to the building where the dance was being held.

After a moment the driver opened the carriage door and helped Hannah down the steps. A few other carriages waited in line behind us and despite the depressing conversation I'd just heard, I spun around in excitement. This was so cool!

"Come along, Hannah," Charles said gently as he took her arm. The two of them walked a few steps ahead of their father. "Don't worry, we'll work something out," he said once they were out of earshot.

She turned to him with a grateful smile and dabbed her eyes with a handkerchief. Lacing her other arm through his, she gave it a squeeze. "Thank you." The light slowly returned to her eyes as she faced the entrance doors which stood ajar.

I wondered why they would leave the doors open on such a freezing night, but as soon as we entered the overcrowded ballroom, I understood. The place was packed and stuffy. I watched as Charles helped Hannah remove her wrap.

Her gown was simple, as most of the women's dresses here were. But Hannah made it look elegant and the cornflower blue enhanced the color of her eyes. More than a few male heads turned her direction as she and Charles began mingling among the crowd.

Mr. Walker joined a group of older men near the refreshments. I hoped for Hannah's sake that her father would be preoccupied enough to not keep a hawk-like watch on her all night. Especially so she could have a chance to dance with William.

As a small orchestra began to play, I walked over to Hannah and Charles, curious to see who they would dance with. I was a few feet away from them when I spotted William making his way toward Hannah. His gaze was fixed on her as he moved through the crowd. He looked out-of-this-world handsome in his black formal dress coat, gray breeches and black riding boots.

Hannah turned just in time to meet his gaze before Frederick Hornsby appeared behind her and tapped her shoulder.

"Miss Walker, may I have the pleasure of this dance?" he asked.

Hannah turned to him just as William made it to her side. She cast him a quick, longing glance before giving a small curtsy to Hornsby. She said nothing as he led her on to the dance floor, but I caught her looking over her shoulder at William before she began the dance.

William cursed under his breath. "I was too late. That blasted Hornsby beat me to it."

Charles put a hand on his friend's shoulder. "I'm afraid the trouble goes deeper than that," he said.

William glanced at him with a raised eyebrow. "I don't much care for the sound of that. What is it?"

Charles looked around, probably checking to make sure his father wasn't nearby. He led William to the outskirts of the room and I followed them. When they were apart from the rest of the crowd, Charles looked at William and spoke quietly. "My father has just told us that Hornsby has made his intentions toward Hannah known, and that he has given his approval."

Both men turned to look over their shoulders to where Hannah and Hornsby were dancing. William's mouth hardened into a line. "What did Hannah say?"

Charles gave his friend a sympathetic look. "You know her, William. Frederick Hornsby is the last man she would ever choose to marry, but she won't speak against Father. She's loyal to a fault." He looked down and lowered his voice further, "Not only that, but our plan to have you 'watch over her' for the evening has gone awry. Father has forbidden either of us to dance with any member of the United Brethren. He treats us as though we were children."

William ran a hand through his hair, his brown eyes fierce. "Then why put up with it?" he demanded. "Why not stand up to him?" His words were sharp, but when he looked at Charles, there was defeat in his eyes.

"You know why," Charles responded.

Both of them fell silent as they continued to watch the dancing.

I felt like I was missing something here. I was totally on William's side—why would Charles and Hannah let their father boss them around like this? Hannah had to be at least eighteen, and Charles was even older. There had to be some kind of rule I didn't understand.

"It's not so bad for me," Charles said, his gaze trained on the dance floor. "I have plans to go to America as soon as I've earned passage."

William cast him a sideways glance. "You've earned enough already. Weeks ago."

Charles looked at him and nodded once. "Yes. That's true, but I'll not leave until I've either earned enough to bring Hannah with me—" he paused as William cast him a warning glance, "or until I've seen her happily settled here."

William nodded, but his mind was clearly far off.

After a moment Charles turned to him with a smile. "But enough of this sober talk. We're at a ball, William, and there are plenty of pretty girls about. We'd not be proper gentlemen to let another dance go by without asking for partners." He leaned closer. "Besides, I've heard there's to be a waltz, and I have a plan to ensure that you may dance it with my sister."

William brightened, bringing the light back into his handsome face. "Truly? How so?"

Charles smiled smugly and patted his shoulder. "Just leave it to me. Now come on, another dance is starting."

The two walked back into the crowd and I let them go, looking around instead for Hannah. When I saw that she had already been asked by another young man to dance, I let out a sigh. At least it wasn't Hornsby. The look of relief on her face made it obvious she felt the same way.

After watching Charles and William find dance partners, I looked at the couples on the floor. The way they danced was completely fascinating. Each couple moved about in total choreography, and I longed to wear a pretty gown and join them. Even without watching much of the last dance I knew that this one was different, and I wondered how long it took everyone to learn the steps. What a difference from the dances I'd been to! Everything was so proper and elegant, but it wasn't boring. It was magical. When I saw William catch Hannah's gaze across the floor, my knees almost buckled.

The two of them were clearly in love. It wasn't fair that Hannah's dad was ruining everything. Feeling a surge of injustice, I turned to go find him. If nothing else, I could at least give him a piece of my mind. Someone needed to set the old geezer straight.

I marched through the crowd and saw that Mr. Walker was seated near the refreshments with the same group of men he'd been with earlier. I walked right up to him and placed my hands on my hips. "You big bully!" I said, stomping my foot.

He made no sign of acknowledging my presence as he continued talking to the man next to him, so I waved my hands in front of his face.

"Maybe you don't see me, but you need to know that you're a big, fat, bossy jerk and you should just butt out of your kids' lives." I stared him down and then stuck out my tongue. There. At least I felt better.

"Absurd!" Mr. Walker blurted out.

My eyes widened and I stumbled back a step as I wondered if he'd actually seen me, but then he turned to the man next to him. "An American preacher—here? What purpose could he possibly have in traveling so far?"

The old man next to him lowered a wrinkled eyelid. "There's been talk of a stirrin' up North. Word of some American preachers come to spread tales of angels appearin' and the like. Absurd, ye may say, but from what I hear they've caused quite a flurry. An' now the Benbows have gone an' opened their farm up to one of 'em. Rumor has it he and his wife 'ave already been baptized by this foreigner."

Mr. Walker shook his head in disgust. "John Benbow is a fool. He and the rest of the lot who decided to join this so-called church of the United Brethren; seeking for prophets and apostles and things that were done away with at the time of Christ. It's heresy! And now joining any new religion that comes along? I say they deserve whatever ill befalls them by taking in this preacher." He stamped his cane on the ground for emphasis.

A middle-aged man standing to the side had taken interest in the conversation. He had a full beard and mustache and carried the air of someone important. When he sat down in the chair on the other side of Mr. Walker, both men turned to him.

"That may be so, Thomas, but all religious matters aside, you can't deny that Benbow is a respected figure in the community. If he gives ear to this American preacher, who knows what the outcome may be?" He put a hand on Mr. Walker's shoulder. "As a friend and member of your parish, I would advise that you not take the matter too lightly. There is a religious fervor in this county, just waiting for a spark to set it aflame. You saw what happened with the Brethren."

Thomas' mouth turned down. "You have a point, Constable. One cannot be too cautious in these matters."

Just then Charles approached. He smiled and tipped his head at the men. "Good evening, gentlemen. I have come to inquire as to what subject has you all so thoroughly engrossed." Since there were no more chairs, he stood to the side of the constable and folded his arms expectantly.

The old man gave a dry laugh and raised his drooping head to look at Charles. "'Tis the only subject I can interest yer father in, lad. Religion, of course."

Charles nodded. "You know my father well then, Mr. Green." He smiled faintly and turned to glance at the room near the entrance where tables were set up with card games. Turning back to the men he continued, "But what you may not know, is that Father is also exceedingly fond of Whist. What say you we take this conversation to the tables and enjoy it over a glass of brandy?"

The constable and Mr. Green greeted this suggestion with enthusiasm, but Charles' father eyed him suspiciously. He pulled him aside before following the other men. "Why the sudden interest in Whist? I've never known you to care for the game before."

Charles shrugged. "Perhaps there are many things you don't know about me, Father." There was an unmistakable chill in his tone which he quickly shook off with a smile. "But you're right. I'm not terribly fond of cards and I *did* promise the next dance to Hannah. However, I overheard Frederick Hornsby say he was eager to retire to the game room. Have the cards dealt and I'll send him in as your fourth."

Thomas Walker stared at his son a moment longer before releasing his arm with a grunt. "Very well . . . but be quick about it."

Charles nodded and immediately made his way through the crowd. I followed after him until he reached Hornsby, who was holding Hannah captive in a conversation which she looked eager to escape. As soon as she saw her brother, her face lit up.

"Charles! What a pleasant surprise."

Hornsby turned and offered a stiff bow. "Good evening, Charles."

"Good evening." Charles returned the bow. "I'm sorry to intrude, but I've been sent with an urgent message for you."

"Indeed?" Hornsby raised a skeptical brow.

Charles nodded. "It seems that my father is in need of a partner for Whist. He asked if I would inquire whether you would be willing to complete the table." Leaning closer, he added, "I believe he felt it would be a good chance to get better acquainted . . . something which could only prove in your favor." His eyes darted quickly to Hannah and then back.

"I see," Hornsby said, leaning back on his heels. After a second's hesitation he nodded. "Tell your father I'd be delighted to join him, just as soon as I've had the pleasure of the next dance with your sister."

Hannah's face paled.

Charles slapped him on the shoulder, a tad harder than necessary. "Not to worry, old chap. You see, I've already promised the waltz to Hannah so you're free to join my father immediately." At Hornsby's scowl Charles added, "He had hoped the game would not be detained for long, so I suggest you hurry."

I laughed out loud at the look on Hornsby's face. His jaw was working but he turned to Hannah and bowed. "Excuse me, Miss Walker. I shall return as soon as we've played our hand."

Hannah gave a weak smile. "Please don't rush on my account, Mr. Hornsby."

He looked at her under his hooded brow and then gave Charles a final glare before he spun on his heel to head for the game room. Once he was out of sight, Hannah reached for her brother's arm.

"Oh Charles, you've saved me! I was sure I couldn't bear to dance with him again—especially the waltz." Her gaze lowered to the floor. "In fact, if it's alright with you I'd like to go home now. Will you take me?" Moisture glistened in the corners of her eyes.

Charles put his finger below her chin and titled her face up to meet his. "Cheer up, Hannah. I'll take you home if you wish, but let's see if this next dance doesn't make you feel better first."

The orchestra began to play the flowing strains of the waltz, but just before Charles took Hannah in his arms, he looked over her shoulder and grinned. Snapping his fingers, he said, "You know, I've completely forgotten I already promised this dance to Miss Taggart. However, I see another gentleman who is willing to take my place."

Hannah's mouth dropped open in surprise. Before she could protest, Charles took her by the hand and spun her around until she faced William who was standing directly behind her.

"William," she gasped, her face instantly blushing.

He took a step forward and bent his head down to kiss her hand, his warm brown eyes never leaving hers. "M'lady." He straightened again and I sighed at the look that passed between them. "May I have the pleasure of this dance?"

Hannah nodded, her face slowly breaking into a smile. William swept her into his arms and the two of them seemed to glide across the room in a world all their own. It reminded me of when Luke and Eliza had danced at their wedding, and I found myself wishing that someday I could be twirled across a ballroom floor with the man I loved.

Unlike the other dances which had been choreographed and formal, the waltz was a different kind of beautiful. For one thing, the couples danced much closer together than they did in the other dances, and there weren't organized steps. Just the elegant and romantic swirling of the movement as the couples moved about.

When the music ended, I made my way over to Hannah and William. He was clearly reluctant to let her go, and she didn't seem to want to leave his embrace. After they exchanged a few comments about the ball, William took her hand. "It's getting quite hot in here. Might I interest you in a turn about the garden?"

She laughed. "We'll catch our death of cold."

He tilted his head toward hers and a mischievous look entered his eyes. "I'll lend you my coat."

Hannah bit her lip and glanced around before smiling. "Only for a moment," she whispered.

William grinned and clasped her hand as they moved through the crowd toward a door near the back of the ballroom. He looked around to make sure no one was watching before he opened it a crack and the two of them slipped outside.

Just for fun, I waited until the door closed behind them and then walked through it. The shock of leaving the stuffy dance hall for the frigid night air made me shiver. I wrapped my arms tightly around myself and saw that Hannah was shivering as well.

William stripped off his dress coat, leaving only his vest and shirtsleeves as he placed the coat around Hannah's shoulders. "I'm sorry to bring you out into the cold like this, but I had to speak with you." He allowed his arm to rest across her shoulders for just a moment before letting it drop to his side.

Hannah tilted her face up at him. "What is it, William?"

He stared mesmerized at her for a moment before looking away and raking a hand through his dark hair. "I wish I could have done this properly—courted you in the way you deserve before declaring my feelings. But there simply isn't time." He looked at her again and his eyes were intense in the moonlight.

Hannah seemed to barely breathe as she waited for him to continue.

William stepped forward and took both of her hands in his. "I love you, Hannah Walker. I've loved you for as long as I can remember. With all that I am and all that I have, I long for you most desperately."

Hannah made a small gasping sound as her blue eyes shone with tears. "William, I—"

He shook his head and squeezed her hands. "No, please, let me continue or I'll never be able to say it." He took a deep breath and glanced up at her from beneath his lashes. "Forgive me for being so forward, especially when you've not made your feelings clear, but I know of Hornsby's intentions and I couldn't bear to stand by and watch without letting you know of my own." His brown eyes were filled with warmth as he tenderly stroked her cheek. "I wish to make you my wife, Hannah."

Her eyes widened a moment before more tears filled them. She placed a hand to the side of his cheek as she tilted her face up to his. "I love you too, William."

The air was completely still as he stared at her in wonder. He took her face in both of his hands, a smile curving his mouth as he bent down to kiss her. Hannah stood still for a moment and then wrapped her arms tightly about his neck, returning the kiss with fervor. A small moan escaped William as he circled his arms around her waist and drew her in closer.

I watched the two of them completely wrapped up in their love. It was so beautiful I almost didn't dare to breathe for fear of ruining the moment. But I noticed that tears were still streaming down Hannah's face.

William noticed too. He pulled away from her, gently wiping away the moisture with the back of his hand. "Here now, what's this? Tears of joy, I hope?" he asked softly.

Hannah looked down and stepped back. "Oh, William, what's to be done? It's true—Mr. Hornsby has made his intentions known, and Father has given his approval." She twisted her lace-gloved hands. "But if that were our only obstacle, it would be nothing." Her face filled with sadness as her eyes searched his. "You know Father would never approve of our courtship, much less marriage. His pride was deeply wounded when you left the parish to join the United Brethren."

William's brow furrowed. "But surely once he knows of our love for each other, he can be made to see reason?"

Hannah shook her head, her features twisting in pain. "Not Father. Not about this. You don't know him like I do."

He took her hand in his. "Hannah, I would do anything to gain his favor again, you know that. But I can't pretend to believe in something I don't."

"Nor would I wish you to." She let her hand drop from his. "Which is why we must . . ." her lip trembled as she struggled to maintain composure. Taking a deep breath, she straightened her shoulders. "Why we must not entertain these feelings for one another any longer. It's not a possibility, William. Not for us."

He reared back as though he'd been slapped before his face slowly hardened. "No. I won't accept that." He stepped forward, taking her by the arms. "We'll run away if we have to. Now that I know you return my feelings, I'll not let your father or anyone else stand in the way of our being together."

Hannah's tears fell faster. "Please don't make this harder than it has to be. Father has already lost my mother, and as soon as Charles earns passage he'll leave for America. If Father continues to lose members of his parish he'll have to let Mrs. White go, and where would that leave him? I couldn't possibly abandon him."

William tilted his head down until his eyes met hers. "Charles intends to take you to America with him. He won't leave without taking you, or making sure you're happily settled here."

Her brows knit together in confusion. "Charles hasn't said a word to me about it."

William nodded. "And he'll have my hide for telling you, but you must see reason." He lowered his voice. "Hannah, I've been saving too. With my job at the mill, soon I'll have enough for us to settle here, or take you with me to America. Whatever you wish."

She looked up at him, but uncertainty still creased her brow. Before she could say anything, the door to the dance hall burst open.

"What is the meaning of this?" Mr. Walker boomed. Charles appeared behind him looking breathless.

William dropped his hands from Hannah's arms. Her face turned white as she spun around to face her father.

CHAPTER nineteen

I startled awake, my heart pounding. It took me a second to shake the image of Mr. Walker and the murderous look that had been in his eyes. I desperately hoped Hannah and William would be okay, but then I realized they weren't even real. It was all a dream. Just a crazy, overly-vivid dream.

My alarm went off and I jumped again, slamming down on the clock harder than usual. It was Friday. My last and only chance to practice before the halftime performance tonight.

I hopped out of bed and changed into my dance clothes, forcing thoughts of my dream to the back of my mind. I had to stay focused, but there was no denying now that this series of dreams was weird to say the least. I'd never dreamt a full-on story before, especially one in sequence. I found myself thinking about Hannah during the day and hoping to dream more about her life during the night. Was I losing it?

On the snowy drive to school my thoughts turned in a different direction—one that involved my current boy issues. This would be my first time facing Serena since that rotten Instagram post, and I was not looking forward to it.

"Just focus on dancing," I reminded myself. For this morning, I needed to push everything else aside and remember why I had tried out for the drill team in the first place: I loved to dance.

I shouldered my bags and made my way into the gym where only a handful of girls were present. I'd made it a point to be on time today. Any small thing to show Coach I was serious about wanting to do my best.

Everyone turned and stared at me as I walked in, but thankfully Serena wasn't among them. I ignored the stares and stowed my bags in the locker room before returning to the gym to stretch out.

I sensed the moment Serena walked in because every square inch of the large gym suddenly filled with tension. I looked up and saw her watching me. Her eyes were cold and calculating as we stared at each other, then she flipped her hair and joined a group of her friends who were whispering in the corner.

Coach Weaver walked in. "Alright girls, circle up. I have a couple of announcements before we start today," she said.

We formed a circle and she stood in the middle. Janie suddenly appeared at my side and Coach eyed her. "Janie, that was cutting it close. Another thirty seconds and I would have had to mark you as tardy."

"Sorry, Coach. It won't happen again," Janie said.

Coach Weaver nodded and turned to me. "Courtney has something to share with you guys, and then I have a few reminders about tonight's performance."

I swallowed as all eyes suddenly turned to me. "Um, yeah." I shifted onto my other foot. "I was absent yesterday because my mom was in the hospital with some pregnancy complications. Everything is okay, but because it was a family emergency Coach is allowing me to perform tonight."

Most of the girls nodded in understanding, but Serena looked ready to draw blood.

Coach scanned the group. "Everyone should be clear that this was an extenuating circumstance. I very rarely make exceptions. If I felt that Courtney's dancing wasn't up to par, I wouldn't be allowing her to perform tonight." She glanced down at her clipboard and began the reminders about our costumes and what time we would need to show up tonight.

I sighed in relief as the topic had moved away from me and Janie gave me a quick, comforting pat on the back. We listened as Coach ran through the rest of her announcements, but just before she excused us to begin warm ups, Serena raised her hand.

"Coach?"

She lifted her gaze from the clipboard. "Yes?"

"I understand that you're making an exception for Courtney, but to set an example I think it's only fair that she still have some accountability. Something like—having to move to the back line for the performance."

Coach lowered her clipboard. "I appreciate the suggestion, Serena, and I know it stems from your desire to keep things fair, but to move Courtney would mean to change up some of the choreography. That's something we don't have time for at this point."

Serena shrugged. "I understand. I just don't want anyone to feel like Courtney's getting special treatment."

Tension pooled around the gym again and I felt my face burn.

Janie fidgeted beside me and finally spoke up, "I don't think anyone feels that way. Her mom was in the *hospital*." She gave Serena a cool stare. "I'm sure we can all understand that."

Serena glared at her and Coach held up her hands to intervene. "Alright, girls, let's not make this a big deal. I've worked things out with Courtney and that's the end of it. Understood?" She looked at Serena who shrugged and checked her nails.

Coach nodded. "Alright then, let's warm up!"

We began our laps around the gym and Janie fell into step beside me. "You okay?" she asked.

I nodded and swallowed the thickness in my throat. That whole situation had been mortifying. "I'm fine. I knew Serena wasn't going to want to be best pals anymore," I said with an edge of sarcasm. "At least I still get to perform tonight."

Janie looked over to where Serena was jogging. "Yeah. Let's just hope we've seen the worst of what she's going to do."

I didn't like the foreboding sound in her tone.

After our laps and stretches, we finally got to the part I loved—the dance. We lined up in formation and waited for the music to start.

"Don't forget to watch your spot partner and give any pointers you think would be helpful," Coach reminded a split second before the music keyed up.

As I fell into the routine, I couldn't keep the smile off of my face. I loved the choreography of this dance, which was a take on futuristic robots.

"Sharper! I want precision! Girls on the left, tighten up that line . . . tighter!" Coach called out as we danced.

I glanced at my spot partner, Katie. She was a great dancer, but I did notice she was a second behind the rest of us during one particular leg lift. I'd sandwich my feedback with compliments, the way we'd been taught to do for our spotters. I was sure she'd have some good pointers for me too.

I held my end pose as the final notes ended. Adrenaline coursed through me and I knew I'd done well.

Coach had been watching me closely, and her curt nod of approval told me she was pleased. "Okay, girls, quick comments from spotters and then let's run through it again," she said.

I turned to Katie and gave her a high five. "Great job! Your movements were totally sharp. Maybe just watch that leg lift right before we break out of formation; it seemed just a second behind. But other than that you totally nailed it. I can't believe how high you can kick!"

She smiled. "Thanks. Yeah, that one spot always throws me, but I'll get it this time."

Before she could give me my feedback, Serena called across from a few rows over, "Courtney, remember we're not supposed to smile during this number—it's straight-faced. And your arm work was really sloppy."

My face flushed as the girls around me stared.

"Okay. I'll work on it," I said. It was humiliating to be called out like that in front of everyone, especially since Serena wasn't even my spotter.

Katie turned to me and raised an eyebrow. "I think you did awesome. Sure, you were smiling, but your arms were *not* sloppy," she said.

"Thanks." I tried to pretend that Serena's comment didn't faze me. "Was there anything else you think I should work on?"

She shrugged. "You know I'd tell you if there was, but honestly you did great. You're ready for tonight."

I smiled uncertainly, hating that Serena's comments made me doubt Katie's praise.

The music began again and we ran through the number twice more, breaking it down into a few segments Coach felt needed extra practice. Each time we had a break, Serena criticized my dancing, but she was quiet about it. She knew Coach would call her out for picking on me if she got caught.

Although I tried to push the negative comments from my mind, it was becoming harder and harder for me to focus. As much as I tried to fight it, Serena was getting in my head. By the time practice was over it was all I could do to keep my tears in check.

"Courtney, is everything all right?" Coach asked.

I glanced at Serena who wore a smug smile. Janie looked at me curiously from across the room. If she knew what was going on, she would have told Coach, but I wasn't about to give Serena the satisfaction.

"I'm fine," I lied.

Coach's lips tightened. "The first few times you did the number it was flawless, but the last few needed improvement. Make sure you bring your best to the performance tonight."

"I will." When I turned to head to the locker room, Katie gave me a sympathetic look. I knew if she talked to me about Serena right now I'd lose my battle with the tears so I rushed in to change.

Janie came in as I was pulling clothes out of my bag. "Are you alright?"

"Yeah. Just lost focus there at the end." I turned my back and sat down on the wooden bench to pull my jeans on. Thankfully Janie didn't press for more information. She was good at giving me space when she sensed I needed it.

After getting ready I had a few extra minutes to eat a yogurt and granola bar before heading to biology. I rounded the corner in the hallway and slowed down, waiting for Tate in what had become our usual meeting place.

As I waited, I noticed two guys look at each other's phones. One of them glanced at me and his eyes got wide a second before he bumped his friend in the arm and gestured my way. The other boy looked at me and then back at his phone. They laughed and looked over their shoulders at me again before walking down the hall.

Weird. I didn't even know those guys. When I started getting more looks and hearing more snickers from people walking by, my stomach turned. Something was up, and I had a feeling it wasn't good. I pulled out my phone and saw there was a new message on Snapchat. I opened it and felt a surge of bile rise to my throat.

It was a picture of me in my bra and underwear in the locker room. My jeans were halfway up my leg, and someone had Photo Shopped the image to make it look like I was sitting on a toilet. As if the picture wasn't horrible enough, the caption underneath was even nastier, involving my name and bowel movements. And it had been sent to the entire student body.

Tears swam in my eyes as I put my phone back into my pocket and ran for the nearest restroom. The stares and snickers that followed me down the hall were like needles jabbing me from every direction.

I found the nearest open bathroom stall and shut myself inside, covering my mouth with my hands so no one would hear me crying. I wanted to crawl into a dark hole and die. I would never live down this humiliation. Even though the message was gone by now, the shame I felt was branded into me. One little picture had crushed me until I felt nothing but hollow despair.

As my mind still tried to grasp the enormity of someone's cruelty at doing this, a burning anger crept into my heart. Not *someone*. It had been Serena. She had done this out of her petty jealousy. I welcomed the hatred that grew inside of me. Anger was the only thing that seemed to ease my torment at the moment. Serena was going to pay for this.

Tears poured down my cheeks and I didn't even bother wiping them away until the bell rang. I had to get to class. Mr. Sanchez was allowing me to make up the test and I didn't dare mess that up by being absent again.

Using a wad of toilet paper, I dabbed at my tears and dried off my face as best I could. I knew there was no chance of hiding the fact that I'd been crying, but at this point I didn't care. If this was going to be the worst day of my life, I might as well have the tear stains to prove it.

I took a deep, shaky breath and opened the stall door. When I exited the bathroom, there were still a few stragglers rushing to get to class. One acne-ridden boy smirked at me as he passed. "Hey potty girl—get caught with your pants down?"

I clenched my teeth and pretended not to hear him as I made my way to class. Several pairs of eyes looked my way as I entered the room. Eli sat at our table, watching me with an expression so sympathetic it made me want to cry all over again.

I looked away from him and headed straight for Mr. Sanchez's desk. He barely glanced up. "You're late, Miss Moore."

"I know. Sorry. Can I still make up the test?"

He raised his eyes from the paper he was marking and must have noticed my puffy eyes, because his face softened. "Everything all right with your mom?"

I swallowed and nodded. He looked at me a second longer before handing me a few sheets of paper stapled together. "Go ahead and have a seat at that empty table in the back. You can take the full hour, but you'll have to get notes from your lab partner about what we cover today."

"Thank you." I headed to the table and tried to force my brain to switch gears into test mode. Which, at this point, was laughable. I used to always pray before taking a test, but I couldn't bring myself to do it. I sank into my chair and pulled out a pencil, using my hand to shield my face from the curious glances darting my way.

I was so going to fail this test.

Eli was waiting for me when class was over. I didn't feel like talking to anyone, but there was no way of getting around it. I approached him with a pathetic attempt at a smile. "How's it going?"

He stepped close and looked down at me, gently taking hold of my arms. "Courtney, are you okay?"

I let out a mirthless laugh and shook my head, avoiding eye contact. "It's no big deal. Just your everyday cyberbullying at its finest."

He squeezed my arms slightly. "Well whoever it was, they only made themselves look stupid. Even with the lame toilet in the picture, you looked . . ." His words trailed off and I finally dared a glance up at him.

He rubbed a hand across the back of his neck and I saw the hint of a blush beneath his bronze skin. He cleared his throat. "I'm sorry it happened, but the only thing people will remember is how gorgeous you are, and what a jerk whoever sent it was."

His warm hazel eyes started to melt the pain away from my insides, but I could only nod in response. He dropped his hands but his gaze stayed locked with mine. "I'm sure it will be forgotten by tomorrow, but if anyone gives you crap about it, they answer to me, okay?"

"Thanks, Eli." Tears pooled in my eyes again so I wiped at them and changed the subject as we walked toward the door. "That test was pretty intense. I'm not sure I passed."

He shook his head and smiled. "You always say that."

"Well, this time I mean it. I couldn't focus, let alone remember what I studied the day before yesterday."

"That's because you had the wrong study partner."

I turned to him in surprise but there was no hint of humor in his face.

"Oh, you think so?" I said with a wry smile.

"Let's just say you might want to study with me next time."

I scoffed and he gave me a charming sideways grin.

"So, you're performing at the game tonight, right?" he asked.

"Yeah." My stomach turned sour just thinking about being in the same room with Serena.

"Does that mean you're sticking around for the dance after?" He glanced at me out of the corner of his eye.

I bit my lip. I'd planned on going to the dance, but after what had happened the last thing I wanted to do was hang around people from school. "I don't think so."

Eli stopped walking and touched my elbow, sending electric little shivers dancing down my spine. "Look, Courtney, I don't blame you if you don't feel up to it. But I really hope you won't let whoever sent that picture win by putting yourself in hiding." He paused and looked away. "Besides, I'll be really disappointed if you're not there."

When he glanced back at me the look in his eyes made me forget how to breathe. I swallowed and shook my head. "That's really sweet, but I don't think tonight's a good night for me."

He tilted his head. "Come on, don't make me use that 'you owe me' thing on this."

I couldn't help but smile at his impish grin. "You wouldn't waste it on something so lame. You're too smart for that."

He shrugged. "I don't know . . . it's sounding better by the minute."

A group of girls walked by and laughed when they saw me. Eli gave them a dark look before putting his arm around my shoulder. Even though I knew it was a pity gesture, I was too broken to protest. His arm was the only thing holding me together at the moment.

He leaned in. "Don't pay any attention to them. I'll walk you to class."

CHAPTER

twenty

By the time I made it to lunch, I was ready to leave school and never come back. My last class had been torture, with a few girls whispering and laughing behind me almost the entire period. Suddenly it seemed like no one would talk to me or look me in the eye, even the people whom I'd thought had been my friends before.

I remembered Eli's comment that anyone who gave me a hard time would answer to him. Those words, which had been comforting then, now made me cringe with embarrassment. He would pretty much have to take on the whole school at this point.

There was one person whose avoidance hurt more than anyone else's. Tate hadn't tried to find or text me since this morning. I didn't blame him for being ashamed to be seen with me, especially on his big game day. But that didn't make the pain any less intense.

Rather than giving in to the tears that constantly threatened, I allowed anger to wash over me and cover me like a force field as I gathered books from my locker. I could put on an indifferent face for a few more minutes until I made it out of this nightmare place.

"Courtney."

At the sound of Lexi's voice, my face crumpled. I turned and she immediately threw her arms around me. I couldn't keep the tears from streaming down my face as she gave me a tight hug.

After several seconds she pulled away and looked me in the eyes. "You haven't replied to any of my texts. I've been so worried."

I wiped my tears with the edge of my sleeve and looked away. "Sorry. I just—need to get out of here, you know?" Alexis and Janie had been sending me texts all morning, but I couldn't bring myself to answer them. Getting sympathy would cause the floodgates to open, and I couldn't afford to break down like that here. After watching other kids get bullied, I knew the key was to act like it didn't affect me at all. But that was so much harder to do than I'd ever realized.

Lexi's green eyes softened as she watched me close my locker. "I don't blame you for wanting to go home, but come to lunch with me first. You'll feel better if we talk."

I shouldered my backpack and hesitated. I did want to talk to someone, and I knew I could tell Alexis anything. She saw that I was waffling so she touched my arm.

"We'll go somewhere off the grid. I'm buying."

I gave her a watery smile. "Thanks, Lex."

"Should I text Janie and invite her to come? I saw her heading to the cafeteria but she probably hasn't gotten her food yet."

I shook my head. "No. I'll talk to her later. I'd rather it be just you and me this time."

Alexis nodded. "Let's go."

We set our trays of food down at a small, out-of-the-way café that Lexi suggested. I hadn't had much appetite, but the bowl of creamy homemade mac n' cheese and Oreo milkshake were calling my name. Normally on performance days I nitpicked about what I ate, but today I just wanted to drown in comfort food.

I took a spoonful of the pasta and sighed. "This is really good."

Lexi smiled. "Told you. My mom bought brownies from here last week and I haven't stopped dreaming about them since."

"Well thanks, it was exactly what I needed." I sipped on my ice water and then took several more bites. Lexi was letting me lead the way in the conversation, and I knew she was waiting for me to open up, but I didn't want to talk about the Snapchat post. Not while I was enjoying my macaroni.

"So tell me about the temple the other night—did you and Connor talk much?"

Her eyes lit up. "Courtney, it was so awesome. I wish you could have come. There was this amazing sunset and as I sat outside reading my scriptures, I just felt so much peace, you know?"

I nodded and looked down, taking another bite. Actually I didn't know. I hadn't felt that kind of peace in a long time. "And Connor?" I prodded, hoping to steer the topic back to something I was comfortable with.

Her smile widened. "He came out to sit with me after he was done doing baptisms and we had a few minutes alone to talk."

I raised an eyebrow. "What did you talk about?"

"Just our goals and school, and a bunch of other random stuff—but it was perfect." She took a bite of her chicken salad croissant and I could tell by the light in her eyes that there was something else.

"What? There's something you're not telling me," I pried.

"He asked if I was going to the dance tonight," she said, picking at her brownie with a grin.

My mouth dropped open. "Um, hello? I can't believe you didn't tell me that first. Lex, that's so cute! I bet he'll dance every slow song with you."

"Whatever." She shook her head but kept smiling.

"You'll see." I polished off the last of my pasta and started for the milkshake.

Her smile faded as she watched me. "You're coming, right?"

I paused halfway to the straw and my stomach twisted. "To the dance?"

"I don't blame you if you don't want to go. We can watch movies and eat chocolate instead." Her eyes were pleading.

I swallowed the milkshake which suddenly felt thick in my throat. "You could go with Janie. I'm sure she's planning on it."

The light drained from Lexi's eyes but she smiled. "No, it's totally cool. We'll have a girls' night in."

I looked down and swirled the straw in my shake. "It's just that I don't know if I can handle—"

She reached out and touched my hand, giving it a quick squeeze. "It's okay, Court. I understand."

I hated that I couldn't just suck it up and tell her I'd go to the dance. I'd considered going again after Eli's subtle invitation, but after dealing with so many cruel looks and whispers for the first half of the day I wasn't sure I was up for more.

"Do you want to talk about what happened?" Alexis hedged. "It was Serena, wasn't it?"

My blood boiled just hearing her name. "Yes, but I don't really feel like talking about it. Unless you want to help me plot how to get revenge."

Lexi's eyes widened. "Wow. Really?"

I felt a bit annoyed that she wasn't immediately on board. "Um, yeah. You don't think I'm going to sit by and do nothing when she practically destroyed my reputation, do you?"

Lexi dabbed a seasoned fry into her ketchup. "Look, it's not that I don't think she doesn't have it coming, it's just . . . are you sure you want to go there?"

I stared at her without blinking. "Yes."

She paused for several seconds before finally nodding. "Okay then."

We cleaned up our table and headed for Lexi's car. When she started the ignition she turned to me. "So what are you going to do? Head home?"

I shook my head. "No. Thanks for talking me into coming to lunch. I'm feeling a little better now. Besides, I already missed yesterday so I'd probably better stick around."

She smiled and put the car in gear. "Good. My evil plan worked."

I laughed. On the way back to school we talked about random silly things, joking around the way we used to. Lexi had a way of bringing me out of a bad mood. By the time we arrived in the parking lot I felt lighter and ready to face the rest of the day, so I was surprised when she turned to me before getting out of the car.

"Courtney . . . is everything alright?" Her expression had turned serious.

I raised an eyebrow. "Yeah. What do you mean?"

She shifted in her seat. "I don't know. It probably sounds lame, but I've been kind of worried about you. You haven't seemed like yourself for the past few weeks and I just wanted to make sure that everything is okay."

"Haven't been myself?" I repeated, instantly feeling guarded.

She shrugged and gave a small laugh. "I told you it was lame. It's just that even before this whole Snapchat thing you haven't seemed—happy. At least not like you used to be, and I wanted to let you know that if you ever want to talk—"

"Lex, I'm fine," I cut her off, looking her square in the eyes for emphasis. "But thanks for worrying. I couldn't ask for a better BFF." I titled my head to the side and gave her a cheesy grin.

She laughed. "Okay." She opened her door and grabbed her bag. "Well, I'm off to seminary."

"You seem pretty eager about it." I grabbed my backpack, closing the car door as I fell into step beside her.

"Our whole class has done one hundred percent on daily scripture study for the past two weeks, so Brother Richards is bringing doughnuts today."

"Wow. That's cool." I tried to sound enthusiastic. Apparently I needed to up my "happy game" around Alexis, who was a little more perceptive than I cared for at the moment.

She nodded. "Yeah. You know, at first I totally dreaded having to read my scriptures every single day. Ten minutes felt like forever, and the first few days I was constantly staring at the clock. But the crazy thing is, you know that gross 'wasted time' feeling you get when you've been watching TV or surfing Instagram too long?"

I shrugged, not sure where she was going with this.

She smiled. "Well I noticed I never feel that way after reading my scriptures. In fact, I feel the opposite. I really can tell a difference in my life since I've been reading. Nothing huge, but it's like I see things more clearly, you know?"

The light in her eyes made me feel about two inches tall. How could I confess that I hadn't read my scriptures in over a month when she was so hyped up about it—and when had my non-LDS best friend become more spiritual than I was?

I nodded and remained silent.

"Even my mom has noticed a difference. The other day she told me that I seemed happier, and asked what new relationship I was in." Alexis laughed and I joined in half-heartedly.

"That's so great, Lexi." *Now let's talk about something else.*

"I know! Brother Richards is always telling us that miracles are not only possible, but if we're doing the right things, we can expect to see them in our lives. It makes me think that if studying my scriptures everyday can make this much difference, who knows what might happen? Maybe my dad will even let me get baptized before I'm eighteen."

I glanced at her out of the corner of my eye and she must have seen the doubt there.

"What? Don't you think it's possible?" Her expression wavered and I instantly felt like a jerk.

"Yeah . . . totally. I think anything is possible. It's just that your dad—" I didn't know how to finish.

Lexi's face twisted. "I know. It would take a miracle for him to change the way he feels about Mormons."

I stared at the ground and hated that I couldn't sound more positive, but I didn't want Lexi to get her hopes up. Her dad had some very strong opinions about the LDS church, and I couldn't see him softening on the issue—no matter how much Alexis read her scriptures. Her older brothers were the same way, and with all of those cards stacked against her I didn't want her to be disappointed when the miracle she hoped for didn't happen. Besides, she was sixteen and could choose to be baptized in two years. What was the rush?

I put my hand on her shoulder. "I gotta head to my next class. Enjoy the doughnuts, okay?"

She gave me a half-hearted smile. "I will. And you be thinking of what you want to do for our girls' night. It'll be awesome."

"Epic." I smiled at her and then headed inside the school, bracing myself for whatever cyberbullying after-shocks awaited me.

CHAPTER twenty-one

The bleachers were packed but I refused to think about that as I waited in beginning pose for the music to start. As the first beats filled the gym, I put all other thoughts out of my head and got lost in the dance.

The music pulsed through me as I performed each step with precision. Adrenaline always helped me perform better and it was all I could do to maintain the robotic expression we were supposed to wear when my natural impulse was to smile at the pure energy I felt.

A few seconds before the end of the routine, I spotted Tate standing on the edge of the gym floor. He was watching me with a huge grin on his face. I hadn't expected to see him since the basketball team was supposed to be in the locker room during halftime. The sight of his smile almost made me forget the choreography, but I quickly recovered and forced myself to focus on the final few steps.

After holding the end pose to the sound of applause and cheers, I dared another peek in his direction. He was clapping and looking straight at me. I looked back at him and smiled, feeling a whole different surge of adrenaline. Did this mean that he wasn't going to be embarrassed to be seen with me, in spite of that Snapchat message?

Serena noticed our exchange. I saw her watching Tate and then turn to give me the evil eye.

Our team filed back off the gym floor and out into the hallway. I lifted my head and smiled confidently, finding Janie as soon as we made it through the gym doors.

"You rocked it, Moore!" she said as we gave each other high fives.

"You too, Janie."

We giggled and skipped arm-in-arm to the locker room to change. I loved meeting up with Janie after a performance; we always fed off of each other's energy.

"Now we finally have some extra time to get ready," she said as she opened her locker. "Can I borrow some of your new eye shadow? I love the way it shimmers and I want to look hot for the dance. You're coming, right?"

I grinned and tossed it to her. "You bet." After seeing the way Tate had smiled at me, I was determined to go. Not to mention I'd spotted Eli watching the game with a group of his friends. Besides, it would make Alexis happy.

I sent her a quick text: *Be out in a sec. Good thing you wore that new cute shirt—cuz we're goin' dancing!*

Alexis: *Woo-hoo! I'm so glad you changed your mind. Better get out here quick—Tate is on fire making baskets & we're killing the other team. You won't want to miss it!*

I grinned at Lexi's enthusiastic reply, feeling a little smug when I glanced down the locker room to where Serena was getting ready. She had failed. Tate, the basketball star, and one of the hottest guys in school liked me, and there was nothing she could do about it.

Janie and I walked into the darkened gym which was now thumping with dance music. There was an added notch of excitement in the air after the amazing game that our team had won. And there was no denying, Tate had been the star. He'd scored an insane amount of points and I'd watched a good majority of them, feeling my pulse rise with every basket.

He looked incredible on the court, effortlessly sinking shot after shot. He'd sought me out of the crowd a few times and given me these gorgeous grins until I felt like I was going to melt into a puddle on the bleachers. How was I so lucky? I could hardly wait to see him.

As my friends pulled me into the crowd to dance, I glanced around the room. Lexi laughed and grabbed my arm. "You're going to give yourself whiplash. Don't worry—he'll come looking for you when he shows. Now let's dance!"

Janie was already busting some moves and the three of us danced to the next two fast songs. I danced along with them, but when a slow song finally played, I couldn't help but glance around again.

Connor quickly found Alexis and asked her to dance, leaving Janie and me to move a little farther off the dance floor. Then a guy I didn't know asked Janie to dance. She gave me an uncertain smile and I nodded in encouragement before he led her onto the floor.

Awesome. I was flying solo. As hard as I tried to banish them, thoughts of the Snapchat text started wiggling into my mind. I didn't usually have a hard time getting asked to dance, but I began to wonder if tonight would be different. Folding my arms across my chest, I slowly began edging farther off the dance floor.

A commotion near the entrance doors caught my attention and I spotted Tate. People cheered as he walked in with a group of guys from the basketball team. My heartrate sped up in anticipation as I felt the anxiety melt away. He was going to find me and ask me to dance, or maybe I would be brave and ask him.

A hand touched my shoulder and I whipped around to see Eli standing there. He gave me a charming sideways smile.

"Can I have this dance?"

The way he extended his hand suddenly gave me a flashback from my dreams. He stood so tall and handsome I could almost picture him in Regency clothing.

I beamed and took his hand. "Yes."

He led me a few steps onto the dance floor before putting his arms around me. "Is this okay, or would you rather dance the 'old fashioned way'?"

I laughed, trying to switch my thoughts from Tate to Eli. The familiar scent of Eli's body wash and the feel of his arms around my waist were making it easier than I dared to admit.

"This is good," I said, glancing up at him. The moment our eyes met I knew I shouldn't have made eye contact. Something happened whenever Eli's gaze met mine—something way too unsettling.

"You did a great job dancing at halftime."

I tilted my head and raised a teasing eyebrow. "You were watching me?"

His lips quirked as he shrugged. "I may have noticed you here and there."

I smiled and shook my head. "Whatever."

His eyes searched mine and then tightened. "That was a pretty awesome game." He looked away as an unspoken thought seemed to form between both of us. I was almost surprised he would bring up the game at all.

"Yeah, it was." I couldn't help glancing over his shoulder to where Tate was still surrounded by a crowd.

If Eli noticed where my attention was directed, he made no sign. "A few of us were thinking about going to my place to watch a movie after the dance." He had been looking over the top of my head and then suddenly he glanced at me. His hazel eyes warmed as they met mine. "Do you want to come?"

My mouth felt dry. *Yes! No . . . maybe?* I stared at his shoulder. "That sounds really fun. I'll just have to check and see what my friends want to do first."

He nodded. "They can come too if they want. It's just going to be a bunch of us hanging out."

"Okay." The song was winding down. For a moment I allowed myself to bask in the feel of Eli's arms around me. There was something comforting about being held by him. I almost wished he'd pull me in tighter.

"Well, thanks for the dance."

Disappointment rose within me as he let go before the final few notes, but I smiled. "Yeah, thanks." I stepped back slightly and hooked my thumbs through the belt loops in my jeans. "I'll talk to Lexi and Janie about the movie and let you know."

"Sounds good." His eyes lingered on mine for a moment before he turned and walked away.

I watched him go before seeking out my friends. I found them near the center of the crowded floor, already dancing to the fast song. I joined them and felt carefree as we moved to the music, just having fun.

When I spotted Serena dancing a few yards over I didn't let it get to me. She and a group of her friends were surrounded by some of the popular guys in school. I did my best to ignore her, but I could feel her eyes on me every now and again.

As another fast song started, I felt someone come up behind me. He pulled me up against him and starting dancing in a way I'd never been comfortable with. I was about to move away when I turned and noticed it was Tate.

"Hey there, gorgeous. I've been looking for you," he whispered in my ear.

My face flushed as I wondered what to do. Janie and Alexis were still dancing, but from their wide-eyed expressions, I knew they were surprised to see me dancing this way. Then my attention was directed to Serena, who was watching while pretending not to.

In an instant I didn't care how it looked. This was my chance for revenge and I was going to take it. Besides, what girl in her right mind wouldn't want to dance with Tate Williams up close and personal?

I allowed him to continue to hold me as we moved together to the music, pushing guilt and the words from *For the Strength of Youth* out of my mind. Strangely, I kept thinking about Hannah and the way the people had danced at the ball. They would be shocked to see how teenagers danced these days.

Alexis turned away, dancing half-heartedly. Janie was still bug-eyed, but I didn't care. I wanted to get back at Serena and the rest of the school who'd tormented me all day. Let them see who the most sought-after guy was crushing on now.

Tate continued to hold me close and wrapped his arms around my waist, pressing his cheek against mine. I smiled as I inhaled the scent of his cologne, and then the smile on my face froze. Eli was standing in the crowd, watching us. The look in his eyes made my throat constrict. When his gaze met mine he shook his head in disgust before turning and walking away.

I stopped dancing but Tate continued holding me. "Everything okay?" he asked low into my ear.

I nodded and swallowed. "Yeah. I just need a drink of water. I'll be right back."

He released his grip around my waist, an almost hungry look in his eyes as he held my hand a second longer. "Don't be long. I'm saving the next slow song for you."

"Okay." I smiled back at him and then quickly weaved through the crowd. I didn't know why I felt the need to find Eli. I had only been dancing, but I couldn't stand the look of disappointment I'd seen on his face.

I searched all around but didn't see him anywhere. Finally I found one of his friends and went up to him. "Have you seen Eli?"

He shook his head. "He took off a few minutes ago."

I bit my lip. "I thought you guys were going to watch a movie at his house."

He shrugged. "He said he wasn't feeling good."

My shoulders slumped. "Okay. Thanks."

I made my way out into the hall for the drinking fountain and considered sending Eli a text, but then decided against it. I didn't want to make the situation a bigger deal than it needed to be—and what *was* the big deal anyway? It wasn't like I'd been making out with Tate on the dance floor.

"Courtney." I turned at the sound of Lexi's voice behind me. If the sharpness of her tone didn't surprise me, the anger on her face did. "What was up with that?" she demanded.

"With what?" I folded my arms across my chest.

She reached my side and raised an eyebrow. "You know what. We've always made fun of people who dance like dogs in heat. What were you thinking?"

I rolled my eyes and looked away. "Come on, Lexi. It's no big deal. I just wanted to make Serena jealous."

She frowned. "Since when are your standards 'no big deal'?"

I blew out a breath. "Okay, first of all, you're taking all of this church stuff *way* too seriously lately." I waved my hand. "Look around; the majority of the kids in our school are LDS, and how many of them dance like that? It doesn't matter."

When her eyes widened and her mouth dropped open I felt my irritation rising. "I can't believe you're standing there judging me on such a stupid thing. Why can't you just be happy for me that Tate likes me?"

Her expression faded from shock to sadness. "I'm not judging you, Courtney. I just don't get the way you've been acting lately. You're not yourself, and I'm worried about you."

I jutted out my chin. "Well maybe I don't like the way you've been acting lately either, all goody-goody and critical." I glared at her and then shook my head. "Just quit worrying about me. I'm fine. Okay?"

Without waiting for her reaction I burst through the gym doors and back to the dance. I'd had enough for one night. A slow song was playing as I made my way past dancing couples. I would find Tate and come up with an excuse for why I was leaving.

I saw him searching through the crowd. When he saw me, he smiled and moved toward me. My heart warmed and suddenly all I wanted to do was be with someone who liked me without casting judgments.

Tate pulled me into his arms and we began dancing to the slow song. He held me tight, the way I'd wanted Eli to before. I held him back and rested my head on his shoulder.

"How did you like the game?" he asked.

I pulled back long enough to face him. "You were completely amazing. I seriously cannot believe what an awesome basketball player you are." I was gushing like a fangirl, but I couldn't help it.

His eyes brightened as he straightened a little. "Thanks. I was really glad you were there to see us play." We made another slow turn before he added, "And you did a great job at halftime. You looked totally hot in your outfit."

I blushed, but didn't say anything. As the song ended, he tilted my face to look up at him. "Hey, is everything okay?"

I nodded, but as wonderful as it was to dance with Tate, I didn't want to be there anymore. "Yeah, but . . . I think I might head home soon."

He frowned. "Why? The dance barely started. It won't be any fun if you leave."

I looked at the floor. "It's just been kind of a rough day." I looked back up at him and tried to brave a smile.

He put his arm around me. "In that case, you might need a shoulder to cry on. Let's go to my place and watch a movie or something."

I glanced up. "What about the dance?"

He shrugged. "I'd rather be with you anyway."

My heart stuttered as his blue eyes stared into mine. "Me too," I whispered.

He gave my arm a squeeze. "Let's get out of here."

"Okay. I just have to tell my friends I'm leaving first." By "friends" I mostly meant Janie. I went to find her, and cringed slightly to see that she was standing by Lexi.

I walked up to her, ignoring Alexis. "Hey, I'm taking off, okay?"

She turned to me in surprise. "Why?"

I glanced at Lexi who had apparently kept our little hallway exchange to herself. "Tate invited me to his house to watch a movie. You don't mind, right? I mean, you still have Lexi to hang out with," I said.

Janie glanced between Alexis and me, obviously confused that I was only addressing her, but she looked back at me with a smile. "Are you kidding? You have a chance to hang out with Tate. Go!"

I gave her a hug. "Thanks. Have fun tonight." I briefly made eye contact with Lexi as if to say, *See? This is how real friendship is done.* Part of me knew I was being juvenile, but I didn't care.

Tate was waiting for me by the exit doors. He smiled and his eyes travelled over me before he took my hand and we walked outside.

CHAPTER
twenty-two

"Well, here we are," Tate said as we pulled into the driveway of a nice-looking two-story. He parked in the garage and turned off the ignition.

I waited for a brief second to see if he would get my door, but when he headed for the house, I quickly unbuckled and got out. He flipped on the light in the mudroom.

"Is anyone home?" I asked, feeling nervous to meet his family.

"Nope. My parents and sisters were at the game, but they're catching dinner and a late movie after, so we have the place to ourselves." He smiled and took my hand, sending shivers along my arm.

"Oh." Suddenly I was even more nervous. Being all alone with Tate in this unfamiliar house made me feel strangely vulnerable.

"Come on. I'll pop some popcorn and then we can head to the family room."

I nodded and followed him into the kitchen. He grabbed popcorn from the pantry and a couple cans of soda from the fridge. I watched him unwrap the popcorn and stick it in the microwave before he turned to face me. "So, what's this 'rough day' all about?"

I had my back against the counter and shifted my weight, looking away for a moment. He hadn't brought up the Snapchat message yet, and I was hoping it was because: A) He didn't know, or B) He was too considerate to bring up a painful subject. Either way, I really didn't want to be the one to talk about it.

I shrugged. "It's nothing. Just not my favorite day, let's put it that way."

He tilted his head to the side. "Was it something to do with that post this morning?"

My face flushed. "You saw it?"

He nodded and made his way over to me, placing his hands on either side of my hips and boxing me into the counter. His marine eyes leveled with mine. "Yeah, but trust me—you have nothing to be embarrassed about. In fact," his gaze travelled over me the way it had at the dance, "I've had a hard time getting that image out of my head. I only wish it hadn't disappeared so fast."

I scoffed and pushed against his chest, trying not to notice how firm it was beneath my hands as I playfully shoved him back. "Oh wow. Seriously?"

"What? I mean it." He grinned at my deepening blush as he went to get the popcorn from the microwave.

I bit my lip, debating whether to keep going. "You know Serena sent it, right?"

His back was to me as he emptied the popcorn into a large bowl. I watched his broad shoulders lift and then lower before he turned to me. "Look. How about we forget about Serena and the text? We won the game, you're here with me—let's just have fun."

I nodded, feeling bad for spoiling Tate's victory night with my personal drama. He could be out celebrating with his friends but instead he'd chosen to spend time with *me*. Time to act like a big girl for once.

I gave him my most charming smile and reached for the sodas. "You're right. I'll carry the drinks and you lead the way to the family room."

His face relaxed into a smile. "Follow me."

I walked behind him through a hallway and down into the basement. The family room had a large sectional and a cozy gas fireplace in one corner. When I saw the size of the flat screen on the wall, I gawked.

Tate glanced over his shoulder and smiled at my reaction. "Wait till you hear the sound."

I closed my mouth so I wouldn't look like an idiot. "Um, this is amazing."

"What do you want to watch? We have a pretty good selection."

"How about an action movie? That way I can get the full effect."

He quirked an eyebrow. "Really? Because if you're serious, that pretty much makes you the perfect girl."

I laughed. "Don't get me wrong, I still like chick flicks, but with this setup it's gotta be something more intense."

He regarded me and the glimmer in his eyes suddenly made my stomach muscles tighten. If I was completely honest, I was also a little nervous to be alone with Tate and hoped an action movie would help keep things in check. The memory of how he'd danced with me made me slightly uneasy about where his boundaries were standards-wise . . . or where he thought mine were.

The lights dimmed automatically as the movie started and Tate and I sat next to each other on the couch. He put a blanket across our laps. When the speakers came alive I turned to him with wide eyes. "This sounds better than an actual theater."

He nodded and put his arm around my shoulder as we ate our popcorn. I was grateful to have the snack to keep my hands occupied as we watched the first part of the show, but it wasn't long before the bowl was empty, so I quickly picked up my soda to have something to hold.

After a few more minutes, Tate leaned over, offering me a piece of gum. It felt like some unwritten rule that you had to accept gum from someone when they offered it, because what if it was a subtle hint?

"Thanks." I took the gum and he smiled as he lifted the soda from my hands, placing it in a nearby cup holder in the sofa. He pulled me in a little closer and I snuggled into his shoulder, feeling the warmth of his body as I breathed in his cologne. My heart rate sped up in sync with the race car zooming across the screen. I could sense that Tate wanted to kiss me. The tension in the air between us was as thick as syrup.

After a few more seconds, Tate put his hand beneath my chin, tilting my face up to his. Our lips met, releasing the tension while building a whole new level of it. I felt excited and nervous and a thousand other things all at once as he continued to kiss me.

After what seemed like seconds, but must have been at least a while later, our kissing intensified. Feelings swarmed inside of me that I hadn't experienced since I'd been with Kellen. But they were more intense with Tate. I felt the warnings go off and the familiar battle rage within myself. This was Tate, the hottest most popular guy in school. I loved the fact that he wanted to be with me, and I was enjoying making out with him way more than I should have. I thought of how I'd broken up with Kellen and promised myself I wouldn't do anything like that again. I tried to remember how sick I'd felt ever since, but then my hormones took over and drowned out any thoughts to resist.

Tate didn't seem to have any issues with what was going on as he slowly pulled me back until we were lying next to each other. We continued kissing but the warning sirens in my head were blaring. His hands began travelling from my face to my hair, and then down my back where they toyed with the hem of my shirt. I knew if I didn't do something soon, the warning I felt would fade and I would give in to desire. I had to make a choice.

Just as his fingers touched the skin at my waist, I sat up. "I think I'd better go," I said breathlessly.

Tate stayed where he was and ran his hand along on my arm. "Come on. The movie's not over yet," he said with a cajoling smile. His eyes devoured me as his handsome face was illuminated by the light of the screen.

The fever still raced inside of me and I wanted nothing more than to lie back down next to him. I wanted to be his girlfriend. I wanted to let go of all the pain I'd felt today and feel nothing but the closeness of being with Tate.

He reached up, tracing his hand along my cheek. "You're so gorgeous, you know that?" He placed his hand on the back of my neck and gently bent me down until we were kissing again.

In that moment I decided to stop fighting.

I turned off any thought other than Tate and lay back down beside him.

CHAPTER twenty-three

Snow was blowing outside the windshield of Tate's Mustang as he pulled up alongside my car in the deserted school parking lot. I felt as numb and empty as the storm raging outside.

He put the car in Park but made no move to get out and open my door this time. "Thanks for hanging out tonight. Text me tomorrow, okay?" he said, turning to give me one final kiss.

I kissed him back half-heartedly, trying to hide how sick I felt. All of the earlier excitement and giddiness I'd experienced in being with him had evaporated, and in their place were guilt and shame. I pulled away after a moment and avoided looking at him. "Okay. Talk to you later."

I climbed out of the warm car, bracing myself against the biting wind and snow. Tate waited until I was in my car, and then he was gone.

My windshield was covered with icy snow, so I attempted the wipers. They removed powder on top, leaving a frozen layer of ice behind. Of course I didn't remember to put a scraper in my car, so I was going to have to wait until the heater warmed up enough to melt the ice.

I sat numbly, wishing the cold could freeze the sick emptiness I felt inside. I'd let things go further tonight with Tate than they had with Kellen, lowering my standards to a point I'd never thought I would. And just like Kellen, Tate didn't seem to feel any remorse about what had happened. It no longer mattered that he was the school basketball star and wildly popular. I felt a self-loathing I'd never experienced before.

And completely alone.

As if affected by the horrible thoughts tormenting my soul, my car suddenly sputtered and died. I tried the ignition again, but nothing happened.

"Oh no. No, no, no," I said, desperately attempting to turn the engine again with no luck. I was going to freeze to death here in the school parking lot. Maybe that's what I deserved.

I pulled out my phone and looked at the time. I had exactly twelve minutes to make curfew. I was about to dial my dad's number when another idea came to me. Eli. He was great with cars, and in that moment, there was no one else I'd rather talk to. But would he want to talk to me?

I pictured the look on his face when he'd seen me dancing with Tate. Eli would never have danced with me like that, or pushed boundaries when it came to standards. He was like the gentlemen in Hannah's world, and suddenly I realized what an idiot I'd been that I hadn't noticed it sooner. An urgent need to see him filled me as I sent him a text.

Hey, I'm sorry to bug you so late but I really need to talk.

I paused and squeezed my eyes shut before typing again.

Also, my car is dead and I'm kind of stranded in the school parking lot.

After several minutes passed I decided he wasn't going to reply. I was about to dial my dad when a pair of headlights turned into the parking lot and approached where I was parked. My hand hovered over the automatic lock until I recognized Eli's car. A flood of relief washed through me.

Eli left his car running and got out, his face expressionless. I opened my door and pulled the collar of my coat up. "I'm really sorry. Thank you so much for coming," I said nervously.

He gave only a slight nod in return, moving past me to sit in the driver's seat of my car. After a few attempts to start it, he popped the hood and got back out.

"This might take a few minutes. You can wait in my car." His tone was detached as he moved to the front of my Buick and looked under the hood.

Feeling like an imbecile, I hesitated for a moment before climbing into his car. The heat was delicious as it enveloped me, but I felt guilty for enjoying it while Eli was out braving the elements for my sake. He was clearly still mad, and I didn't blame him.

As I watched him working to revive my car my heart squeezed with remorse. If only I'd hung out with him tonight instead of Tate. If only I'd recognized sooner what an amazing guy Eli was. Now I knew that what I'd felt for Tate had been a combination of physical attraction, pride, and wanting to get revenge on Serena. My obsession with him hadn't been based on anything deeper than that. After tonight I'd lost respect for him, as he had undoubtedly lost respect for me . . . if he'd had any to begin with.

With Eli things were completely different, but now I was afraid I'd messed things up too much to deserve another chance.

Several minutes went by, and I got a text from my dad when it was past curfew.

Are you on your way? I don't like you being out in this weather.

I tapped a quick reply: *My car died in the school parking lot. Eli is working to get it started, but if he can't I'll ask him to give me a ride.*

Dad: *I'm coming to get you.*

My mouth twisted. His response didn't surprise me, but the last thing I wanted was my dad showing up when I needed a heart-to-heart with Eli. The sound of my car starting made me glance up in surprise.

Me: *Hang on—he just got it started. I'll be there in a few.*

Dad: *Ok. I'll be waiting.*

My stomach twisted. I didn't want to see my dad after what had happened tonight. It had been hard enough trying to act like everything was normal for the past month, but now? I swear my parents had a sixth sense when things weren't right.

The car door opened, startling me as Eli brushed snow off of his coat and climbed in. He didn't look at me but I saw him do an involuntary shake as he held his bare hands up to the heater vent.

"Your hands must be freezing! Why didn't you wear gloves?" I asked.

"It's kind of hard to work on an engine with gloves on." He spared me a sideways glance, but his tone was flat.

"Oh . . . right," I said, feeling even worse about asking him to come. "I can't believe you got it started. What was the problem?"

"The battery connection was bad. It should be fine now, but once your car gets warm I'll follow you home to make sure it doesn't die again." He stared outside.

"Thank you so much. I would have frozen to death if you hadn't come." I watched him, willing him to look at me.

He frowned, still staring out the windshield. "What were you doing out here all by yourself?"

I swallowed, feeling the sickness in the pit of my stomach as I contemplated how best to answer. "A friend dropped me off and I was waiting for my car to defrost when it died."

Finally Eli turned and looked at me, his hazel eyes questioning and guarded at the same time. "Why would someone drop you off? Weren't you already at the dance?"

I sucked in a quick breath. I could lie about what happened tonight, but I already felt crummy enough. Besides, this was my chance to try to mend things with Eli. I twisted my hands and looked down. "Tate invited me to watch a movie at his house."

At the mention of Tate's name, Eli jerked a nod and looked out the driver's side window. Though I could tell he was trying to hide it, irritation practically radiated from the stiffness of his posture. "So why didn't you call him to come help you?"

An unexpected tear formed in my eye. "Because I wanted to see you."

Eli turned, his face a mask but there was a crease between his eyes. "Courtney, look . . . I don't know what kind of game you're trying to play, but I've realized some things tonight." His jaw tightened as he looked down at his hands and then back at me. "I think you know that I liked you." He ran a hand through his hair and my heart stung at his use of the past tense.

"But my feelings have changed after seeing you with Tate tonight. You guys are clearly together—"

"We're not," I interrupted.

He lowered his eyes, searching mine before he shook his head. "Whatever. It's really none of my business. I think maybe it's just best if you and I don't hang out anymore."

The tear that had been pooling finally slid down my cheek as I reached for his arm. "Eli, I've been such an idiot. I've realized some things tonight too—mostly that Tate is not the person I want to be with." I swallowed and looked down before locking my gaze with his. "I want to be with you."

His eyes softened, revealing some of the warmth I had missed before he looked out the window again.

I rushed on, "I know I don't deserve it, but can't you give me another chance? Please?"

He blew out a breath and rubbed a hand over his eyes before finally facing me. The mask was back in place. "Courtney, as badly as I want to say yes, the truth is—you're not the girl I thought you were. I think it's best if we just stay friends."

His words stung like a whip to the face. He was right. I wasn't myself.

I hadn't felt like myself in a long time, and the way I'd danced with Tate had proved it. Eli didn't even know what had happened after. I didn't deserve him.

Several more tears escaped, but I brushed them away as I nodded and took a quick breath. "I think my car is warm enough now. Thanks again for your help. I'll—find a way to pay you back." Before he could answer I quickly got out of his car and into mine. The heater was on full blast and the windshield was clear enough that I could see.

Putting it into gear, I started making my way home. Even with Eli's headlights in my mirror I felt more alone and empty than I ever had before. For some reason, I thought about the conversation I'd overheard at the Tasty Freeze the other day. I knew now that Kiersten had been lying. Forget how much she loved her boyfriend, there was no way she didn't feel guilt about the choices she was making. There was no such thing as escaping the consequences of sin, no matter how hard you tried to deny it.

I thought about the way I'd been treating my friends, especially Alexis. I hadn't been happy for weeks and had ended up taking it out on her. Mostly, I was just tired of carrying around the weight of my sins. It had been hard enough to carry with Kellen, but after tonight it was practically crushing me. I hated myself in that moment. I hated who I was becoming.

Tears were falling uncontrollably now. I felt the need to pray like a drowning person needed oxygen, but I fought against it.

You can't pray. Not after what you've done, the thoughts insisted, crushing any hope.

I pulled into my garage and Eli drove past, flashing his lights once before continuing down the street. I closed the automatic door and took a few deep breaths, trying to stop the flow of tears but they kept coming. There was no way I was hiding this sob-fest from Dad, so I had to come up with an excuse.

I thought of something that wasn't a lie and then made my way quietly into the house. Dad was sitting at the kitchen table with the light on. He turned to me with a small smile that froze as soon as he saw my face.

"Courtney, what happened?" He got up from the table and pulled me into a tight hug. "I was just about to call. Is everything okay?"

My tears fell faster as I leaned my face into his shoulder, but I nodded. "Yeah. Sorry."

He pulled back and searched my eyes, concern etched deep into his features as he waited.

"I just . . ." I bit my lip to keep it from trembling. "I told Eli that I liked him and he said he just wanted to be friends." My face crumpled as another small sob escaped. Saying it out loud sounded so pathetic.

Dad's shoulders visibly relaxed. He was clearly relieved, though I could tell he wanted to look sympathetic. "Honey, I'm so sorry." He put his arm around me. "Want me to make you some hot chocolate? I don't know much about women, but I do know that chocolate is somehow supposed to make things better."

I gave a small laugh and wiped my nose with the edge of my shirt sleeve. *If only.* "No thanks. I'm just tired and want to go to bed. Is Mom still up?"

He shook his head. "She wanted to stay up and ask you about your performance and the dance, but she had to take some more medicine tonight and it wiped her out. I'm happy to stay up and talk though, if that would help?"

I smiled weakly. "Thanks, but I'll be okay. I just need to sleep it off."

He gave my shoulder a squeeze before letting his arm drop. "Things will look better in the morning. Besides, tomorrow's Saturday." He glanced at his watch and then at me. "Make that today. No more being late for curfew, understood?"

I nodded and then headed up to my room. How I wished what he said was true, that I could wake up in the morning and all the mistakes I'd made would magically disappear. But I knew better.

The guilt squeezed like a vice as I got ready for bed, threatening to suffocate me from the inside. I was about to climb under the covers when I couldn't take it anymore. I needed help, and there was no one else I could turn to.

Forcing myself onto my knees, I folded my arms and let my tears silently fall.

Heavenly Father, I know I'm not worthy to pray right now, but I'm a mess and don't know what else to do. Please. Please help me.

I knelt there for several minutes. Surprisingly I wasn't struck down by lightning and I didn't feel worse for praying. As I continued to pour out my heart, a tiny thread of light seemed to penetrate the wall of ice around my heart. It felt like something I hadn't felt in a long time. It felt like hope.

After ending my prayer I lay down on my pillow. My tears began to subside as I clung to that thread of light, feeling just enough peace to allow me to drift off to sleep.

CHAPTER
twenty-four

Hannah stood by the window in her bedroom. Her face was drawn as she gazed at nothing and held her Bible to her chest. Unlike the pretty ball gown I'd seen her in last, she wore a plain dress of deep gray. The color seemed to match her sullen mood.

A soft knock sounded at the door a moment before Charles entered. His mouth pulled down in concern as soon as he saw his sister. "I think this is the first morning I've not found you out reading in the barn. Was it too cold?"

Hannah turned to face him with a feeble smile. "No. I just wasn't feeling . . . quite up to it this morning."

He took a few steps into the room and reached to feel her forehead. "You look pale. Are you certain you feel well enough to attend church?"

She nodded. "It's nothing. Just a restless night."

His eyes darkened. "I imagine so. How could you sleep after Father's irrational behavior at the ball last night?"

Hannah looked down. "It's best if we don't speak of it, Charles." Her brow wrinkled as she struggled to keep her emotions in check. "Has he left yet?"

He frowned. "Yes. He's gone to prepare for his sermon. We should probably be on our way."

She gave a quick nod and Charles took her arm. "Hannah," he waited until she looked up at him before continuing, "I can't bear to see you suffer like this. Father cannot force you to marry that wretched Hornsby. We'll find a way to make him see reason, but if he won't, I'm taking you to America with me."

"Please, Charles," Hannah's blue eyes glistened with tears, "please, let's not talk of it just now. I must try to maintain some measure of decorum or I'll never make it through the meeting." She reached up and kissed his cheek, giving him a tender smile as she pulled away. "But thank you for looking after me. You've always been my protector."

His brow was still creased as he took her by the arm and led her from the room. I followed them to the front door where Mrs. White was waiting to help them with their coats.

"Have a nice time at the service, loves," she said as she opened the door.

Hannah turned to her in surprise. "Will you not be at the meeting, Mrs. White?"

The older woman smiled as she folded her arms across the apron around her ample middle. "Not today, dearie. I'm off to hear the preacher from America. Never seen an American up close before—not in these parts. It's quite all anyone can talk about." Her cheerful eyes danced with excitement.

Hannah paused a moment before nodding. "Enjoy yourself then."

"Thank you, Miss." She looked a bit contrite as she paused and lowered her head. "I'd 'oped you might not mention my whereabouts to the master. You know 'ow he can be over things like this."

Hannah and Charles exchanged quick glances before Hannah put a reassuring hand on the woman's arm. "I'll not tell."

She visibly relaxed. "Thank you, Miss Hannah. I'll be back 'afore afternoon tea, so's I'm not missed." Her smile broadened as she held the door for them. I followed right on their heels, more curious than ever about this American missionary.

We walked out into the cold, clear morning. After a few paces, Charles said, "I confess I'm intrigued by the news of this foreign preacher. William has spoken of little else since hearing of his arrival at Benbow farm."

Hannah shot him a warning look. "Charles, don't you dare."

He stopped and gave her an impish grin. "Father will scarcely notice I'm gone with so many in his congregation—and if he does, you'll vouch for me, won't you, Hannah?"

She put her hands on her hips. "Charles Walker, if you expect me to lie for you—"

"You'd do as much for Mrs. White, then why not your own brother?" He raised his eyebrows in a challenge.

"I never said I'd lie for her! Just that I wouldn't tell Father where she was if he asked," Hannah retorted. She tried to look stern but when Charles gave her a puppy dog look the corners of her mouth lifted. "Very well, you scallywag. But only because I'm curious too."

Charles grinned and lifted her in a quick hug. "You're a saint, Hannah."

She laughed as he set her back down, then lowered her voice as she looked toward the church. "Father is sure to notice your absence. What shall I tell him?"

He shrugged. "Tell him I wasn't feeling up to attending this morning. I'll deal with his questions later."

She bit her lip a moment before nodding. "Hurry along then. How will you know where to find the American?"

"William told me he's to preach at Frome's Hill this morning. If I hurry, I should be able to make it." Charles began walking backward. "I'll be home before Father returns from church."

Hannah shooed him off and then watched after him for several moments. The longing to join him was painfully evident in her face before she turned back toward the church.

I wasn't sure what to do; run after Charles to find out more about the American missionary, or follow Hannah. I was really curious about the missionary, but felt a slight pull to follow after Hannah. Deciding to go with it, I caught up with her just as she entered the old building.

Organ music played and Hannah stopped in surprise as she looked around the room. It was nearly empty, with maybe a dozen or so people scattered among the pews. She glanced over her shoulder, but it was clear no one else was coming.

I heard footsteps approaching and turned. "Watch out—it's Hornsby," I whispered, but even if Hannah could have heard me, it was too late.

"Good morning, Miss Walker. May I have the pleasure of sitting beside you during the sermon?" Hornsby asked, tipping his head in a bow.

Hannah turned, her face paling as she nodded.

He took her by the arm and guided her to a pew near the front of the church. Hannah's father sat at the front of the room, near the organist. He was dressed in his rector's garb and wore a sour expression as he watched Hannah sit next to Mr. Hornsby. He was clearly trying to catch her attention, probably wondering where Charles was.

Hannah trained her gaze on the open Bible in her lap. I felt so sorry for her. She was stuck sitting by a man she could never love and her dad was going to be through-the-roof mad if he found out where Charles was. I had a feeling the near-empty congregation wasn't going to help his mood either.

There was an awkward shifting in the room as people kept looking at each other and glancing toward the doors. I counted fifteen in attendance, including the constable and Mr. Green who had been at the ball, but the chapel was clearly built for a much larger group.

Hornsby pulled out his pocket watch and checked the time. "I'm sure he will begin soon," he mumbled.

Hannah's face flushed. "Yes. He's just given the signal to Mrs. Pierce to finish her prelude."

The room fell silent as Mr. Walker approached the podium. He began a sermon, which would have bored me to tears in seconds if not for the fact that he was so flustered. Even though the chapel was drafty, he stopped several times to wipe his face with a handkerchief.

Hannah sat stiffly, clutching her gloves throughout the entire sermon. Pity filled her eyes as she watched her father sit down before the closing hymn began. Hornsby adjusted his collar before singing out loud, painfully off-key notes. Hannah politely pretended not to notice. Her lovely, clear voice joined in, helping to drown out the tone deaf strains of her companion.

As the congregation began to leave, Hornsby stood and offered his arm to Hannah. "May I escort you home, Miss Walker?"

She shrank slightly against the pew. He towered over her, staring intently beneath his hooded brow like a vulture. I glared at him as Hannah accepted his arm. She glanced to where her father stood speaking with the constable before allowing Hornsby to lead her from the chapel. I followed behind and then walked on Hannah's opposite side, wishing I could find a way to help her escape.

Hornsby cleared his throat. "Your father's sermon was inspiring, as always," he said, moving at an overly slow pace.

"Indeed," Hannah replied. She kept her eyes trained on her house down the road and I could tell she wanted to walk faster.

"Pray, where is Charles this morning? Not ill, I hope."

"I'm afraid he wasn't up to attending the meeting." Hannah's face reddened slightly before she changed the subject. "It's nice to see the sun out. Perhaps spring will find its way to Castle Frome after all."

Hornsby made a non-committal sound and then glanced over his shoulder before stopping to face Hannah. "Miss Walker, I confess I'm grateful for the opportunity to have this moment alone. I've already spoken with your father and now wish to express my inten—"

"Won't you join us for tea, Mr. Hornsby?" Hannah quickly interrupted. Her blue eyes were desperate as she let go of his arm and continued walking. "I am sure Father would be glad to have your company, seeing as the two of you have so much to talk about."

I smiled at the chill in her tone, but Hornsby furrowed his thick brows. It took only a few of his lumbering strides to catch up to her. "But I'm afraid you misunderstand. It's not your father's company I wish to—"

"Charles!"

I turned to see where Hannah was looking and saw Charles nearly running toward the house a few yards ahead of us. He stopped and turned at the sound of Hannah's voice. She rushed to meet him. "You must get back to your bed at once," she scolded with a backward glance a Hornsby.

Charles slowed his breathing and nodded. "I will. Thank you."

Hornsby regarded him. "Are you sure that's necessary? I'd say you look the picture of perfect health, old chap." He glanced suspiciously in the direction Charles had come from. "Out for a morning stroll?"

Charles straightened his shoulders, ignoring the comment as he offered Hannah his arm. "How was Father's sermon?"

"It was . . ." she seemed to struggle for the right words. "He did a fine job, though sadly there were very few in attendance to hear it."

Charles seemed deep in thought as he nodded.

"I fear the lack of attendance may have had something to do with that American missionary. Perhaps you've heard, Charles?" Hornsby sneered. "I understand he was to preach to a group of the United Brethren this morning." He glanced meaningfully in the direction Charles had come from.

"Thank you for accompanying my sister from church," Charles answered, his jaw tightening. "I can escort her from here."

"I've invited Mr. Hornsby for tea." The regret in Hannah's tone was barely perceptible. She and Charles exchanged quick glances before Charles nodded.

He turned to Hornsby. "I'm sure Father will be delighted." Then he held tighter to Hannah's arm and began a conversation as he led her toward the house.

Hornsby glowered as he followed behind them. I laughed at his expression before hurrying to catch up to the others.

Mrs. White was bustling about the room preparing the tea service. She jumped as the door opened and placed a hand over her chest. "Oh, Charles—you made it back! I was afraid it was the master."

"Mr. Hornsby will be joining Hannah and Father for tea," Charles said before Hornsby came through the door.

At the sight of the unexpected guest, Mrs. White swallowed whatever she'd been about to say and dipped her head in a curtsy. "May I take your coat, sir?"

Hornsby allowed her to take his things as Hannah turned to her brother.

"Now, Charles. Off to bed with you. I'll send your regrets to Father." She gave him a pointed look.

He seemed conflicted before finally nodding. He gave a slight bow to Hornsby. "Forgive me for not joining you. I'm afraid I must rest now."

Hornsby bowed back. "Oh yes . . . I do hope you'll feel better soon." A sneer formed across his thin lips as his eyes challenged Charles.

Charles straightened his shoulders, his expression hard as he maintained eye contact. Hannah immediately jumped in to help break up the tension.

"Mr. Hornsby, won't you join me in the sitting room?" she asked.

He turned his attention to her as Mrs. White shooed Charles up to his room with a promise to bring him some tea. Charles threw Hannah one last look and she gave an imperceptible nod with pleading in her eyes. He sighed and shook his head before heading up the stairs.

Mr. Hornsby followed Hannah into the small sitting room where they made polite conversation for a few minutes. I stifled a yawn and drummed my nails on the empty chair I sat in, wishing Hornsby would get lost. Not only was he creepy, but also incredibly boring. I was grateful Mrs. White was there pretending to tidy up the room. I had a feeling if he was alone with Hannah he would have tried bringing up his "intentions" again.

The door opened and Mr. Walker stormed into the house. "Confound it all—something must be done!"

The constable entered behind him. "I agree, Thomas. After the report we've just heard, I think it's best to put an end to this before things get out of hand."

Hannah's brow creased in alarm as she stood to help the men with their coats. "What is it, Father? What are you talking about?"

"That infernal American, that's what!" Mr. Walker said as he shuffled out of his coat. "I've just had it from the Hopkins lad that nearly my entire congregation attended his sermon at Frome's Hill this morning—all but the fifteen who were in the church. Fifteen! I've never been so insulted in all my life."

Hannah and Mrs. White exchanged nervous glances as Mr. Walker paced the room.

"And rumor has it that John Benbow and his wife have already been baptized, along with four other preachers of the United Brethren. It's absolute madness, I tell you! The feebleness of mind and conviction to join some unknown, obscure religion just because a Yankee preacher has made an appearance in town." He slumped into a chair and rubbed a hand across his eyes before looking up at the constable. "Something must be done."

"This is startling news indeed," Hornsby said.

Mr. Walker jumped. "Frederick. I didn't see you there."

Hornsby rose from his chair and moved into the living room to join the men. "Your daughter was kind enough to extend an invitation to tea."

Mr. Walker gave an approving grunt. "As well she should. It's nice to know I've not been completely deserted by my parish." He narrowed his eyes as he looked about the room before turning to Hannah. "Where is Charles? Why was he not in attendance this morning?"

"He wasn't feeling up to it, Father. He's in his room." She cast a quick warning glance at Hornsby who gave her a wry smile.

Mr. Walker grunted as Mrs. White handed him a cup of tea. He turned his attention to her with a scowl, but she hurried into the kitchen before he could comment over her absence at church.

"Well, what are you proposing, Thomas?" the constable asked before taking a sip of tea.

"Won't you sit down?" Hannah attempted to defuse the tension as she gestured to the empty chair at her father's side. The constable nodded and sank into it.

Mr. Walker forcefully set his teacup and saucer on the table in front of him, causing some of the warm liquid to slosh onto the wooden surface. "What do I propose? The only thing that can be done at this point—a warrant, for the man's arrest. This so-called missionary's preaching ends tonight."

The blood drained from Hannah's face as the constable set down his tea cup. The room was still for several seconds before he nodded. "It'll take some time to get the warrant."

Hannah's father used his cane to rise to his feet. "Then I suggest we get started. There's no time to waste." He turned to Hornsby. "Will you join us? As one who will soon be a part of this family, I would appreciate your support."

Hornsby's neck flushed to match the color of his hair as he glanced under his hooded brows at Hannah. She stared at the floor with pursed lips. When she refused to look up, he tipped his head at Mr. Walker. "I'd be honored, sir."

The men moved to the door and had their coats on before Mrs. White could offer assistance.

"Hannah, tell that brother of yours that I'd like a word when I return," Mr. Walker said with a stern look before following the other two men out the door. It closed with a loud thud.

I blew out a long breath as Mrs. White put a comforting arm around Hannah. "My dear, could I have misunderstood? Are you engaged to that young fellow?"

She shook her head. "No, there is no understanding between us, and there never will be." A fiery determination filled her eyes as she turned to face the older woman. "Mrs. White, you were at the American's sermon this morning . . . do you think him worthy of arrest?"

Mrs. White dropped her arm and made a tsking sound. "Indeed I do not. I know an honest man when I see one, and that Mr. Woodruff is a good man." Her eyes took on a light as she seemed lost in thought. "I felt a stirrin' at his words I've never felt before—somethin' I can't explain." She looked at Hannah and smiled. "I still need time to think it over, mind, but I'd like to hear him preach again. It would be a shame if he were to be arrested. A right shame."

Hannah nodded and hurried to the coat rack for her things. "Where will he be preaching next?"

Mrs. White's eyes widened. "What are you thinking, child? You can't go. Heaven knows what your father would do if he found you there." She moved as if to stop Hannah from putting on her coat, but Hannah waved her off.

"Someone must warn him. It will take time for Father to obtain the warrant, so I'll likely have ample opportunity to warn the missionary and get back home."

"You must send Charles then. This is no errand for a lady."

Hannah shook her head. "No, and you mustn't tell him about the warrant or where I've gone. Otherwise he'll insist on finding me or warning the missionary himself. Things will be much worse if Father finds Charles at the meeting instead of me. He's in enough trouble as it is over missing Father's sermon."

When Mrs. White didn't look convinced, Hannah took hold of her arms. "Promise me, Tilly."

Mrs. White twisted up her mouth in worry before finally nodding.

Hannah dropped her shoulders in relief. "Thank you. Now please—tell me where he's preaching."

Mrs. White sighed. "Very well, but you take care, Miss. I'll not forgive myself if you get into trouble." When Hannah nodded she lowered her voice and continued, "He was at Castle Frome this morning, and was to preach at Standley Hill this afternoon." She glanced at the grandfather clock in the sitting room. "I believe after that he's to preach at Benbow Farm this evening."

Hannah tipped up on her toes and kissed Mrs. White on the cheek. "Don't worry. I'll find him and be back before you know it." She smiled and Mrs. White held open the door as Hannah finished putting on her gloves.

"See that you hurry, child. I do hope you find him before Constable does."

Hannah nodded and rushed off down the path.

I was close on her heels, excited to finally get a glimpse of this missionary and see what all the fuss was about.

Hannah seemed deep in thought as she walked quickly down the dirt road. I found myself wishing I could talk to her, but even though she had no clue I was there, I felt a sort of companionship as we walked together.

I loved seeing more of the countryside and passing farms and houses as we walked. Life was so simple here. No cars on the road, no phones or TV. If I was stuck here forever I would probably be bored out of my mind, but it was nice to visit for a while. Something about the way people gave their full attention to each other when they talked was refreshing.

After what must have been almost an hour, we arrived at a large building where a few people were standing around. Hannah approached a couple of girls her age.

"Pardon me."

Both girls stopped talking and turned to her curiously. Their dresses were almost threadbare and they looked like they'd seen plenty of time in the sun.

Hannah bobbed her head in a quick curtsy. "I'm looking for the missionary from America. Is he inside?"

One of the girls shook her head. "He finished not twenty minutes ago and is on 'is way to Benbow Farm."

The other girl watched as Hannah's shoulders drooped. She touched her arm and gave her an encouraging smile. "It's worth the walk, Miss."

Hannah smiled weakly and nodded. "Thank you." She straightened her shoulders and blew out a breath before turning back down the road we'd come from.

"How far away is Benbow Farm?" I asked, not expecting a response. I worried that we wouldn't make it to our destination before Hannah's father showed up with the constable.

Hannah walked as quickly as possible, but after another mile her pace began to slow. I didn't know how she managed walking in those boots. They looked incredibly uncomfortable. Not to mention how cold it must have been wearing a dress instead of pants to keep her legs warm.

I gave her words of encouragement as the sun began setting over the fields. She wrapped her arms about herself and continued on, and I found that I liked talking to her, even if she didn't respond. I told her about school and drill and my boy troubles. I was about to tell her about the emptiness I'd been feeling, when she suddenly stumbled and fell to the ground.

She let out a small cry of pain and tried to stand, but gasped and sat back down. She lifted her skirts and petticoats to look at her foot, and I crouched beside her. Removing her boot, she bit her lip and ran her fingers along the ankle which was already swelling beneath her stocking.

"Just lovely," she said, blowing out a breath. She looked around at the deserted road and rows of empty fields as far as the eye could see.

"What are we going to do?" I asked as I stood and paced in front of her. We were out in the middle of nowhere and there was nothing I could do to help. I'd never felt so powerless as I watched the sun set. Hannah spoke softly behind me and I turned in surprise.

"Lord, please help me. I'm all alone, and can't walk. If this missionary is truly thy servant, help me find a way to warn him."

I stood stunned as I listened to Hannah's fervent prayer. She was in danger of being left alone all night out here and freezing to death, and she was still concerned about this missionary? And the fact that she had thought to pray humbled me. Why wasn't that ever my first thought when I had a problem? I knelt on the ground next to her and bowed my head as I continued listening to her words.

After a few minutes, the light from the sun had almost completely faded. I looked up in dismay as the final rays crested the hillside, but a sound coming down the road caught my attention.

Hannah heard it too. She ended her prayer and looked in the direction of the noise. A horse! I was sure that's what it sounded like. I squinted into the fading light to see a horse and rider trotting down the road.

Hannah's face lit into a smile and tears streamed down her cheeks as she bowed her head and whispered, "Thank you, Lord."

The rider must have spotted her, because the horse broke into a gallop. As he approached, Hannah gasped and her tears fell faster. "William!"

He pulled up a few paces short of where she sat and jumped down from the saddle. "Hannah! What on earth has happened? Are you hurt?" He bent down and took her face in both hands, brushing the tears from her cheeks as he searched her eyes.

"It's my ankle. I think it may be sprained, but I'm not sure." She watched as he dropped his hands and gently felt the bones at her ankle.

"What are you doing out here all alone and on foot?" The worry in his voice made it gruff.

"I was on my way to Benbow Farm. Father is getting a warrant to arrest the American missionary, and I wanted to warn him." Hannah's voice trembled as William gently set her leg back down.

"I don't think it's broken, but we need to get you home and warm as soon as possible." In one swift motion, he lifted her off the ground and set her sideways on top of his horse.

"William, did you hear me? If we don't hurry, the constable will make an arrest. We must go to Benbow Farm at once!"

He didn't look at her as he placed her discarded boot in a saddle bag and climbed into the saddle as well, reaching his arms around her waist to hold the reins. "Your well-being is my first concern. I'll see you safely home and make sure you're tended to. Then I'll address the situation with the constable."

Hannah shook her head and turned to face him, her blue eyes sparking with determination. "No, William. Take me to Benbow Farm or so help me I'll never forgive you. My ankle will be fine. Please, we must hurry or it will be too late."

William's warm brown eyes deepened into a frown as his gaze locked with hers. He was clearly torn, and Hannah seemed to sense his internal conflict.

Reaching up to place a hand on his cheek, she slowly leaned forward until her mouth found his in a gentle kiss. His features softened as he returned the affection. She pulled away, keeping her hand on his face. "Please?"

He sighed and gave her a wry smile, leaning his forehead against hers. "I have a feeling you'll be my undoing, m'lady."

She grinned and held on as he tightened his grip on her waist and spurred the horse on, leaving me standing alone on the long dirt road.

"Hey! Wait for me!" I called. I shook my head in disbelief before taking off at a run after them. I still had William's horse in sight, but as he rounded a bend down the road I realized there was no way I was going to keep up. Darkness was falling quickly and I slowed my pace in weary defeat. What now?

As if in answer to my question, all at once I was standing outside a home. Lights burned brightly inside where a huge crowd was gathering. I spun around in confusion, not recognizing anyone around me. I followed the stream of people into the home and stood in the back to see if I could figure out what was going on.

A man stood at the front of the large room. He had dark hair, with long sideburns. Even from where I stood I was struck by his clear blue eyes. Feeling drawn to him, I made my way through the crowd of people taking their seats until I stood just a few feet from him.

"Sir, my family has heard of your preaching and have traveled some distance to be here tonight. We're most eager to hear your sermon," a man said, shaking hands with him.

"Elder Wilford Woodruff at your service, sir. I'm delighted you've come." His blue eyes shone as he firmly returned the handshake.

I gasped. Wilford Woodruff? I knew the name had sounded familiar! I'd learned the "Latter-Day Prophets" song in primary. This was *the* Wilford Woodruff—the American missionary? I watched him introduce himself to others in the group surrounding him.

A man stepped forward and placed his hand on Elder Woodruff's shoulder. "If you're ready, Mr. Woodruff, I believe the congregation is anxious to get started."

Elder Woodruff smiled. "Thank you, John." He shook a few more hands before the crowd around him moved to find seats. I scanned the room. People seemed to fill every possible space, sitting on chairs, benches and even the floor. Those who couldn't find seats stood along the walls.

The room quieted as Elder Woodruff stood next to an empty chair at the front. Even though I knew no one saw me, I felt self-conscious standing next to him and quietly moved to a spot on the floor nearby.

"I'd like to thank you all for coming here tonight. I know many have traveled far and I assure you the message I have to share will be worth the sacrifice. I'd also like to thank my good friend, John Benbow, and his family for lending us this space to meet in." Elder Woodruff turned to the man and his family seated in chairs behind him, giving them all warm smiles which they returned.

Facing the congregation again, he continued, "My name is Wilford Woodruff, and I am an Elder of the Church of Jesus Christ of Latter-day Saints. I've come with the message of salvation, to preach the gospel of life to any and all willing to hear it."

A stirring in the back of the room drew the attention of Elder Woodruff and the congregation. I followed the direction of the noise and my heart sank to see the constable standing there. He entered and walked down the make-shift aisle toward Elder Woodruff.

"Sir, I am the constable and have been sent by the rector of the local parish with a warrant for your arrest."

The room erupted in quiet murmurs and outcries. I did a quick scan but couldn't see Mr. Walker anywhere.

Elder Woodruff squared his shoulders. "For what crime?" he asked.

The constable took an authoritative stance. "For preaching to the people."

Elder Woodruff smiled. "I, as well as the rector, have a license for preaching the gospel to the people." He gestured to the empty seat beside him. "However, if you'll take a chair, sir, I'll wait upon you after the meeting."

The constable shifted uncomfortably. I could tell he was thrown off by Elder Woodruff's composure. Whatever he'd been expecting, I was pretty sure he was surprised. After clearing his throat and glancing about the room, he nodded. "Very well then." He took a seat and the tension slowly dissipated.

Without missing a beat, Elder Woodruff began his sermon. He taught about the gospel of Christ's time being restored through the Prophet Joseph Smith, of the Book of Mormon, and modern day revelation.

I sat captivated by his words, feeling a stirring I hadn't felt in a long time—maybe never. As I looked around, I noticed many people in tears. Something powerful was taking place here, but it was Hannah's face that caught my attention most of all. She and William must have snuck in the back sometime during the sermon, too late to warn Elder Woodruff.

She leaned on William's arm and her eyes shone as tears poured down her cheeks. Her face was practically glowing as she seemed to drink in every word.

William supported her so she wouldn't have to put weight on her ankle, but he was also listening intently.

This was something I'd never experienced before. Elder Woodruff's teachings were all things I had known about for as long as I could remember. But sitting here and watching a roomful of people hearing about the Restored Gospel for the first time—it was humbling.

Elder Woodruff ended by reading from the Book of Mormon, the promise in Moroni that if the people would seek to know for themselves the truthfulness of the message, God would reveal it to them. Something struck my heart in that moment. I'd grown up in the Church and had heard this lesson taught all my life, but I'd never really asked. I'd gone along with what was taught because that's what everyone else did. But I didn't truly know.

Elder Woodruff bore his testimony. After a prayer was offered the room still held a feeling of reverence. Every eye seemed to be on the constable as he slowly stood from his chair. He straightened his shoulders before extending his hand. "Mr. Woodruff, I would like to be baptized."

A few laughed and the tension in the room evaporated as Elder Woodruff smiled and clapped him on the shoulder. I watched as several more approached and asked to be baptized. I was so surprised by the reaction that I didn't notice Hannah approaching. She held on to William's arm for support. She was careful to keep the weight off of her injured ankle as she balanced long enough to tap Elder Woodruff on the shoulder.

When he turned to her she took a deep breath.

"Pardon me for interrupting, sir, but I wondered . . . might I possibly purchase a copy of that book you were reading?"

He offered an apologetic smile and held up the Book of Mormon in his hand. "Unfortunately I've already given out all but this copy which I must keep for my study."

"Of course." Hannah dipped her head as disappointment filled her eyes.

Seeing her crestfallen expression, he continued, "I will do all I can to obtain more copies. Perhaps you could leave information where you may be reached once we have them?"

Hannah's face lit up. "Thank you, sir. I would like that very much."

William squeezed her arm as she gave the information to Elder Woodruff, her gaze never leaving the book in his hand.

"Forgive me, but might I just hold it for a moment?" she asked.

Elder Woodruff nodded. "Certainly. Why don't you have a seat while I speak with some of the others?" He handed the Book of Mormon to her and gestured to the empty chair beside him.

"Thank you, sir." William said as he helped Hannah to the chair.

She seemed speechless as she held the book and sank into the seat. She ran her hands reverently over the cover before opening it and scanning the pages, her eyes filled with hunger as she read. She held the book out far enough for William to see as he looked over her shoulder.

I smiled at how engrossed they were, and then got chills realizing this was the first time either of them had read the Book of Mormon.

The line of people waiting to speak with Elder Woodruff was long. I could see the eagerness in their faces and wanted to understand the excitement they felt. I'd been baptized long ago, but suddenly I yearned for what these people had.

I wanted to know for myself.

CHAPTER twenty-five

When I awoke the next morning my eyes felt like sandpaper. I lay in bed as I thought back on my dream. Something was going on here—I knew that without a doubt. For some strange reason I was dreaming about Hannah and Wilford Woodruff and sensed that it had something to do with me. The answer seemed to be tugging at my mind, but was just out of reach.

One thing was for sure though, the yearning I'd had at the end of my dream was still in my heart. I wanted to feel like my old self again, and more than that—I wanted answers. Needed answers. The sick feeling from last night with Tate lingered inside me and I knew it would be lodged there until I did something about it.

I glanced at the clock and saw that it was still early. Dad had forgotten to take my phone again, so I picked it up off the nightstand, distractedly aware there were no new text messages, but that wasn't what I was looking for anyway.

I needed to pray. I knelt by my bed, relieved that the words came more freely this time as I asked for guidance and forgiveness and answers. The tiny sliver of hope cracking the ice around my heart seemed to widen with each word. I continued praying for longer than I could ever remember doing, clinging to this new hope with everything I had. Finally, when I couldn't think of any more words to say, I asked for an answer again. I wanted to know for myself whether this church I belonged to was true.

Taking a deep breath, I ended the prayer and opened the scripture app on my phone. I turned to Moroni's promise at the end of the Book of Mormon that Elder Woodruff had shared with the congregation. I read the words several times before squeezing my eyes shut.

Okay, I've done my part. I'm asking. Please give me the answer.

I sat for several minutes, willing some kind of light to burst forth from the heavens, or an undeniable burning in my bosom, or a voice in my head.

Nothing.

Opening my eyes again I blew out a breath and stared at the screen. This was crazy. Even if an answer was out there, I didn't feel worthy to receive it. But this time I wasn't giving up. I decided to just start at the beginning, so I went back to First Nephi and began reading.

A few seconds into the chapter, I got a text. It was Tate. As soon as I saw his face on the screen my stomach twinged. Without reading the message I locked the screen and tossed my phone on my pillow. This wasn't working. There was no way I'd be able to focus on scriptures if I kept getting texts and Instagram notifications.

I thought about Hannah and the way she'd longed for a copy of the Book of Mormon. I slid open my nightstand drawer and pulled out the scripture quad I hadn't used in months. I ran my hand over the cover like Hannah had done, and then found the spot in Nephi where I'd left off.

It had been a while since I'd read my scriptures, but I tried not to sigh as I forced myself to pay attention to the words. I spent the next thirty minutes reading, and something strange started happening. I actually found myself paying attention to the story.

Nephi, Laman and Lemuel were all brothers, but they were as different as night and day. In a way, it reminded me of the difference between Eliza and me.

Nephi was so perfect, and his brothers were constantly being compared to him. I could sympathize with that. But the thing I realized was that Laman and Lemuel could have been righteous, if they had done one crucial thing when their father Lehi told them to leave Jerusalem. They could have prayed like Nephi did and asked God if their father's teachings were correct.

Maybe if they had done that, they wouldn't have complained so much. Maybe they would have gained testimonies that their father was a prophet and the whole story would have been different, changing the lives of generations.

There was a difference between testimony and true conversion. Laman and Lemuel had angels appear to them, and in a sense they had testimonies. They admitted they knew the Lord was guiding them. But they weren't converted because they refused to live what they knew. They were too lazy or too stubborn to live the gospel.

Thoughts like this began flooding my mind, and then one thought set to repeat. And it was a doozy. It was something I'd known I needed to do all along, but had been too scared. I was still scared—almost terrified. I said another prayer, expressing gratitude for the guidance I'd been given and asking for strength to do what I knew I had to.

When I closed my prayer, my stomach grumbled so I headed down for breakfast. I was surprised to find Dad already making eggs, hash browns and fruit smoothies. He turned to me and smiled as I walked into the kitchen.

"How'd you sleep, Blondie? Feeling any better this morning?"

I nodded. "Yeah, much better actually." Now that I knew what I had to do, I did feel better. Scared, but better. I was taking control of my life again. "Can I help with anything?"

He shook his head, but before he could answer I heard Mom call from the living room. "Courtney, is that you?"

Dad gestured with a spatula for me to go, and I walked in to find her lying on the couch. "Hey, Mom. How are you doing this morning?"

She smiled and patted the space on the couch beside her. "I'm fine, but I've been anxious to talk to you. I want to hear all about your performance last night and what you did afterward."

I sank down beside her and told her about my night—carefully omitting all the unpleasant details of my time with Tate. Part of me wanted to open up and tell her everything, but a bigger part of me was too afraid. Besides, it would probably send her into early labor for real if she knew. After vaguely mentioning that I'd watched a movie at a friend's house and ending with my car trouble, I fell silent.

Mom regarded me with her blue eyes and then pretended to adjust the blanket over her round belly. "Your dad mentioned that you were upset when you got home. Something about telling Eli you liked him . . . ?" I could tell she knew the rest but was trying to be cautious. "Do you want to talk about it?"

I felt the corners of my mouth lift in an attempted smile. "Not really. I've thought about it and I realized it's better this way. I was just tired last night and overly emotional."

She patted my hand. "Being a teenager can be so rough on the heartstrings. It's hard to put your feelings out there. Even if he's not dating material, from what I've heard of Eli, it sounds like he's a good friend. And while it may seem disappointing, sometimes that's more valuable than you realize."

I nodded and turned toward the kitchen, ready to change the subject. "I think Dad has breakfast almost ready. Want me to bring you a plate?"

"That would be wonderful." She smiled as I stood up. "What are your plans for the day?"

I shrugged. "I was hoping to hang out with Lexi before I go to work this afternoon, but if there are chores that need to be done I'm happy to help."

She waved a hand. "That's sweet, but I think we're doing just fine. The sisters in the ward have made sure of that." She shook her head in wonder.

"Yeah, I've noticed that the house is practically gleaming. It's so cool the way everyone has been helping out. They really love you." I smiled at her. "Just let me know if you need anything, okay?" Before I could head to the kitchen, she stopped me.

"Actually, if you have a few extra minutes to spare after breakfast, there's something I'd like to show you."

I turned, surprised by the sudden animation in her voice as she continued, "I've decided to use some of this down-time to work on family history and I was hoping to show you what I've learned so far."

I mustered the most enthusiastic smile I could manage. "Sure." When I turned back around, my smile wilted.

I was pretty sure scrubbing a few toilets would be more fun.

I said a quick good-bye to my parents who were both leaning over a laptop in the family room. They waved without looking up and I made a beeline for the garage. I was happy Mom had found something to distract her, and I'd tried to be patient during her Family Search tutorial, but I'd only lasted about fifteen minutes before using the excuse that I was meeting up with Lexi.

Me: *Hey, I'm really sorry about last night. Can I come over? I want to talk.*
Alexis: *Sure, but let's go for a drive instead.*

My lips flattened into a line. I knew what that meant: her dad had been drinking again and she was embarrassed to have me over.

Me: *K. I'll be there in 5.*

Unsure whether or not I'd make it home before work, I'd changed into my polo and slid the nametag into my pocket. Nervousness and anticipation filled me at the thought of seeing Eli tonight. There were still things I felt I needed to say to him—I just hoped he would be willing to listen.

After squeezing my eyes shut for luck, I turned over the ignition and sighed in relief when my Buick sputtered to life. I patted the steering wheel and then backed out of the garage, hearing the crusty snow crunch beneath my tires as I pulled onto the street and headed for Lexi's.

She must have been watching for me, because I'd barely pulled up to the curb when she opened her front door and headed down the walk. Her expression was unreadable and I took a deep breath, hoping she'd be willing to forgive me and that I'd be able to cheer her up the way she'd done for me so many times.

"Hey," I said as she climbed in and aimed a heater vent in her direction.

"Hey."

"Where do you want to go?"

She stared out the windshield and chewed on her bottom lip for a moment. "Do you mind if we park by the temple?"

My face softened. "Sounds perfect." I put the car in gear and we drove for another minute before I broke the silence. "Lex, I'm so sorry about last night. I was totally out-of-line and said things I didn't mean. You were just being a good friend, and you were right about everything. I just . . . wasn't ready to hear it yet."

"It's okay." She looked out the passenger window and traced a star in the steam on the glass.

"No, it's not." I made eye contact with her briefly before returning my attention to the road. I took a deep breath. "I haven't been myself for a while, Lexi. And it's because I lost track of my priorities."

She turned from the window. "What do you mean?"

The temple spires came into view as I rounded a corner. "I hadn't read my scriptures in forever. I stopped praying altogether—I was lost. I wasn't sure if I had a testimony anymore."

She didn't answer, but I could see the understanding mixed with alarm in her eyes when I glanced her way. After what seemed like an eternity, she finally spoke. "Courtney, you've always been the strong one. You were there with me when I took the missionary discussions, you invited me to church and activities, and you've born your testimony . . ." She shook her head and I could hear the strain in her voice. "I've clung to your example for the past four years. If you're telling me that you don't believe it anymore, I don't know what I'll do."

I parked along the curb outside the temple but kept the engine running so we wouldn't freeze to death. I turned to face her and put my hand on her arm. "That's not what I'm saying. I've just been in a bad place." My voice choked on the words. I dropped my hand and took a deep breath. "I don't want to feel the darkness anymore. I'm trying to find my faith and my testimony again, but I know I've got to get my priorities straight before I can do that."

Her green eyes turned to me, filled with questions. "What happened to make you start doubting everything?"

I looked away and studied the spires of the temple. Somehow I knew I could confide in my best friend. "I made mistakes . . . first with Kellen, and then again last night with Tate."

I heard her sharp intake of breath, but she didn't say anything.

Tears began squeezing from the corners of my eyes as I relived the heartache. "I fell head over heels for Kellen, and it got to a point that I thought being in love was more important than trying to keep my standards." I rubbed my hands across the grooves in the steering wheel. "Honestly, it seemed like I knew so many people our age who were doing things like that and acting like it was no big deal, so I told myself it didn't matter. But I was wrong."

I blew out a breath. "It got to the point where I felt so sick and empty that I finally broke up with him. I told myself that if I just stopped that was all I had to do to repent, but the emptiness never left. Instead of going to the bishop, I buried it and stayed as busy as I could. I didn't feel worthy to pray, and the last thing I wanted was to read my scriptures. Going to church was torture, and I became the worst version of myself."

Lexi looked at her hands and didn't say anything.

"Last night, I knew I shouldn't have let Tate dance with me like that, but I wanted revenge on Serena. I told myself I didn't care, and then at his house later, it was like I just turned completely away from the Spirit and gave in to the cravings inside. I thought it would be worth it, dating the most popular guy in school, but the way I felt after . . . Lex, I never want to feel like this again." Tears poured down my cheeks as I broke into a sob.

Alexis reached over and let me cry on her shoulder as she patted my back. "It's going to be okay. We'll get through this."

After my tears began to subside I pulled away and gave an embarrassed laugh, attempting to wipe away the moisture from my face. Alexis smiled and opened the glove box where she knew I kept a stash of napkins. "Here you go."

"Thanks." I gave another half-hearted laugh. "Sorry to come unglued like that. You're the only person I've told."

She shook her head. "I'm just relieved that you're finally opening up. I knew something was going on, and I've been worried. It was like you started acting the way my brothers do sometimes and that scared me."

I cringed. Lexi's brothers were pretty wild. I must have been doing worse than I thought.

She seemed to stare at nothing as she gazed out the window. "I've seen both sides of the coin, Courtney. You know my past. I've seen what can happen to people when they stop caring. It was only when you and I became friends and I started coming to church that I realized there was another way to live—a happier way. I've wanted that in my life ever since."

I wiped my eyes one last time and touched her hand until she was facing me. "Lexi, I'm so sorry that I've dropped the ball in being a good example. But you know what? This time, you were the one lifting me."

She raised an eyebrow. "What are you talking about?"

I laughed. "You! You've been glowing with this crazy light lately. You're studying your scriptures, coming to church, doing all the right things. When I saw how fast you were growing, the nasty part of me felt bugged, but it's because deep down I knew it was what I wanted again. Whether or not you realize it, you've been the one carrying me the past few weeks. I have a feeling that even if I'd gone way off the deep end, you would have stayed strong. Even though your dad won't let you get baptized right now, you've got a testimony. You just haven't realized it yet."

She titled her head to one side as her face broke into a slow smile. "I think you might be right."

I nodded and sat back in my seat. "I know I am," I paused and furrowed my brow, "and I was wrong to discourage you from expecting a miracle. Your desire to get baptized is a good thing, and I don't see any reason why the Lord couldn't soften your dad's heart, so I'll be praying for you."

"Thanks, Court." Lexi's voice was thick with emotion. After a few seconds of letting this soak in, she turned to me again. "So what are you going to do now? Meet with the bishop?"

My stomach twisted. "Yeah. I know it's what I have to do if I want to get rid of this pain." My eyes tightened. "But I'm scared. What if my dad finds out?"

"Don't worry about that. If you know it's what you need to do, you just have to get it over with."

I nodded, staring up at the temple.

"So . . .?"

"So, what?" I asked.

"Make the call."

I glanced at her and took a deep breath. She gave me an encouraging smile as I took my phone out of my purse and looked up the number for the ward executive secretary. My fingers were trembling but I hit Dial. I held my breath as the phone rang several times. Part of me hoped I'd get voicemail.

"Hello?"

I squeezed my stomach muscles, forcing enough air into my lungs to respond. "Hi . . . Brother Mills?"

"Yes?"

"This is Courtney Moore. I'd like to schedule an appointment to meet with Bishop Reynolds."

CHAPTER twenty-six

I walked into the movie theater, feeling better than I had in weeks. I was still nervous to meet with the bishop but I knew I was taking a step toward repentance and peace. I was doing the right thing, and it felt good.

Alexis and I were back on track, and life in general was looking brighter. I was anxious to see Eli and hopefully have the chance to talk to him in between the weekend rush. I glanced at the concession stand before heading to the employee room. My heart sank when I saw Ashley serving a line of customers.

Where was Eli? I knew he'd been on the schedule for tonight. I put my things in the break room and headed back out to serve the crowd that seemed to be growing larger by the minute.

"About time." Ashley barely spared me a glance before ringing up an obscenely large bucket of popcorn.

"Sorry," I muttered, even though I was right on time. I stepped up to the counter, plastering a friendly smile on my face for the man who was too busy typing something in his phone to make eye contact.

"Give me two packages of Red Vines, some nachos, three popcorns and six large sodas," he rattled off without looking up.

"Um, okay . . . was that one order of nachos?" I asked as I reached for the licorice.

"Yep." A slight hint of impatience in his tone.

"And what size popcorn?"

He pried his eyes from his phone long enough to give me an annoyed stare. "Large. Like I already told you." He glanced over his shoulder and then back at me. "I've been waiting in this line for almost fifteen minutes and I'm missing the start of my movie because you guys are so slow."

"I-I'm sorry." My face flushed at the unexpected verbal attack. "I'll get your order as quickly as I can."

My hands shook as I scrambled to get the food. I was making good time, but in my hurry to fill the sodas I accidentally knocked the entire stack of plastic lids onto the floor. Ashley wheeled around and stared wide-eyed at the mess. Her mouth worked in soundless fury a moment before she finally found her voice.

"What did you *do*?" Before I could respond, she shook her head. "Go get more lids from the break room. Now!"

I darted out from behind the counter and ran for the break room. It took me a few minutes to find where the supplies were stored, and every second felt like eternity. When I finally rushed back out with the lids, I sensed the people in line getting agitated. The guy I was helping looked like he was ready to blow a gasket by the time I had his order and was ringing it up.

"That comes to fifty-eight dollars." Now I was the one avoiding eye contact as I stared hard at the register.

"What? You've gotta be kidding me."

I dared a look in his direction, and then wished I hadn't. His face was contorting in all sorts of scary ways.

"You're obviously still training. You must have rung it up wrong. There's no way that total is right," he snapped.

Angry mutters sounded from the line behind him and I fought back the urge to cry as I did my best to sound confident. "I can go through each item for you if you'd like."

He eyed me for several seconds before letting out an exasperated sigh. "Never mind. Just hurry and run this."

He shoved his VISA at me and I swiped it through the scanner. A strange beep sounded from the cash register and suddenly the charge screen went blank. My throat constricted in panic as I tried to push the total button again, but nothing happened.

"What's the problem?" A vein pulsed in the man's temple as frustration practically oozed off of him.

Instead of answering, I swallowed and turned to Ashley. "Um, can you help me with something real quick?"

The man blew out a loud breath and threw his hands up in the air as Ashley turned to me with fire in her eyes. "What is it now?"

Before I could answer, the man cut in. "This is the worst service I've ever had! I've missed half the movie already. I want a refund for my ticket."

"I apologize, sir. I'll be happy to serve you and then I can arrange for you to speak with the manager if you'd like," Ashley said. She turned and shoved an empty popcorn bucket at me. "Think you can handle filling this up while I take care of your mess?"

A fresh wave of heat filled my face as I nodded and moved to the popcorn machine. I refused to cry over this. Instead, I worked my humiliation into indignation at how rude some people could be. It wasn't like anyone was forcing him to eat popcorn during the movie—and couldn't he have guessed how long the wait was going to be when he got in line? No one had any patience these days.

I rang up the customer that Ashley had been serving and held my breath until the psychopath I'd been helping finally left. There was no time to think about him as I worked non-stop until the line of customers slowly thinned and then finally trickled to a stop. I leaned back against the counter, stretching my shoulders and trying to roll off the stress of the past few hours.

Ashley ignored me as she took a drink of water and pulled out a mirror to check her makeup. I watched her for a second as I debated whether or not to ask about Eli. Finally, curiosity got the better of me, but I figured I'd better try to soften her up first.

"Sorry about messing things up earlier. I guess I still have a lot of training to do." I gave a small laugh, glad I could talk about the incident now without wanting to cry.

Ashley rolled her eyes as she applied a fresh coat of lip gloss. "You just better hope he didn't actually go talk to Bryce. If he did, you'll be lucky if you still have your job after tonight."

I made a small choking sound. "You think I'll get fired?"

She pressed her lips together and smirked into the mirror. My shoulders relaxed when I realized she was joking. At least I hoped she was.

"So how come you ended up having to work tonight? I thought I saw Eli's name on the schedule."

Her face soured. "Believe me, we *both* wish he was here. Getting stuck with a trainee on the busiest night of the week is like a death sentence. This is the last time I'm doing him any favors."

I let the snide comment roll off as I waited for her to continue. She glanced at me and closed her compact with a snap. "He called this morning and practically begged me to trade with him for tonight."

"Did he tell you why?" A sick feeling formed in the pit of my stomach.

"No. He was totally cryptic. But if I had to guess . . ." She looked at me smugly and let the implication hang.

I turned away and pretended to busy myself arranging a cup full of straws. That was that, then. Eli couldn't stand seeing me to the point that he'd traded schedules to avoid it. The realization hurt like a kick to the gut. Maybe it would be better if I did get fired.

"Look, I have no idea what's up between you two, but whatever it is, you'd be a total idiot if you didn't go crawling back to him. He's the complete package."

I spun around and faced her, working to hide any emotion. "There's nothing going on between us."

"Whatever." She rolled her eyes and tapped a French-tipped nail on the counter. "For some reason he's obviously into you. He practically bent over backwards to get you this job. I'm just saying you're messed up if you don't see how amazing he is."

I swallowed and looked away from her accusatory glare. "So why don't *you* go after him then?"

She scoffed. "Trust me, I have. All the girls who work here have . . . not to mention the girls who come to buy popcorn even though they aren't staying for a movie. He's never shown interest in anyone—until you showed up. And you're too stupid to realize what a catch he is." She shook her head. "Oh the irony."

I stiffened. "Hey, I'm not stupid, okay?" She gave me a look and my shoulders sagged as I accepted defeat. "Okay. I am. I'm a total idiot. I didn't realize he liked me so much; we'd always just been good friends. And now I've messed everything up and I'm afraid he doesn't even want to be that anymore."

She glanced at me sideways before lifting a brow. "All I know is, if I had a chance with Eli Jackson, I wouldn't be giving up so easily." She flipped her blonde ponytail and moved to the counter to help a customer.

I chewed my bottom lip as I considered her words. Maybe she was right . . . maybe it was time for me to quit feeling sorry for myself and make a move. But if I wanted to deserve a guy like Eli, I was going to have to get my life back on track first.

CHAPTER
twenty-seven

"I can walk, Charles." Hannah batted away her brother's attempt to lift her after William helped her down from his horse.

It was dark and all three of them stood near the barn, with Charles and William's horses at their sides.

Charles frowned and then draped Hannah's arm across his shoulder. "You shouldn't put weight on your foot until we've had it looked at properly."

"He's right. Let me carry you in, Hannah," William said.

She shook her head and glanced in the direction of the house. "Absolutely not. We'll have enough to deal with once Father discovers we've been to Benbow Farm." She turned to her brother and shook a finger. "I still can't believe you came. Mrs. White gave me her word not to tell you where I'd gone."

Charles smiled mischievously. "You know I can get Mrs. White to tell me anything; the poor soul couldn't keep a secret if her life depended on it. Besides, she was worried about you and rightly so. You should have sent me in the first place." He shifted his weight to support her with his shoulder. "Now stop being stubborn and let's get you into the house."

Hannah lifted her chin but nodded. "Very well. But you let me take the blame for this. You're in enough trouble with Father after being absent from church this morning."

Charles grunted and William moved to take Hannah's other arm, but she stopped him.

"Charles can help me in, William. If you'll take his horse into the barn that would be most helpful, but after that I think it's best if you go home. It's starting to snow, and you'll want to beat the storm."

I'd been so absorbed in the scene I hadn't noticed the fat snowflakes that were gradually becoming thicker in the darkness. I gave an involuntary shiver.

William's brow creased as he reached out and tenderly stroked her cheek. "Very well. But I'll be by to check on you in the morning."

"Perhaps you could fetch the doctor in the morning. I think she'll be alright until then?" Charles glanced at his sister.

Hannah nodded. "Of course. In fact, I don't see any need to trouble the doctor over such a trifle. I'm sure by tomorrow I'll be right as rain."

The two men exchanged glances and William nodded. "I'll fetch him in the morning." Before Hannah could argue he added, "It will give me an excuse to stop by." He leaned in and gave her a quick kiss on the cheek. "Good night, my love."

She smiled at him as Charles handed over the reins and he led both horses toward the barn.

Charles winked at Hannah. "Well, let's get you inside. If luck is with us, Father will be too distracted over your ankle to ask where we've been."

She gave him a weak smile in return as he helped her hobble toward the house. I followed behind and saw Mr. Walker's angry face appear in the doorway before they reached the front step.

"Where in heaven's name have you been? Roaming over the countryside at all hours without a word—"

His tirade was cut short at the sound of an approaching rider. The man pulled up just short of the front walk. I recognized the constable's full beard as he dismounted.

"At last." Mr. Walker rushed out to meet him, calling over his shoulder, "Charles, take the constable's horse at once! I'll deal with you later."

"Father, I must help Hannah—"

"At once, boy!" he barked.

Charles' jaw tightened but the constable held up his hand. "Thomas, there's no need for me to come inside. I'll only be a moment."

"Nonsense!" Mr. Walker cried. "I've been pacing the floors these past three hours waiting for the news. Come in and warm yourself by the fire. Charles will see to your horse." He turned and glared in Charles' direction, waiting impatiently as his son finished helping Hannah inside and then returned for the horse.

The constable gave Charles a weighted look before offering him the reins. I was sure he'd seen them at Benbow Farm. Granted, he'd obviously had a change of heart about Elder Woodruff, but I wondered if he would still rat them out to their father.

Thomas ushered the constable into the house, oblivious to his daughter as he led him to a chair by the fire. "Now, tell me what happened. Is the man in holding?"

The constable declined to sit and squared his shoulders. "Thomas, if you want Mr. Woodruff taken up for preaching the gospel, you must go yourself and serve the writ. For he has preached the only true gospel sermon I have ever listened to in my life."

The room became deathly still. I watched as Mr. Walker's face changed from pale shock to a slow, angry red. "What did you say?"

The constable nodded. "He's an honorable man if ever there was one. I've heard him preach the truth and have asked to be baptized."

I darted a glance at Hannah. She stared at the constable in admiration, but her back was rigid as she waited for her father's reaction.

Mr. Walker's face was almost purple before he erupted, "Priestcraft! 'Tis the work of the devil and you've been fooled, just like the rest of 'em!"

"Father!" Hannah cried.

He thrust out a warning hand to silence her as he faced the constable. "I want you out of my house." The sudden quiet of his tone was almost more chilling than the yelling.

The constable raised his hands. "Now, Thomas—"

"OUT!"

The constable replaced his hat. "Very well. But I hope after a time you'll reconsider. It'd be a shame to part on such terms."

Hannah's eyes filled with apology as the constable tipped his hat at her and headed for the door.

"Leaving so soon, Constable?" Charles asked as he came into the house. "Shall I fetch your horse?"

"He can fetch his own blasted horse!" Mr. Walker bellowed.

Charles' eyes widened as the constable patted him on the shoulder.

"Good night, Charles." He closed the door behind him and for a few moments the room fell silent again.

Charles looked between his father and sister, trying to gauge what had happened. I wanted to warn him to run right back outside, but it was too late.

"Where have the two of you been?" Mr. Walker paced back and forth in front of the fireplace, like a feline ready to attack.

Charles looked warily at Hannah. Something unspoken passed between them before she slowly nodded. He straightened his shoulders. "We've been to Benbow Farm to hear the American missionary, Father."

Thomas stood still with his back to them as he watched the fire. He said nothing for several moments, but I watched in alarm as he shoulders began to shake with rage.

"Uh-oh," I breathed, wishing I could somehow shelter Charles and Hannah from the wrath I was sure was about to be unleashed.

"Don't blame Hannah. It was all my fault . . . I was simply curious what all the talk was about," Charles continued.

Hannah shook her head. "No, the fault was mine. Charles knew I had gone and he was simply trying to bring me home." She twisted her hands in her lap.

Mr. Walker laughed, a deep menacing sound before he spun around to face his son. "Curious? Were you indeed?" He rushed forward and jabbed a gnarled finger into Charles' chest. "Do you have any idea what your curiosity has cost me? My own children, attending the preaching of a foreigner! How does that make me look to my parish?" He shoved harder and Charles stumbled back.

Hurt and anger swam across his face, but his voice remained calm. "Father, we meant no harm. Besides . . . we're of age to make our own decisions about what we believe." He paused to square his shoulders. "I heard Elder Woodruff's sermon this morning. I believe what he taught and wish to join his church."

Thomas swung out his hand and struck Charles across the face. Hannah cried out and tried to stand, but her injured foot caused her to fall back into her seat.

"You've shamed me long enough," Thomas growled. "You're no son of mine and no longer welcome in this house."

"Father, no!" Hannah pleaded.

Charles raised his head slowly, an angry red mark visible on his face. He set his jaw and looked away from his father, attempting a smile for his sister. "It's alright, Hannah. It's better this way." He took a step toward her and touched her shoulder. "I'll be back for you."

"The devil you will!" Thomas cried. "The minute you leave, your name will not be spoken of again. You're dead to me."

Hannah sobbed as she reached for Charles' hand. "Don't go." Turning to her father, she tried to stand again but failed. "Father, you don't mean it. Tell him you don't mean it."

Charles reached down and gave her a kiss on the cheek before turning to head for the door.

"I do mean it. And we'll be better off without him!"

Charles never looked back at his father as he closed the door behind him. Tears streamed down my cheeks as Hannah put her face in her hands and cried.

"Enough! I won't have you wasting tears over this," Thomas growled. "I blame your brother for what happened tonight, but it's clear you've been under his example too long. You are willful and stubborn and it's time you learned your place."

Hannah put a hand over her mouth as she looked up at her father. He glared at her.

"Tomorrow you shall be married to Mr. Hornsby. I won't see you shame this family the way your brother did. He was always too soft—just like his mother."

She dropped her hand and rose to her feet, wincing with pain. "No, Father."

He turned and faced her with steel in his eyes.

She met his gaze and squared her shoulders as tears continued to wet her face. "I'll stay here and look after you, but I won't marry Mr. Hornsby. You cannot force me."

The slap came so fast I never saw it coming. Hannah fell back into her chair and immediately covered her face with her hand.

Rage welled up inside my chest, choking me. I had to bite my fist to keep from screaming at him. It wouldn't do any good.

He pointed a trembling finger at her as his chest heaved. "You will do as you're told. You and Frederick will be married tomorrow and that will be the end of it. He's more husband than you deserve and I pray he can teach you some respect."

He spun and left the room, slamming the door to his bedroom down the hall.

Hannah sat in shock for several moments. She seemed too stunned to move as she stared at nothing.

I knelt down in front of her. "It will be okay. Don't worry . . . Charles won't let this happen. He'll come for you and take you off to America."

My face brightened as I had a thought. "Oh! Even better—William is coming with the doctor in the morning, remember? He'll save you from your horrible father."

Hannah's shoulders slowly straightened. A resolute look filled her watery eyes as she gingerly stood from the chair. She wobbled a moment, trying to maintain her balance before carefully hobbling to the stairs.

"Whoa now, take it easy," I said as I followed her. "You're going to hurt yourself if you're not careful. Maybe you'd better just sleep down here tonight."

She grasped onto the railing and hopped up each step on one foot, pausing halfway up to catch her breath. I had to admire her determination. Besides, I couldn't blame her for wanting to get as far away from her father as possible.

Once she reached the landing, she hobbled into her bedroom and lit the lantern before sitting at her desk. She took out a piece of paper and dipped her quill into an inkwell. I watched in anticipation as she began to write.

Dear Father,

It is with deep sorrow that I write this letter. Not sorrow for myself, but for you. I wish I could have loved you as I wanted to. Selfishly, I wish you could have loved me enough to truly know my thoughts and the desires of my heart. I see now that this can never be. I am leaving to marry the man I truly love. I hope you find happiness, Father. It is all I can wish for you now.

> *I also wish to tell you that Mr. Woodruff's words touched me tonight. I felt something in that meeting that was strange and wonderful. I hope you will perhaps consider at least learning what message he has to share. It may bring peace to your soul as I felt it did to mine.*
>
> *Please know I harbor no ill will toward you, and wish you to know that in spite of the distressing circumstances of our parting, I will always love you.*
>
> Your loving daughter,
Hannah

She finished the letter and then blew on it to dry the ink. I felt new tears spring to my eyes at what I'd read. How could she forgive him after everything he'd done to her?

She left the letter lying on the desk and stood with the help of the chair. Her face was filled with sadness as she looked around the room and then blew out the lantern.

"Hannah, what are you doing?" I whispered as she hobbled to the door. "You can't leave right now. You can hardly even walk—and it's snowing outside." My voice rose in alarm as I followed her back down the stairs. "You could die out there! William will come in the morning, just think this through for a minute."

She made her way to the front door and put on her shawl. She paused for a moment and then grabbed her father's walking stick. She glanced around the dark house before quietly opening the door.

"Don't you do it! I'm warning you, I'll—" I tried to think of something, "I'll wake up your father!" I folded my arms and raised an eyebrow, then sighed and followed her out the door.

She was halfway down the front walk, using the cane to shuffle through the quickly accumulating snow.

"Hannah!"

She paused and then turned around. The hairs stood up on the back of my neck as she looked at me. I glanced over my shoulder, certain there must be someone behind me, but no one was there. She continued to look at me as she moved slowly forward and I held my breath.

Was she truly seeing me? Before I could say anything, she reached out with her free hand and touched my arm.

"Find me."

CHAPTER twenty-eight

I sat up in bed before I was fully awake. Hannah had spoken to me. I ran a hand across my face and then lay back down, feeling a sense of desperation to go back into my dream. But after almost twenty minutes of lying in my bed, I knew I wasn't falling back asleep. As much as I wanted to go back and follow her—to find out if she was okay and try to talk to her—something else was already weighing on my mind.

Today I was going to talk to the bishop.

My stomach was tight with nerves as I got ready for church. I had zero appetite. My appointment to meet with him was scheduled a half hour before church started. By the time I was ready and went down to the kitchen, Dad had already left for his morning meetings. Since he was a counselor in the bishopric we hardly ever saw him on Sundays. I got a sick feeling in the pit of my stomach as I wondered if he would see me going into the bishop's office. The thought of my parents finding out what I'd done terrified me.

"Good morning, sweetheart."

I jumped at the sound of Mom's voice. I'd been so caught up in my anxiety that I hadn't seen her sitting at the kitchen table.

"Mom. You scared me."

She smiled. "You seem a little jumpy this morning. Everything alright?"

I nodded and sat down beside her. "How are you feeling today? Shouldn't you put your feet up?"

She sighed and shifted on the hard chair. "I probably should. Just needed a change of scenery for a bit. How was work last night?"

I grimaced. "A total train wreck. We were super busy and I kept making mistakes. I'm worried I'm going to get fired."

She patted my hand and made a sympathetic sound. "I'm sure you won't get fired. You're still learning the job; everyone knows that takes time."

I shrugged. "I hope so. The girl I worked with was pretty bratty so she could have been exaggerating things, but I don't know . . . I'm wondering if maybe I should quit and go work for Dad instead."

She frowned. "I think you should give it more time before you make that decision. You don't want to be the kind of girl who runs at the first obstacle she comes across. Besides, I thought you enjoyed working with Eli."

I looked down at my nails. "Yeah, that's kind of the problem."

She leaned back in her chair and studied me. "You still haven't talked to him since the other night?"

I shook my head. "He changed his schedule so he wouldn't have to work with me." The words felt sour on my tongue.

"Oh, honey." Mom leaned over and gave me a hug. I willed myself not to cry. After a minute she pulled back and looked me in the eyes. "You just need to have a talk with him. See if you two can't at least be friends. I know he means a lot to you."

I swallowed and nodded. "Maybe I'll try and stop by his house tonight."

"I think that's a great idea. Eliza and Luke will be coming for dinner after church, but maybe you could go sometime after that."

I perked up. "Really? I can't wait to see them! It feels like they've been on their honeymoon forever."

She laughed. "It does, doesn't it? Amazing how much can happen in one week."

I smiled, but when I glanced at the clock, my smile faded. It was time. I stood from the table. "Well, I'm headed out. Can I get you anything before I go? Maybe I should get you situated on the couch first."

She shook her head. "I'm fine. I've got everything set up in there already and I have my phone in case I need you or your dad. Enjoy the meetings and send everyone my love and gratitude."

"I will." I smiled at her before heading to the garage. I normally left early to pick up Alexis before church, but I was glad Mom hadn't asked why I was leaving extra early today.

Since Lexi knew about my appointment, she'd arranged to have her mom drop her off instead. She had offered to come with me and wait while I met with the bishop, but I'd told her it would only make me more nervous. Now I was kind of wishing she was here. The drive to church seemed even shorter than usual. I was so nervous that my palms were sweaty despite the fact that it was only twelve degrees outside.

My black boots made a crunching sound on the ice as I walked toward the building. I had a brief flashback of Hannah walking into the snowstorm with only a shawl and bonnet for protection. What had she meant by "Find me"? Had she walked to her death and I was the only one who knew about it?

I opened the heavy glass doors and took a deep breath to steady my racing heart. Three years ago I had come in to speak to the bishop when I'd been stupid and had tried a beer. I'd been nervous then, but nothing like this. What would he think of me? How could I talk to him about the things I'd done? Every step felt weighed down by my anxiety to the point that I almost turned around and bolted back out the door, but I was committed now. As scary as talking to the bishop was, could it be any worse than the sick emptiness I'd been carrying around so long?

"Good morning, Courtney."

I looked up to see Brother Mills standing outside the bishop's office. He was the one I'd called to make the appointment. My face flushed with embarrassment. "Good morning."

He smiled. "Bishop Reynolds is just finishing up with another appointment, and then he'll be ready to meet with you. Why don't you have a seat?"

"Thanks." I sat down in the chair, too nervous to even take off my coat. I kept looking around, worried my dad would appear any second and ask what I was doing.

After what felt like an eternity but was probably only a few minutes, the bishop's door opened. A deacon I didn't know very well walked out of the office and didn't look up as he continued down the hall.

"Hello, Courtney." Bishop Reynolds stood in the doorway with a warm smile. His eyes held nothing but kindness as he gestured for me to enter.

I swallowed and stood from my chair, offering a silent prayer for strength as I walked into the office and closed the door behind me.

The February afternoon seemed especially mild as I walked to my car after church. The sun streaming through my windshield was like a warm hug, and I sighed in relief as I turned on the ignition.

A smile—the first genuine smile I'd felt in over a month—slowly spread across my face. I had been a prisoner under the weight of guilt and shame, but I felt that weight beginning to lift.

Tears of gratitude filled my eyes as I thought about my meeting with the bishop. He had been so kind and compassionate. I hadn't felt judged at all, only loved as I'd cried and confessed what I'd done. It hadn't been easy. I still had the road of repentance ahead, but as I'd looked at the picture of the Savior behind his desk I was humbled while at the same time filled with hope. I had never needed the Atonement so desperately, and had never been so grateful that its healing power was available to me.

Our lesson in Young Women had been about grace. I'd listened to every word and realized how personal the Atonement really was. Sister Larsen challenged us to work on a Personal Progress value experience as a follow-up to the lesson.

It had been over a year since I'd done any Personal Progress, but I was determined to make it a focus again. I was going to earn my Young Woman Recognition award and wear my medallion every day, just like Eliza did. Once I was worthy to use my temple recommend, I was never going to lose that privilege again.

I turned on the radio to church music and felt more tears as a song about the Savior came on. A silent prayer of gratitude filled my heart as I drove. It felt so good to be praying again that I found myself saying little prayers all the time. Now I was praying for strength and courage to tell my parents.

Bishop Reynolds had told me that he would keep our meeting confidential, but he had encouraged me to talk to my parents about what had happened. The idea was like poison in my system. Telling Mom and Dad would be even harder than talking to the bishop had been, but I knew I had to do it. I was going to follow his counsel to the letter to prove to the Lord that I was serious about wanting to repent.

As I neared my house, I saw Luke and Eliza's truck in the driveway. I was about to pull in when I changed my mind. My dad wouldn't be home for at least an hour, so this was probably the best time to go see Eli. Besides, I had no idea if I'd be able to see him after talking to my parents. There was a chance I'd be grounded for a while, and Dad was going to be more paranoid about boys than ever.

My mouth twisted in distaste as I realized what still lay ahead, but there would be time to think about that later. I drove past my house and headed for Eli's.

I pulled into the parking lot of the condominium complex where he lived and spied his car parked out front. I tried not to think too hard about what I was doing. It was a tactic I was becoming good at when I wanted to chicken out of something: don't think, just do. I blew out a breath and said another quick prayer as I walked up to his door and knocked.

A dog barked and I heard footsteps approaching before the door opened. Eli's mother stared at me a second before a smile lit up her face. "Courtney, right?"

I nodded, surprised she would remember me. "Hi, Mrs. Jackson. Is Eli home?"

"Yes. Please, come in." Her smile widened as she gestured for me to enter. The little dog danced excitedly around my heels. "Roscoe, behave," she scolded the puffball.

I laughed as the dog immediately backed up a few steps and sat down, his tail wagging wildly.

"Mom, can I *please* just watch one show?"

I looked into the living room and saw Eli's younger brother Caleb sitting on the couch. Eli was nowhere to be seen but I heard guitar music coming from down the hall.

"Caleb, you know our Sunday rules," his mother said before starting in on a string of Spanish words.

Caleb grimaced before rising from the couch. He walked over and held out his hand. "It's nice to see you again, Courtney."

I shook his hand, surprised and impressed by the manners his mom was forcing on him. Most kids his age wouldn't have acknowledged my presence, but it made me feel welcome. "It's nice to see you too."

Mrs. Jackson filled the pause that followed. "Caleb was just about to help me prepare dinner." She gave her son a teasing smile before looking back at me and nodding her head toward the hallway. "Eli is in his room practicing. You should listen at the door before you knock; he'll stop playing as soon as he knows he has an audience." She winked.

I smiled and nodded before heading down the hall. The music was slightly muffled so I put my ear to the door to listen. My breath caught as I heard Eli's smooth voice above the skilled chords of his guitar. He was playing a song I'd never heard before, and it was beautiful. I'd had no idea he could play so well, or that he had such an amazing voice.

I stood there until the song came to an end, and then waited to make sure he wasn't going to play something else. I hated for it to stop, but slowly raised my hand to knock once.

"Come in," he called.

When I opened the door he didn't look up as he adjusted one of the strings. "What is it?"

"Um, how's it going?"

His hand froze on the strings. "Courtney." He looked up and his hazel eyes met mine, filled with questions. "What are you doing here?"

I shifted my weight, glancing around the room. Suddenly I was unable to look him in the eye. "I just . . . wanted to come talk to you."

He stood slowly and gestured to the spot on the bed beside him. My eyes widened as I glanced over my shoulder. Was he seriously inviting me into his room?

He laughed. "It's okay. Just leave the door open. There's not much privacy around here anyway."

I smiled, loving the sound of his laugh. It had been too long since I'd heard it. I came to sit next to him and nodded toward his guitar. "You never told me you played."

"You never asked." His mouth twitched as he rested the instrument across his lap. The movement was natural, as if the guitar was a part of him.

"Will you play for me?"

He shook his head. "You came here to talk. What's up?"

I watched as the friendliness quickly gave way to the mask of indifference he'd worn the night he'd fixed my car. My heart stung at the change. "Eli, I hated the way we left things the other night." I looked down and pinched the fabric of my skirt between my fingers. "I just wanted to say that I'm sorry. I don't blame you for feeling the way you do about me, but I really, really hope we can still be friends."

There were several seconds of silence and I didn't dare to look up at him. I forced myself to ignore how nice it felt to be sitting next to him, how natural to smell the faint scent of his body wash and his leather jacket that was draped across the bed beside me. I loved the picture of the motorcycle and the shelf filled with books. There was also a framed picture of the Savior, and I noticed with a twinge of admiration that his temple recommend was sticking out beneath the scriptures on his nightstand. This room was all Eli, and I loved every part of it.

"Courtney, is that what you really want?"

I looked up into his warm eyes and my heartrate stuttered. *No, actually I'd like to be a lot more than that.* I bit down on my lip. Now was not the time. I couldn't keep running from relationship to relationship; I needed to find myself first.

I swallowed. "Yes. That's what I really want."

His gaze searched mine for another moment before he nodded and looked away. "Okay then. I'll be your friend."

I touched his knee, quickly pulling my hand away as I felt him tense. "Thanks. You don't know how much that means."

His lip quirked up at the corner. "Just remember you still owe me. Don't think that because we're friends you can just come here and charm your way out of it."

I smiled and rolled my eyes. "Of course you wouldn't forget. I'm pretty sure you owe *me* now after bailing on me at work last night."

He winced. "Yeah . . . sorry about that. I saw Bryce at church today and he told me it was a pretty hectic night."

I bit my lip. "Did he talk about firing me?"

Eli laughed. "Why would you think that?"

"There was this angry customer and I kept messing everything up, and Ashley implied that I might get the boot."

"Don't listen to Ashley. She can be a bit dramatic sometimes." He shook his head. "I'm sorry I wasn't there. I just thought it might be easier for both of us if I traded with someone else." He paused and looked down at his hands. "Easier for me at least."

"Eli, I can find another job. I don't want you to—"

"No." He touched my hand and then quickly pulled it back again. "I was being an idiot. Let's just forget about everything we talked about the other night and start over, okay? As friends."

I met his gaze and then slowly nodded. "Sounds good."

Eli's mom stuck her head through the open doorway and knocked on the doorframe. When we both looked up she smiled. "Courtney, would you like to join us for dinner? I'm making one of Eli's favorite Argentine dishes."

"Asado?" his eyes brightened.

She nodded.

"Oh, it smells delicious," I said, "but my sister and brother-in-law are back from their honeymoon and are having dinner with us." I checked my phone and saw that I had a missed text from Mom. "I'd better get going, but thanks so much for inviting me." I stood up to leave.

"Another time, then."

"I'd like that."

She smiled, making her exotic features even more striking and I wondered again how Eli's dad could have left such a kind, gorgeous woman. Maybe sometime I'd work up the courage to ask Eli about his father.

"I'll walk you out to your car," he said. I nodded and we followed his mom out into the hallway.

"Your house is beautiful. I can see why you chose to be an interior designer," I told her. I wasn't sucking up. Now that I was past my nervousness about talking to Eli, I was free to notice how nicely the condo was decorated. It wasn't over-the-top, just simple and pretty.

We'd passed pictures of Eli and his brothers in the hallway, and a large framed picture of the temple rested on the mantle above the fireplace.

"Thank you. I enjoy my work," Mrs. Jackson said with a genuine smile.

Eli's brother Gabriel had joined Caleb in the kitchen. He turned and gave me a flirtatious grin. "Hey, Courtney. Are you eating with us? Please say yes—otherwise Eli will go back to his room and write more songs about you to try and get over his broken heart."

"Gabriel!" Mrs. Jackson gasped and swatted him on the back of the head.

I raised an eyebrow at Eli, but he was looking at his brother like he wanted to wring his neck. He let out a low string of words in Spanish and Caleb looked up from where he was setting the table, his mouth dropping open, but Gabriel only laughed.

Mrs. Jackson intervened. "That's enough, Gabriel. Elijah, you behave." She turned to me and shook her head helplessly. "These two."

I smiled as Eli ushered me out the door. "Don't pay any attention to my brother . . . he's delusional. We're trying to get him help." He cast a dark look over his shoulder.

Gabriel protested before Eli closed the door.

As we walked to my car I couldn't resist. "So, *Elijah* . . . you wrote a song about me?" I gave him a sly smile.

Eli ran a hand along the back of his dark hair as his face turned slightly pink. "She only calls me that when I'm in trouble."

I grinned. "It suits you. Maybe I'll start calling you Elijah from now on."

He gave me a withering look and I laughed.

"And the song . . . ?"

He looked away. "Gabe only said that because he's mad and trying to get back at me."

I tilted my head to the side. "Mad about what?"

"I found out he had a girlfriend and told my mom."

My eyes widened. "No wonder he's mad. What did your mom do?" I couldn't help but feel a little bad for Gabriel. I still remembered when Eliza had told my parents I was going out with Nathan Adams three years ago. I'd been furious.

"She grounded him, but I'm afraid it won't make much difference. He's too girl crazy for his own good." Eli shook his head, his forehead creasing. "I worry about him."

I saw it then, the reason Eli had told his mom. He wasn't just Gabriel's older brother, he was more like his father. The man of the house. He carried more weight on his shoulders than any sixteen-year-old boy should have to. Something about this realization made me want to reach out and give him a hug, but I knew I couldn't.

I looked at him and smiled. "With a big brother like you, I'm sure he's going to turn out just fine."

"I hope so." He opened my car door and nodded toward the hood. "How's she running now?"

"Like a wheezing tin can." I shook my head and climbed into the driver's seat. "Hopefully my first paycheck will be enough to get this beast towed to the dump next time it dies."

He laughed. "Don't worry, most Buicks can run forever."

"That's what I'm afraid of."

When he laughed again I found myself absorbed in the way his dimple made his smile so enticing.

Ugh. Being just friends was going to be tough. Especially when I wanted nothing more than to reach up and kiss that smiling mouth of his. But that was exactly the kind of thought I needed to force from my mind. I shook my head to clear it away.

"What is it?" Eli's hazel eyes met mine.

"Nothing," I answered too quickly, grateful he couldn't read my thoughts. "I was just thinking I'd better go before my mom wonders where I am."

A slight look of disappointment flitted across his face, but he smiled. "Okay. Thanks for stopping by."

"I'll see you in class tomorrow."

"Let me know if you have any more car trouble." He winked and something in his expression made my pulse speed up.

I nodded and closed the car door, secretly hoping the engine wouldn't start again so I'd have an excuse to spend more time with Eli. The traitorous heap of metal started up as soon as I turned the key though. Figured.

Eli waved and then slid his hands into his pockets as he watched me pull out of the parking space. I smiled at him and the grin stayed in place for several blocks. A few snow flurries began to fall, breaking me out of my thoughts. My mind instantly went back to my troubling dream from the night before.

What had happened to Hannah? Could it be that she was a real person who was somehow trying to communicate with me through my dreams? It seemed impossible, but those dreams had definitely been more than ordinary. She felt real to me. I'd even tried Googling the name 'Hannah Walker', but the search had only resulted with people on Facebook or Twitter. Besides, I didn't even know when she had lived . . . *if* she had lived.

The thought occurred to me that I could Google Wilford Woodruff and try to find out more about him. Maybe that would give me some clues. Or maybe these really were just dreams and I needed to stop worrying about it. The memory of Hannah's face as she'd asked me for help last night haunted me though. I had to at least try.

It was only after I'd pulled into the garage that I remembered to read my text from Mom.

Where are you? Eliza and Luke are here.

I smiled and got out of the car. My dad's SUV was parked beside me, so they would probably be eating soon. The smell of a roast in the crockpot made my stomach rumble as I stepped into the kitchen. The table was all set, but no one was there. I heard voices coming from the direction of the family room, so I made my way in.

"Courtney!" Eliza stood from her place beside Mom on the couch. She grinned and pulled me in for a hug.

"Hey, Liza." I hugged her back before pulling away. "How was your trip?"

"Oh my goodness, it was amazing! We just finished showing Mom and Dad the pictures, but I'll show you after dinner, okay? Come see what Mom's looking at." Her bright blue eyes shone with excitement as she sat back down, so I plopped down on the other side of my mom as she sat working on her laptop.

"Where have you been?" Mom asked without looking up from the screen.

"I decided to hurry and visit Eli before dinner," I explained.

That got her attention. She stopped what she was doing and looked at me. "How did it go?"

Eliza picked up on the tone and looked over at me with raised eyebrows. "Who's Eli?"

I smiled. "He's a friend," I looked pointedly at my mom, "and the talk went well."

"Good." She nodded and turned her attention back to the screen.

I saw what she was looking at and instantly had to stifle a yawn. Family history. Again. This is what Eliza had been so excited about?

"Where are Luke and Dad?" I asked, trying not to sound as bored as I felt.

"They're boxing up our wedding gifts so we can take them home," Eliza explained.

"Well we should go help them, don't you think?" Anything to spare me from one of Mom's discourses on 'Great Uncle such-and-such'.

"We can in a minute, but first you have to see this," Eliza said, pointing to the screen. "It's Great Grandma Eliza Porter! Mom is trying to find our ancestors from England."

"Cool." My eyes glazed over. What was Eliza so worked up about? Great Grandma had died before she was even born.

"Yes, of course we have her parents' records, but the line ends here." Mom tapped the screen and shook her head. "We have the name of her grandfather, but that's it. Maybe if we try to search through another genealogical website . . ." her voice trailed off as she and Eliza leaned in closer.

My gaze fell on the name pulled up on the screen and the hairs on the back of my neck stood up. Mom was about to open a new window when I reached for her hand.

"Wait."

She turned to me in surprise. I tried to keep my voice steady. "This is Great Grandma's grandfather? What do you know about him?"

Mom studied me for a moment before answering. "Well . . . very little actually. We know that he joined the Church in England and married another convert he met on the ship to America. He died a short time after reaching Nauvoo, leaving his wife and little daughter behind—that would be your Great-great Grandmother Gertrude—"

"Anything else? Do you know anything else about him?"

Mom and Eliza both turned to gape at me. "Courtney, what's gotten into you?" Mom asked.

"Please, I know it sounds crazy, but think . . . is there anything else you know? Any pictures?"

Mom looked puzzled as she tapped her fingers on her lips. "Well, I did hear your Great Grandma tell my mother once that he made that dresser she passed down to me. You know—the one in the attic?"

CHAPTER twenty-nine

Now I knew why that little heart-shaped knot had looked familiar.

"No. Way." I felt the blood drain from my face as I stared at the name again: Charles Walker. It had to be the same person. Without a word I bolted from the family room and ran toward the stairs.

"Where's the fire?" Dad asked as I blazed past him and Luke carrying loads of boxes down the hallway.

I didn't answer as I continued on up the next set of steps to the attic. My heart thumped against my ribcage as I pulled the string to the lightbulb and walked slowly over to the dresser. It was covered in a layer of dust, and had clearly seen a new coat of varnish or two, but it was the same dresser I'd seen in my dream.

My fingers shook as I opened the top drawer. I tossed out the old clothes inside and felt around in the bottom. There was just the tiniest divot in the back of the wood; you wouldn't know what it was if you weren't looking for it. I held my breath and curled my fingernail underneath, lifting gently. There was a scraping sound as the thin board lifted, revealing the hidden compartment below.

I blew out a shaky breath and carefully set the board down before looking into the compartment. Tears filled my eyes as I recognized Hannah's journal, her Bible, and all of the notes and trinkets from William. It was all there—worn with age, but it was there. As well as something I hadn't seen before. I carefully picked up a small leather-bound journal and opened it. The name Charles Walker was scrawled inside the cover. My eyes widened as I saw page after page filled with his handwriting. This was Charles' journal!

I sank to the floor and began reading, drinking in the words as quickly as I could.

September 3, 1841

Though I've never kept a journal, I write this at Hannah's request. She always could goad me into getting her way, even now, from beyond the grave. She was the finest sister a brother could ever wish for, and I guess she knew I'd move the earth and stars if she asked me to. So here now, is my record for which I can only hope her daughter will one day find a use.

Little Gertrude, your mother, Hannah Alice Walker married your father William David Lucas in Gadfield Elm Chapel on the ninth day of March, in the year of our Lord Eighteen Hundred and Forty. She and your father shared a love few people on this earth will ever know.

Hannah was frail at the time of their marriage. She'd fallen ill after walking to William's home in a snowstorm the night before they were married, but stubborn as she was, she insisted on marrying him before she'd allow herself to be seen by the doctor. William cared for her day and night until she was well again. I visited her often and we were all encouraged by her progress. However, when she became pregnant it grew apparent she had yet not fully recovered. It was a difficult pregnancy and she died during childbirth.

Here, the handwriting became shaky and the ink was slightly smudged on the page. I set the journal down and wiped at my own tears which were streaming down my face. My heart was broken as I mourned for this woman I'd only known through my dreams, yet she was as real as any dear friend.

Not just friend. Family.

Through blurry tears I continued to read.

> *Don't ever feel burdened by this fact, Gertie. Your mother loved you fiercely, and the two of you shared a special bond before you were even born. I know my sister, and if she had it all to do over again, she would have chosen the same course. Your father loved you too. After Hannah died, William grieved to the depths of his soul. You became the center of his universe and he cherished you up until the day of his death, on the twelfth day of May, Eighteen Hundred and Forty-One. Three months to the day after you were born. The cause of death was consumption. Your mother and father are buried in the cemetery at Castle Frome, near the hill where they played as children.*
>
> *This past year has been difficult for me. I lost my beloved sister and closest friend. I carried bitterness in my soul as I blamed my father for these events, but through the goodness of the restored Gospel, I've found forgiveness in my heart. I was baptized on August the Ninth, 1841 in Benbow pond. I've found a new light in my life, a light which I'm sure your mother and father felt as well. They were interested in learning more of the doctrine which they heard preached by Elder Woodruff, and I feel certain they too would have been baptized if circumstances had allowed.*
>
> *The other light I've found came through you, Gertrude. You are like my own daughter and the day I took you in as my own was one of the most important days of my life. You're just an infant and won't remember this time in England, but perhaps that's just as well. We're looking forward now and*

will leave in a few days to join with the saints in Zion.

"Courtney? Is everything all right?"

Eliza's voice startled me and I looked up to see her approaching. She took in my tear stained face and sat next to me on the floor, gathering me in her arms. "What is it? What are you doing up here?"

I turned and cried into her shoulder, finally releasing all the tears I'd been holding back. Tears of disbelief over what I'd found, tears of sorrow for what had been lost. Eliza just held me and let me cry.

Finally, I sniffed and pulled away from her, careful not to bump the journal. I held it out for her to see.

"This belonged to Charles Walker. It was hidden here in this dresser. He wasn't our Great-great Grandma Gertrude's father—he was her uncle. Eliza, I know this is going to sound crazy, but I've had these dreams . . . they showed me—" I shook my head, not even sure how to finish.

Eliza's eyes widened and then filled with tears. She smiled and touched my arm, glancing up at the portrait of Great Grandma Porter before looking at me again. "I understand better than you think."

CHAPTER

My head swam with thoughts as I drove to practice the next morning. I couldn't get over my conversation with Eliza, when she'd confided in me about the special dreams she'd had with Great Grandma Porter. We'd talked and looked through the contents in the drawer until we realized Mom needed to share in the excitement.

My dad and Luke had helped her into the attic and we'd all cried over the miracle that led us to the discovery of our lost ancestors. The door had opened for us to do their temple work, to seal Hannah and William together and then to their daughter Gertrude. Mom had been so excited over the new line of possibilities I was afraid she was going to go into labor, but the joy and peace that filled our attic was something I'd never forget.

Mom had even told me I could be baptized for Hannah. I was too emotional to respond. I wanted nothing more than to be baptized on her behalf, but I'd pulled my parents aside and explained why I would have to wait to go to the temple.

We cried together, but it hadn't been as awful as I'd expected. My parents weren't angry—they were sad. I could see the sorrow for me in their eyes. Their disappointment hurt more than any angry words could have. As expected, I was grounded for a while, but I felt their support and knew they were proud of me for taking the steps to repent. After dreaming about the way Hannah's father treated her, I'd never been more thankful for my own loving parents.

In my prayers this morning, I'd expressed all the gratitude I felt. My life was getting back on track, and I was remembering what it felt like to be happy again. I entered the gym with a smile on my face and headed straight for Serena.

She didn't see me as she stretched out on the floor, so I dropped down beside her.

"Hey."

When she looked up, an instant scowl twisted her picture-perfect features.

"What do you want?"

"I just wanted to apologize."

Her eyes widened and her mouth fell open before she slid the dirty look back into place. "Apologize for what? Lying about you and Tate? Because it doesn't even matter. It's not like I'm with him anymore."

I nodded. "I know. He might not be your boyfriend, but I think maybe you still have feelings for him. I should have been honest with you about hanging out with him, and I'm sorry. I guess I was just, sort of . . . scared of you."

She snorted. "Seriously?"

"Yeah." I smiled and stood when I saw Janie enter the gym. Before making my way over to her, I glanced back down at Serena. "This has nothing to do with you, but I thought you might want to know anyway—I'm not seeing Tate anymore. It didn't work out."

Serena raised her eyebrows. "That was fast."

I shrugged and then turned to find Janie.

"Courtney?" Serena said.

I stopped and glanced over my shoulder at her.

"I'm sorry too."

I gave her a small smile and nodded. She didn't say anything else and looked away as she leaned into a stretch. She didn't have to explain; we both knew what she was apologizing for.

After practice I made my way to biology. There was still one more conversation I needed to have, and I wasn't looking forward to it. Tate had sent me several texts yesterday, but I hadn't replied to any of them. I knew I had to talk to him, but I wanted to do it face-to-face. I wasn't sure if he was going to meet me in the hall after I hadn't answered his texts, so when I rounded the corner and saw him waiting for me, my heart kicked into a gallop.

"There you are," he said with a sideways smile. "I wasn't sure if you were going to meet me today or not. How come you didn't answer my texts?" He reached out and pulled me in for a hug, kissing the top of my head. "I missed you yesterday," he whispered.

My tongue felt stuck in my throat as I pulled away from him. "Tate, we need to talk."

"Uh-oh. Those are never good words." He lifted my chin with his finger until I was facing him. "What's up?"

"Um," I looked around for a place that would give us a little privacy, and nodded toward an alcove near a glass case displaying art projects. He took the hint and followed me out of the crowded hallway.

I took a deep breath and forced myself to meet his eyes. "Look, I think you're an amazing guy and I'm really flattered that you like me, but I can't see you anymore."

He frowned. "What's this about, Courtney?"

I bit my lip and looked away. "What happened after the dance on Saturday was wrong. I shouldn't have made those choices, and I'm really sorry. I talked to my bishop yesterday," I willed myself to look back at him, "and I think you should too."

He shifted his weight uncomfortably and shoved his hands in his pockets.

"Listen, I feel bad about that too, but it doesn't mean we have to break up. We just won't do anything like that anymore."

I shook my head. "I wish it were that simple, but it's not. I've learned that with stuff like this it's not enough to just say it won't happen anymore. The only way to truly repent is to meet with the bishop and go through the repentance process. It's hard, but it's the right thing to do." I touched his arm. "You said you wanted to serve a mission. I don't think you should wait until you're filling out your papers to get ready for it."

He regarded me with his marine colored eyes for a moment. "You're the first girl who's ever said anything like this to me before."

I sucked in a breath, feeling sick inside. Sick because I realized I wasn't the first girl he'd done things like this with. It helped me know I was making the right decision.

"Good luck, Tate. I wish you all the best." I turned and started heading for class.

"So it's really over, huh?" he called.

I turned. "Yeah. It really is." I smiled sadly, hoping he knew I didn't hold any bad feelings. He shook his head and looked at the floor before turning to walk away.

I watched him for a moment and then made my way to class, feeling peace in knowing I'd done the right thing.

CHAPTER thirty-one

As I stepped down into the water of the font, I felt warmth seep into every part of my body. It wasn't just the warm water, but a warmth of my spirit that filled every one of my senses. I knew Hannah was with me, and that I'd finally found her. Tears spilled down my cheeks as Dad said the words of the ordinance and dipped me under the water.

When I came back up, the warmth intensified. I hugged Dad and then wiped my face as I turned to smile at the rest of my family and Eli who were watching from behind the glass. With my parents' permission, I'd asked Eli to be baptized for William. We were also baptized for Hannah's parents and other ancestors Mom and I had been able to find with the help of Hannah and Charles' journals, and records we'd discovered online.

Once Eli and I did the baptisms and confirmations, Luke, Eliza and my parents were going to be proxy for the rest of the temple ordinances. We planned to meet up and celebrate over dinner. This was a special day for our family, one I'd been waiting anxiously for. I knew Hannah had been waiting too.

After the baptisms and confirmations were finished, Mom found me in the dressing room and gave me a hug. It was nice to be able to get my arms around her now that baby Hannah had arrived safe and sound. Alexis was tending her so our family could share this special day together.

Mom kissed the top of my head. "I'm so proud of you, honey."

I knew what she meant and gave her an extra squeeze. "Thanks, Mom."

She pulled away with eyes glistening. "You know that feeling you had while doing this temple work?"

I nodded. "It felt like they were here with us; all of them." Part of me had wondered about Thomas Walker and whether he'd had a change of heart on the other side. I liked to think so.

She pulled back and smiled. "I felt it too. But there was also another special spirit I've felt during this entire, miraculous process—the spirit of Elijah."

I tilted my head and she continued, "'He shall turn the hearts of the fathers to the children and the hearts of the children to the fathers.' That's what the scriptures tell us about temple work in the last days. You are a part of that, Courtney."

I smiled, feeling the warmth fill me again. "That's awesome. I'll have to tell Eli about it."

"Yes, you should. Although it seems your Elijah has a pretty firm grasp on living up to his name. I found out from his mom that he's been going to the temple before school once a week since he was a deacon."

My eyes widened. "Seriously? He never told me that."

Mom winked. "You'd better keep your eye on that one. Speaking of which—you've probably kept him waiting long enough. We'll meet you both at the restaurant later."

I grinned and nodded before turning to leave the dressing room. I found Eli sitting on a chair in his suit and tie, waiting for me. He stood as soon as he saw me, his gorgeous smile lighting up his face. For a second it looked like he wanted to reach for my hand, but then he slid his hands into his pockets.

I wanted to reach for his hand too, but decided for the next best thing. "I'm a little clumsy in these heels. Mind if I hold onto your arm?"

His hazel eyes met mine as the dimple I loved appeared. "Of course not." He held out his arm. "M'lady?"

The breath caught in my throat. He couldn't have said anything more perfect in that moment. I had to quickly swallow the lump in my throat as I smiled and took his arm. "Thank you, kind sir."

We walked outside the temple and both turned in unison to look up at its glorious spires.

Eli cleared his throat. "I sort of . . . have something for you." He dropped my arm and reached to an inside coat pocket.

I raised an eyebrow as he brought out a rectangular object wrapped in silver paper. "What's this for?"

He shrugged. "I just knew this was a special day for you, so . . ." He shrugged again and handed me the gift.

I gave him a questioning smile before ripping open the paper, and then gasped at what was inside. "Oh my goodness—it's perfect!" I held the journal to my chest and beamed. "I seriously love it."

The cover was made of deep purple suede and it was just the right size. Ever since I'd found Charles and Hannah's journals I'd told myself I needed to do better at keeping my own, and now I definitely would.

Who knew? Maybe my great-great-great granddaughter would come across it someday.

Eli smiled and seemed to relax. "I'm glad you like it."

"I love it. Thank you so much," I said, taking his arm again.

His eyes slowly took on a sly look. "There's something else I wanted to talk to you about . . . remember how you still owe me something?"

I scrunched up my eyebrows. "Hmm . . . I *think* I remember something about that, but it's a little hazy." He poked me playfully in the ribs and I laughed. "Just kidding. I was just hoping you'd forget."

He smirked, but I could tell he was nervous. "Well I was just thinking . . . I mean, it's no big deal. If you don't want to it's totally cool—"

"Eli, what is it?"

He straightened his shoulders. "A group of us were thinking of getting dates for dinner and laser tag this Friday night, so I was wondering if I could call in that thing you owe me."

I tilted my head and gave him a teasing smile. "You're asking me on a date?"

His gaze met mine. "Yes."

A tiny thrill traveled through me. "Okay."

"Does that mean you'll come?"

"Yes."

"Cool."

We walked a few steps before I said, "You know, you didn't have to call in that favor. I would have said yes anyway."

He gave me a sideways smile. "I didn't want to risk it."

My heart stuttered at the look in his eyes, but I didn't want him to see how much he was affecting me so I changed the subject. "Has anyone ever told you about the Spirit of Elijah?"

He turned, his face mere inches from mine. "I've heard the phrase before. What is it?"

I smiled and held on tighter to his arm. "Let's walk."

As we talked and made our way slowly around the temple grounds, I felt completely free. I admired the outside of the beautiful temple, still carrying the feeling of peace from being inside its walls.

I was so grateful for the Atonement which made it possible for me to be worthy to use my temple recommend again. I knew I would keep the promise I'd made to Eliza on her wedding day. Because being married in the temple was no longer her promise.

It was mine.

☙

That night I dreamed of the pond, the one I'd seen Hannah sitting by so many times before. I hadn't dreamed of her since discovering the dresser, so I was excited to be back in the place where it all began.

Now I knew this was Benbow Pond. In my research I'd discovered that over a thousand English saints had been baptized here before leaving to join the rest of the Latter-day Saints in America. This pond was almost a sacred place and now it made sense why I'd seen Hannah sitting on its banks. But as I looked around, I was disappointed to find that she wasn't there. I was all alone.

A breeze rustled the tall grasses at my feet, sending a ripple across the smooth surface of the water. I felt a hand on my shoulder and turned. My breath caught in surprise.

"Hannah!"

She smiled and her bright eyes danced with joy. Now I could see where Eliza got her blue eyes from, and the mystery of my blonde hair was finally solved. The realization gave me a sense of belonging.

"Thank you, Courtney." She reached out and pulled me into a hug. "Thank you for finding me."

I was instantly filled with the love I'd felt so strongly in the temple. "Thank you for helping me find myself," I said, hugging her tighter.

She pulled back and turned. I followed her gaze and saw William standing a few yards off with baby Gertrude in his arms. He nodded and smiled at me.

I grinned as Hannah went to join her family. Her eternal family. Knowing I'd helped forge that connection in some small way was the best feeling I'd ever had. I knew there were still others who were lost and needed my help to find them.

I couldn't wait to get started.

AUTHOR'S NOTE

About a year ago, I was sitting in a combined Young Men, Young Women lesson on family history work. Out of nowhere, the Spirit nudged me that I needed to write a story involving family history. At the time, I was in the middle of writing a YA sci-fi and did NOT want to put it aside and switch gears.

In the first place, I thought I was done with the Invaluable series. As much as I loved it, I just couldn't see anywhere else to take the story and felt Eliza had her happy ending. And in the second place, I really wanted to finish my current project and try publishing to the national market. But guess what? The Lord had other plans.

It took some humbling—and twelve weeks on bedrest—to make me realize that Courtney's story needed to be told. Once I began, I couldn't stop typing. I knew I wanted Courtney to have dreams about a girl who was one of her lost ancestors. I also had a vague notion that I wanted the girl to be the daughter of a vicar or something similar.

I was led to the historical account of Wilford Woodruff and the conversion of the Saints in Herefordshire England in 1840. Some of the quotes from Courtney's dreams were taken from President Woodruff's biography. I read in his account about the local rector who was upset over the loss of his parish, and suddenly Hannah's story came to life.

Aside from Elder Woodruff, the rector and the constable, the rest of the characters in Courtney's dreams are fictitious. However, I did use names or combinations of names from my own ancestors for the characters. The journal pictured on the front cover is an authentic journal from one of my ancestors as well. I used to think that genealogy and family history work were—well, how can I put it? Boring. With a capital B. But I can't believe how wrong I was!

I had so many cool experiences just from writing this book on family history, that I wish I had room to share them all. Suffice it to say that your ancestors are aware of you, and they want you to be happy. If you're looking for a way to feel good inside, look no further than family history work. Seriously! There is no way you can't feel the power of this work once you get involved. Visit www.familysearch.org to get started, and you'll see what I mean. Go. Go now. You can thank me later.

ABOUT THE AUTHOR

Holly J. Wood is an avid reader. She attended Ricks College and Brigham Young University where she pursued a degree in health science. Holly has a passion for travel and has lived briefly in Israel and Mexico. True to her name, she enjoys watching classic movies and musicals. She currently lives in Mountain Green, Utah, with her husband and four young children.

www.hollyjwood.com
hollyjwoodauthor@gmail.com

SUGGESTED READING

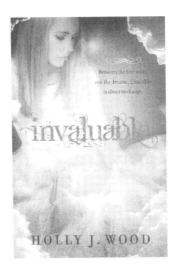

Eliza Moore's sophomore year of high school is turning out to be anything but ordinary. After only half-listening to her mother's lesson on Sunday about the importance of the Young Women values, something strange begins to happen. Eliza begins dreaming about her great-grandmother, who visits her with some important lessons taught by some very special people. Each time Eliza awakens, she finds herself on a treasure hunt of sorts as she begins to understand the significance of the eight Young Women values, and she finds her life changing for the better as she strives to live them. Invaluable is the fun and inspiring story of Eliza's journey of spiritual self-discovery that will have girls of all ages excited to be part of the Young Women program.

Just when Eliza thought she had her future planned out, her heart is thrown a major curveball. With Luke two months away from returning home, she meets Sawyer, who makes her question which path will lead her happily ever after. Relying on help from her unusual dreams, Eliza must make a choice that will affect her future forever. So how will she know which path is right? This inspiring sequel to Invaluable follows Eliza on her journey from Young Women to Relief Society, and will hold readers captive to the very end.